By Raymond Burke

The Starguards - Of Humans, Heroes, and Demigods

The Magna Aura Genesis
The Axalan Revelation
The Terra Chronicles
The Destinia Apocalypse

The Destinia Apocalypse

BOOK FOUR OF

THE STARGUARDS
Of Humans, Heroes, and Demigods

Raymond Burke

THE STARGUARDS

Raymond Burke is a British-born author - The Destinia Apocalypse the fourth in The Starguards series. His background includes an early life in Canada and the US, employment in the British Army as an aircraft technician, an MSc degree in Archaeology from University College London, and short-article writing. He is also a member of The Mars Society. Raymond cunningly lives without a fridge, satellite TV, iPods, and he also can't drive. He's a self-confessed 21st century caveman . . . and loves it! Through all, he has been a keen and aspiring writer. He currently lives in London.

To

Neena & Brian Baker
A late wedding gift

Acknowledgements

My continued grateful thanks to my family and many supporters and friends: John McMillan, Nigel Livingstone, Mark Emsley, Ptolemy Philpott and Tania Johnson, Chris Bellay, Mark Veal, Dave Baseley, Chad Dixon, Lori Buttermark, Anke Marsh, Leigh Mack, Carl Bialik and Lydia Serota. To my fellow writers Paul Arvidson, Peter Ellis, Lance Steen Anthony Nielsen, Nick Cirkovic, David P Perlmutter, Jon-Jon Jones, Stephen Marriott, Anne John-Ligali, Soulla Christodoulou, Anton Marks, Michael Grist, Benjamin Smith, and Nilam A McGrath for their help and guidance. And to the members of the LOTNA sci-fi group - you guys rock!

Cover design by Janet Dado. Formatting by Ivy Port.

Any leftover errors are mine alone to claim.

I can spell; I just like to make words up!

BOOK FOUR

THE DESTINIA APOCALYPSE
The Last War

EVIL pervades.
It hides and it shifts, waiting in eternity,
dancing to the pulse of its impenetrable heart.

But there is an evil which returns from sleepless death.
An evil thought long lost, but through which all things
were born; an evil destined to shine its dark light
from the pre-cosmic dawn until the universal twilight.

No time, no place, is unknown to evil.
No one escapes its bounds.
Evil lives to be supreme.
And it is awakening.

Prologue

Water spilling.

Rock spinning.

Splashing down upon her.

No.

Tumbling through blackness, hurtling toward her, sprinkling her feet.

Life was emerging. Death was coming.

No not exactly - one now. The other not.

An omen of synchronicity? Her mind was not right. It wasn't her own. It was more.

Concentrate!

She saw it now, focussed in blurry flashes, present and future colliding in pain. The birth of death. The end of life.

She screamed. And breathed. Quick precious breaths. But the heavenly behemoth stayed its course.

Silly, she wasn't in space. She was confused, exhilarated, delirious.

She was home. With no way to change its trajectory. But the other miracle of magnitude was certainly on its way, ready or not. She could push that. No problem.

Focus. Breathe. Push.

The night was closing in upon them.

She screamed again. She had to forget about the catastrophe in dark the future.

Because for now, Lynn Kellis had to give birth!

CHAPTER ONE

Mindscream's name echoed on Zane's lips as her tired eyes sprung opened. They were instantly assaulted by bright sunlight. She was flat on her back, her body being subjected to rough movement. She threw a hand over her face to shade her eyes; to see her assailant. She could tell she was somewhere else, definitely not Earth.

Flashes of memory pin-pricked her brain. The explosion. Thane Industries. The attack of the E-Corps. The lorelet inadvertently released by Altair when he had touched the Archwitch's falling Lore stone shattering into energy. Desperately, Zane had somehow opened up a time-portal, spiriting herself and the Starguards away just in time.

Squinting hard, her eyes focused on Aerl. It was he who was shaking her. He stopped when she looked at him. Aerl continued to stare at her. Zane peered around, a bit dazed. The two of them were alone. No sign of the other Starguards Altair, Deb or Urana. Zane coughed and spat dust from her dry mouth.

Where were they? her eyes asked Aerl, who continued to gaze at her in a curious manner.

Aerl had removed his visor; searching brown eyes still studying her very attentively.

"What's wrong, Aerl?" her voice trembled slightly, stifling another cough. His constant stare was becoming more than a little intimidating. Fear rose in the pit of her stomach. "Has something happened to the others?" But his cold eyes told her that was not it.

"Who are you?" Sceptre shouted in her face.

Zane recoiled from his harsh voice.

"What? Aerl, it's me, Zane! What are you on?" She stopped herself as she noticed that her voice had changed. It sounded more mature. She looked at her hands, they seemed a little older, and then she noticed her body; a longer, fuller figure. "Oh, wow, look at me!"

"That's not all, if you are who you say you are." Sceptre fetched out a small crystalator, one the ubiquitous multifunctional crystalline computers, from his blue and gold uniform. He had made a recording, replaying the images to Zane.

Her mouth dropped open in shock at the sight. She was at least ten years older, dyed blonde hair replaced by her natural black hair, longer and fuller. She was a woman. Zane rolled onto her knees and stood up like a new-born foal, legs feeling a bit wobbly beneath her. Dusting herself off she felt and saw well-trimmed muscle; at least she still fit into her purple and black manoeuvre suit, which had automatically accommodated her fuller figure.

What's happened to me? she asked herself.

"Aerl, I swear it's me," she pleaded still finding her new voice a bit disconcerting, "but I don't know what's happened or how we got here, wherever here is . . ." The surrounding landscape was as rocky, hilly, and desolate as a brown moon.

A buzzing from Sceptre's comms cut her off. He adjusted his visor controls to enhance the sound. Listening carefully to make out the signal, he frowned, before his eyes widened in surprise. He replaced his visor and his head spun in the direction of the signal.

And before Zane could get her bearings and register that the call was a mayday, Aerl had homed in on the signal and taken to the air faster than Zane had thought possible.

He left me here! She gaped in dismay after him.

Despite that and disregarding still being disorientated from whatever had just happened, Zane shot after him, a trail of dark dust marking her wake.

Thank god I can still run fast, she thought relieved.

Azure woke up. She yelped as bright sunlight burned her eyes.

Her thoughts raced *Where am I? Where was Classia?* Sword Celectral? *Novan? Was I dreaming?* But it had seemed so real.

The heat, however, was really unbearable after the relative darkness and shade of Celectral City under the coloured mists of the Ribbon System. *Had she really fought the Lore again?* She looked around at her new reality.

There were other things in the heat. Long shadows cast by a score of metal, vaguely humanoid-beings silently standing in a line a hundred meters away. Urana, the blue-haired Starguard, faced them in a stand-off, her hands ready to rain energy upon them. The gap and silence between them was pregnant with violent anticipation.

Alarmed, Azure staggered up to stand to support Urana. That's when she saw another figure, prone, behind her.

"Altair!" Then she noticed the familiar brown and red coloured uniform and mask.

The E-Corps leader, Fusioneer, she thought his name was.

What was he doing here? Where were Altair, Sceptre, and Zane?

Stuck between helping Urana and seeing to Fusioneer, Azure ran a systems check on her manoeuvre suit. Seconds later, she received an all-function clear mode. Keying up comms, she transmitted a mayday call on a Starguards frequency in the hopes Altair or Sceptre would hear it. Just as she did so, the metal beings began to stir and step forth toward them.

Did I trigger that? she questioned herself.

"Rain, what's going on? What are those things?" she commed her fellow Starguard.

If Urana heard her, she didn't answer. She had started firing plasma from her hands at the strange beings, who didn't return fire.

Azure saw they were absorbing Urana's energy. She knew what was coming next, "Rain, stop firing, they're..."

Too late.

The beings had absorbed enough from Urana. They re-channelled the energy and began firing back. They were in battle.

Fabien L'Coyle, leader of the Marquis Edgar de la Valtare's forces on this new world, was bored. He and a good score of soldiers had been sent out to hunt down the traitor-spy known as Guillaume de Roth. Instead they had come across three unconscious figures laying in the wastelands to the west of the Silver City, their strange alien fortress.

"*Voici! Voici!*" a man shouted and pointed; Benoir, L'Coyle heard his distinctive loud voice.

There were cries of excitement at the sight of two women.

"Benoir, leave them! They are prisoners!" L'Coyle knew he needed to calm them down before they got out of hand. But he also knew his men would ignore his orders, Duke or not. They knew some of his past, enough to know it was the nominally lesser-ranked Valtare who gave the orders. And L'Coyle wanted his lands and title restored to him. The only way to do that was to see this war out. And these men weren't going to jeopardise that for him.

"*Allez, Allez,*" called out the excited Benoir, the rest of the men rushing over to the women against L'Coyle's orders, trying to awaken them.

"Bring them back to the fortress for some fun!" another soldier, Roscos, muttered.

"No, are you joking? The Devouts will keep them away from us! Do it here!" Faverini had even started unclipping his breeches.

"How do you know they aren't Devouts, lost out here?" L'Coyle tried to dissuade them.

Faverini grinned. "We'll soon find out!"

Benoir grunted his approval.

L'Coyle cursed himself. The Devouts, the fearsome sisterhood allied to Valtare and Archron, were no fun to be sure, not wanting to sully their bodies and reputations with Valtare's men so the medieval warriors were reverting to their barbarous ways with the two strangers.

But even as they argued over one of them, the blue-haired woman dressed in white and yellow armour awoke.

"Get off me!" she yelled in anger, teeth barred. "Now!" Her eyes glowed bright yellow.

Now scared, the men tried to hold her down, Benoir gripping her armour, to restrain her. At his fervent attempt to force her, the woman erupted.

L'Coyle saw her unleash some form of hot bright yellow magic from her hands. Benoir and his fellow assaulters burned to their crispy deaths in front of L'Coyle.

"Retreat!" L'Coyle ordered in panic; the first to distance himself as more and more of his men were cut down by the mysterious woman's energy.

As he ran for cover, L'Coyle retrieved the crystalator Valtare had given him.

"Three strangers in armour," he panted. "A blue-haired demoness burning my men alive! We need reinforcements!" He described the strangers to Valtare and after a few seconds silence; "Kill them!" came the cold reply: Archron's voice.

"Help is on the way," Valtare confirmed.

Two minutes later, a dozen or so Surge pelted in from the cloudless sky. The metallic beings occupying the female warrior, just as the second woman, who wore all-blue armour began to wake up.

Licking his lips nervously, L'Coyle saw his chance outflanking the otherwise-engaged Urana. He sneaked up behind Azure, who was blinking in the bright sunshine and talking into her forearm comms. L'Coyle prowled up to the still unconscious man, his first target. With his sword raised to deliver a killing blow upon Fusioneer, a bright glint in the sky caught his attention. It sparked brightly from around a group of ridges moving like a golden arc, rapidly closing upon them. A brief flash sparked from the looming rainbow. Before a bedazzled L'Coyle could react, a massive burst of hard golden light had slammed into him hurling him twenty feet through the dusty air.

And there, flying in to unleash more lightning vengeance was Sceptre, a vision of burning livid light, unrelenting, felling L'Coyle's small human army with impunity.

L'Coyle was only saved by dint of a small forcefield pack given to him by Valtare. Hurting all over, cracked bones jarring, jaw twitching, L'Coyle pushed himself up as Sceptre circled to land to assist Urana and Azure. Readying for another attack, L'Coyle charged but was brutally downed again into the red earth, by a force whose speed was a manic burst of colour.

L'Coyle's thin scar along his eye smarted and itched. Everyone thought it was a battle scar. He laughed to himself remembering the gift from his father, the Duke, who had whipped him as his step-mother had watched; punishment to both of them for his then teenaged son's and new wife's transgression in the estate stables. His step-mother's punishment had been worse. Blue eyes wide with fear, she had watched her young lover being stripped of both his clothes and inheritance and whipped while she hung from the stable loft, long blonde hair hiding the rope around her neck. Their eyes had met as she drew her last breath. Funny how he always thought of her when he was in pain.

Just before blacking out, L'Coyle's mind vaguely caught the image of a girl vanishing almost too quick to see. With Azure and Urana occupying the Surge with covering fire, Sceptre picked up Fusioneer followed by Urana and Azure, leaving behind a battle-scarred land and destroyed men.

The impassive Surge did not pursue the strangers. One dull gray-coloured Surge picked up L'Coyle none too gently. He was flown over the dead land back to the fortress, where his collapsed body was presented before a stunned Valtare and Decion, who had been expecting a victorious return.

Needless to say, it was not a very quiet day in the Silver City.

Sceptre had flown erratic courses. Where to he did not know. He flew low avoiding any potential detection systems. Zane in her Windburst costume was almost running beside him. Azure and Urana flanked them. Sceptre kept going until a warren of hills and valleys approached. His visor's sensors detected no movement so he deemed it safe to land on a small plateau. Gasps of relief escaped them as they stopped to check themselves over and regroup. Sceptre made sure Fusioneer was still alive setting him down on a sandy patch of ground.

No sooner had they caught breath when Sceptre's head whipped around sensing movement to their rear. A stranger was scrambling down a rocky hill toward them, brandishing a sword. Before anyone else reacted, the stranger was plowed into by Windburst, sending him flying into unconsciousness as he hit the rock hard wall. His sword landed by Sceptre.

I'm getting good at this shoulder-barging-at-speed thing, thought Zane.

"Is that Zane?" Azure asked in confusion, looking at the older Zane. "She almost looks like me!"

Her stare made Zane feel self-conscious. She milled around the fallen stranger, who was dressed in a stylised medieval warrior's armour.

"Long story, but it seems so," a laser-focused Sceptre answered, warily scanning the area, as the Astral came over.

She looked sheepishly at Urana and Azure and shrugged. "Guess a girl has to grow up at some point," she smiled, trying to feel more comfortable.

"Oh Universe, Zane, what happened?" Urana soothingly hugged Zane.

Zane could only shrug again, "I think we're well out of the Kansas time zone and it's obviously affected me, a natural time-traveller, more than it has you guys," she joked.

She needed the humour. She didn't want to think about what had happened. At least not yet. Then she remembered her strange dream about Mindscream.

"By the way, did any of you have strange dreams before we ended up here?" She spread her arms out wide, frowning. "Wherever here is!"

Aerl and Urana shook their heads. They looked at Azure who seemed frozen in thought.

"Deb?" Zane prompted, keen not to be alone in her freakishness.

Hazily, Azure recalled her dream of being with Novan, Classia and Elysius, and saving the Ribbon System from the Lore.

"Wow!" Zane digested the news. "I think you were really there," Zane said. "Either that was me and my erratic new-found powers or whoever it is manipulating our timeline. I've obviously aged for a reason. Maybe I was somewhere else during that time then I was returned, for whatever reason. Spooky." She shivered at the thought. Temporal-amnesia was not good.

The others thought about it in silence, but had no answers. They were as lost as Zane.

"You're an Astral?" said a new voice from behind them.

The man with the sword had woken up. He sat up casually searching for his sword, located behind Sceptre against a small ledge. Holding out his hand, the sword flew into it. Startled, the Starguards braced defensively.

With a charming smile, the stranger mollified them. He rose to his feet, dusted himself off, and sheathed the sword.

"I mean no harm. I just wanted my sword back. It's saved my life more than once." He caressed the hilt with a practiced movement. "So, an Astral, and from the looks of you three, kin to Alpha Rion and the blackheart Decion." He spat the last name out.

"And you are?" Sceptre politely demanded. He reminded Sceptre of someone, but he couldn't quite place it.

"A friend. I am Gordell Exmoor." The young sharp-faced man had a mane of white hair tied back in a pony-tail with a thin leather strap. His chain mail, which had traces of blue dye was now returning to its original dull gray sheen. It bore wide leather buckled straps on his torso, arms, and thighs. They in turn were studded with small knives and other assorted tools. His wide blue belt was adorned with a dull-red coloured stylised 'H' for the buckle, his sword sheath attached hung from his left hip.

A splutter of surprise greeted his announcement, Azure recovering quickest. "Bastian Exmoor's grandfather! Alpha Rion thought you might be dead!"

"You know my grandson?" Gordell smiled. "How is he? And my son, Charles? Did they or Alpha Rion send you to rescue me?"

"Rescue...?"

Gordell's smile faded from his face as he glanced concerned between them not understanding their confusion.

"We're here by accident," Zane explained. "Where are we?"

"Where?" Now it was Gordell's turn to look confused. "We're on Earth still, but millions of years in the future." He slumped against the ledge, looking like a defeated man. "I thought you were here to rescue me. Take me back to the past, no?" His disappointment seemed to weigh heavily upon each of them. It was almost overwhelming.

Fighting against the stupor, Zane voiced their thoughts. "What? Millions?" Zane scoffed. "No way!" She felt she would have noticed the time transition.

Suspicious, Sceptre added, "More to the point, Alpha Rion didn't mention you had psychic abilities. None of the Exmoors we met exhibited such abilities," he said, pointing to Gordell's sword.

Gordell actually laughed, like it was his own private joke. "I didn't, not until I came here through the portal. It was a trap meant for Alpha Rion and Tera, but I came through by accident, escaped to these hills where I was, for want of a better explanation, mentally kidnapped by remnants of the Chryrians left behind when the human race disappeared millennia ago. Though I don't like them being in my head, they have helped me to survive." A mixture of pride and bitterness edged his tone. "And I can help you defeat Valtare, Decion, and their lord's army." He told them of the gathering forces of humans, Surge, and Devouts. "I also have crystalators for images and storage."

"Devouts, here? They must have travelled time after the explosion," Zane said.

"No," Gordell corrected her, "these Devouts are from my time, sent by their Archwitch, the Lady Van Tager, Valtare's wife. She had disappeared before I had infiltrated Valtare's castle in the distant past."

The name of Valtare's wife transfixed them.

"Van Tager? Wasn't that the name of one of the scientists who created the E-Corps?" Zane pointed to the still prone Fusioneer. "She was Sagerhawk's assistant; it makes sense now why she had the Lore Stone."

"So you think she was sent to the twenty-first century by the Devout's lord to create more Devouts, conquer the world, and rid it of Exmoors, the only ones who could stop them?" Gordell surmised.

Zane nodded. "Sounds reasonable."

"Until the Starguards arrived and ruined their plans," Sceptre finished their thoughts. "That seems to have been our mission, set by the other Astrals," he added.

"But it backfired on all of us," replied Zane, gloomily.

It was a lot to take in. In the sheltered cul de sac they filled Gordell in about what had happened on Earth and to Alpha Rion after he had been brought forward in time.

"*Mon Dieu!* So much has been endured on Earth. I wish the Exmoors had done more to safeguard Earth. Too many sacrifices have been made." He looked around. "And it's led us here. And for what reason?"

"Where are all the humans?" Zane asked.

Gordell looked pained, whether from his memories or reply, it was hard to tell. "I don't know, or rather the Chryrians don't know. The humans had to escape an invasion and the Time Empress helped them," the Exmoor answered.

"Okay, whoa, the Time Empress? I keep hearing of her," Zane said.

"I did in my dream as well," echoed Azure. "Who is she?"

"I don't know," repeated Gordell.

"So what do you know?" Sceptre asked, impatiently, his trust hard to give. "Who is their lord?"

"Ah, that I do know: his name is Archron, another Astral," he replied, turning to Zane.

"Oh great, this makes so much bloody sense, now," Zane huffed, rolling her eyes. "First Netherlord tries to re-arrange the universe and now his brother is playing God in the future. What are they up to?" she asked Gordell, who was about to say 'I don't know'.

But it was Urana who answered. "The Knights Destina. That's who they are. The ancient and heretical Tomes of War stated that the Knights Destina will bring forth the ancient ones in the coming of the Storm, whatever that means. They will unmask the universe bringing war and begin again, so the Tomes say.' Her voice was low and respectful; a little scared.

"You know of the old Tomes, Rain?" Sceptre asked, his face tight and intrigued.

"Just what my father taught Cirrius and I. We grew up on the old legends."

Sceptre nodded. He had never held much stock in the old tales, but an old Celestian Knight like Hyphon the Sky Warrior would have instilled such myths into his younglings.

There was a stirring on the ground beside them. The E-Corps leader was awake. He sat up, rubbed his head. His red mask covered his upper face, his brown hair ruffled above. His manoeuvre suit was dark brown with a red flared jacket, red gloves, and a black belt. His eyes widened like saucers as he saw who surrounded him. In fear, he tried to scramble away, but Sceptre stopped him.

"Hey," he held his hands up in a plea of innocence. "We're not going to hurt you."

"Yeah, right!" a sceptical Fusioneer shot back looking around at them all, his eyes falling upon Gordell and his medieval armour. But he had stopped moving away from them.

"Listen to us!" Sceptre pleaded. "We're friends now. We're a long way from New York and we'll have to work together to get back."

Considering they were in the middle of a wasteland, Fusioneer relaxed a little.

"I need a drink," he aired aloud. "What the hell happened at Thane's?"

Patiently, the Starguards explained to him what had happened since the Starguards had originally arrived on twenty-first century Earth.

Half an hour later...

"You're crazy! Aliens?" Fusioneer scoffed adding a nervous laugh. He backed away slightly.

"Distant kin from another galaxy," replied Sceptre, calmly, not wanting spook the human any further.

"Well, I'm half human, at least," smiled Zane. Her breeziness didn't sit well with Sceptre or Fusioneer, both of whom gave her a look of displeasure.

Fusioneer stared at them all for a long while, not knowing whether to believe them, run, or fight. But one thing was for sure, he was alone.

"I'm not saying I believe you or not, but I would like to know where's the rest of my team: Flaunt, Venture, and Angelfire?" Fusioneer asked, still trying to digest the story he had been told.

"We don't know. We're missing a few members ourselves," Sceptre confirmed. His crystalator had not picked up any signals from Alpha Rion, Altair or Chalant, still.

"Hold on." Gordell closed his eyes and quick psi-scanned the area. He had been getting quite adept at tracking Valtare's troop movements from miles away. He didn't sense anyone. "All I can sense is us here and Valtare's group at Silver City. There's nothing, unless…" he scowled.

"They're not dead! They can't be!" Urana countered. "Why should we have been spared the explosion? We were grouped together."

Zane replied, "Well, maybe if we're being manipulated by this Time Empress, maybe the others are, too." She turned to Fusioneer with some good news. "But I know Kellis and Starshina aren't dead, at least. I met them in the twenty-third century. We were good friends," she added fondly.

"Hell's bells, the twenty-third century!" Fusioneer rubbed his head, making his hair comically stand on end. "So my team were thrown into another time and I'm stuck with you? Great!" Fusioneer bitterly mock her as he shook his head. He sat on a rock and threw his hands up in frustration.

"Sorry," muttered Zane. "I only know of Kellis and Starshina. Not the rest.

Azure snapped, "I don't understand why we're being flung around space and time. What is there to be gained?"

Zane looked at Sceptre. He caught her eyes and Urana's. Their collective pensive mood creating an awkward silence.

"What?" Azure asked, looking around agitated. "What aren't you telling me?"

Zane was suddenly interested in the ground. Urana hugged herself casting a sideways at Sceptre.

Finding himself with the unwanted responsibility, he sighed noisily. She had to know.

"We lost the first time around," Sceptre's quiet voice said.

"What!" Azure said, not sure she had heard him correctly.

"Deb," Sceptre addressed her by birth name, "when your Fath. . . " He corrected himself, "When the Traitor Synther and the Lore, attacked Magna Aura, we all died. All of us. It was only due to Phasia's intervention and the arrival of the Astrals that saved us by re-making the past, which included you. The first time you knew about your powers and your Loremaiden ancestry. It didn't save us. But the second time around it was the nature of your finding out about your father in battle which made the difference."

He smiled kindly at her, which she didn't return. She had her arms wrapped around herself.

"You used me," she said quietly, angrily. Her eyes burned into all of them.

"No," Sceptre replied gently.

Urana tried to back him up with a comforting arm on Azure's shoulder. Azure nudged it away, glaring at Sceptre.

"Without you, we would still be dead. But now I think we are re-fighting wars already lost and this . . . Time Empress is trying to prevent the Knights Destina from winning. We're all being used as cosmic chess pieces, and piece by piece, move by move, we're saving the universe."

"You are kidding me," Fusioneer drawled sarcastically. "What would they want me for?"

Urana said, "You, human, carry the genes of our kin who crashed and survived on Earth thousands of years ago. Your powers were activated by the Lore Stone via those genes."

"You're practically one of us," Zane said, feeling a little sorry for Fusioneer and all the information dumped on him.

"*Dieu*, I thought I had problems!" a fascinated Gordell quipped.

Fusioneer thought better at scoffing at this latest piece of news, realising the full impact of the situation. "I'm part alien." He closed his eyes, rubbing his hands over his temples as a dull ache began to throb.

Uncaring of Fusioneer's anguish, Urana added, "But surely with her powers the Time Empress could have defeated the Lore and Knights Destina by herself and be done with these games?"

Sceptre thought about this. "Then maybe it's not just the Lore and Knights Destina that we're dealing with and everyone has their part to play, even you Fusioneer."

The E-Corps leader stopped nurturing his migraine in time to shrug, resigned to his fate. "So now what?" he asked, depressed about his less-than all-American heritage.

"Well for one, we shouldn't stay out here for too long," Gordell urged. "The sun isn't fully up and it'll get really hot then. I've got a cave hideaway up in those ridges," he pointed over to his far left. "You're quite welcome to stay in there and we can make plans. I'm afraid there's not much food and what there is, is either small and furry, or a bitter green weed. Let's go." He started off up the track he had initially come down.

The Starguards looked to Sceptre. Would he trust another on their word? Would he follow someone else's lead?

The gold-clad Starguard made a quick internal decision, pursed his lips, and glided over to Gordell.

A little surprised, Urana and Azure glanced sideways at each other with sly grins. Zane followed. Fusioneer brought up the rear, a rather sullen figure.

Gordell regarded the newly arrived human. He sensed a great loss within him. Fusioneer hadn't been given a warm welcome and hardly felt part of this team, but if they were going to survive they would have to be more than a team, they would have to be a family. Electing himself as the paternal mentor, he decided to get the ball rolling.

Shouting back over his shoulder, he asked: "So what's your real name then, Fusioneer?"

Fusioneer seemed startled by the question. He'd been in secret-identity mode for years and now someone had asked the question outright. The others stopped, crouching low, along a rocky ridge and glanced back in expectation.

Fusioneer grinned and then laughed. He felt like he was being outed and among fellow superbeings at that. He shook his head in resigned disbelief as he put his hands up to his head and grudgingly removed his mask. He ruffled his brown hair, revealing a handsome thirty-something face with a five-o'clock shadow and piercing brown eyes. He felt naked, but also liberated, able to finally say in public, such as it was:

"My name is Jay Jupiter Lundy, but my friends call me J.J. I am. . . I was the leader of the E-Corps. I manipulate matter, I'm formerly of the U.S. Air Force, and I love seafood." He shrugged, feeling silly, waiting for any response.

Gordell laughed. "*Enchante*, J.J." He walked over and gave J.J. a bear hug, shaking his hand after. "I'm Gordell Exmoor. I, like you, have special genes in me and my family is very long-lived. The Astrals, Zane's people, used us as agents to battle the Devouts. I used to live in the twelfth century, but was unceremoniously dumped here almost two years ago where I now share my mind with psi-creatures called Chryrians who helped me to survive."

J.J. wasn't sure of his story, but couldn't doubt it. "Nice to meet you," was all he could say, stepping forth to shake his hand.

Zane came up to him and put out her hand, which he shook. "I'm Zane, time traveller and one-time advisor to a great mutual friend called Lynn Kellis, who missed you very much, J.J. We'll find her again, I'm sure. Starshina is safe; she's going out with my brother."

J.J. smiled, visibly moved. Then he looked closer at Zane as if remembering something. "You're, no . . . " he second-guessed himself. "Are you the speedy girl I saw Kellis with at Thane's?"

Zane smiled back. "That was me! Younger and blonder."

J.J. shook his head. "Man, this time travel shit is hurting my head. The others laughed then gathered around for their introductions.

"I'm Aerl, the Sceptre, though you knew that. We're going to get out of here and make the people responsible pay for their actions. And we'll need your help."

Aerl also put out his hand, J.J. shaking it enthusiastically.

"Welcome to the Starguards, J.J."

Azure and Urana also introduced themselves, not knowing they had almost met Kellis and Starshina while out clubbing in New York all those aeons ago.

Gordell let the mutual respect and relaxed air sift through them, helped on by a bit of psionic pushing here and there. He let it naturally die down, before announcing they should move on.

The new team trampled onwards and upwards with renewed vigour, any lingering doubts about each other firmly in the back of their minds.

As they neared Gordell's cave, Sceptre devised a new plan. "We need to go on the offensive and demand answers from

Archron and Decion. There are enough of us to take them on and see what we can learn."

"It's a risky idea, they'll surely try to kill us," Gordell added with some hint of humour.

"Well then, we'll know where we stand. We'll know where Decion stands, too. He's a traitor for turning on his own brother and the Starguards. He will die with them if he fights against us." Sceptre looked each of them in the eye, doubt in their faces, before adding, "Besides, they might have some food . . ." That at least got him a few nervous laughs.

>*Such a bad idea*< Gordell heard J.J.'s lamented thought. He patted him on the shoulder.

"Don't worry, we'll be okay. I've got friends in these hills and caves who will help us."

Fusioneer gave him a startled look. "Did you . . . ?" he held his thoughts, not wanting to know. This was all too surreal for him.

The group moved on again, now following a path only Gordell could see.

"Millions of years, my ass," J.J. grumbled, looking around at the barren landscape, "We're in Nevada!"

CHAPTER TWO

"... And that's when I drained the dwarf star of all its energy to recharge my voidspear," Archron eyes widened as he bragged. "You should have seen the looks on the faces of the other Astrals," he bellowed, chortling at his own story. His head lolled back and forth in cherished memory.

In front of him, Valtare and Decion laughed halfheartedly at Archon's tall tale even as Archron's mood darkened.

Valtare knew his lord's mood could change at the flick of a neutrino.

"But seriously, let me tell you a story." Archron emphasised his last words leaning toward them.

His breath smelled of an ancient brewed wine he had transported from Greece. A ceramic jug decorated with Greek warriors fighting a sea monster and three half-empty tall brass cups lay on the table between them. If Archron had not been an Astral, Valtare would have thought him a barbaric heathen for his choice in wines alone.

What made an Astral drink himself into a state? he wondered. *What horror? What memories?*

Valtare had been denied the choice of bringing his own French wines. And who knew what this nectar was Decion spoke of. But Archron was a bore—all stories and bluster washed down with swill. He could tell by the way Decion hid his dark scowl that he thought the same. Decion's mind was full of dark thoughts these days.

How did we end up here? Valtare thought gloomily to himself.

Archron carried on oblivious to Valtare's inner disillusionment as he began another tale. "My brother, Lazeron, and I fought at Troy. That's where our lives changed." His voice was grave. "A strange mystic creature appeared to our families and revealed our true heritage to us. Her name was Phasia. And

23

she fully awakened our powers." His eyes gleamed at the adventures of yesteryears gone by. "We were taken through Earth's history and into the far future learning and training as warriors," he clenched his fists, "as scientists, philosophers, architects, and explorers. We were told we were the temporal counterpart to our kin, the heroic Starguards," he acknowledged Decion with a genuine smile. "We were Astrals— the Star People—and we were the last lineage of the great Celestian Knights.

"But we Astrals changed Earth's history in ways we didn't anticipate or understand. It was I who discovered the Exmoors' secret after coming across the same long-lived family over the centuries, having fought with them by Alexander the Great's side and other battles. My brother and I recruited them as agents, handed them technology ahead of its time, all this to defend Earth from the threats like the Lore and even from fellow kin, the Devouts.

We Astrals then retreated to our own dimension to build our temporal fortress, the Chronopolis. Without us Astrals, the Exmoors and Devouts would have not have know their destinies and would have destroyed the world many times over warring amongst each other. Without us, there would not have been any E-Corps or superhuman wars on Earth. Maybe the Chryrian humans," he pointed casually at Valtare, "would be in charge or maybe the Lore would have consumed Earth."

Cal Xarien, Archron the Astral, paused in his monologue as he paced around his quarters. His blood-red Corinthian-style helmet sat on his desk watching them with hollow eyes. Both Cal Xarien and Lazeron had a love for the Greek and Roman Empires, hence Archron's armour was a stylised mix of Greek and Roman fare. He wore it boldly complete with a preference for a blood-red tunic with pleat-like *pteruges*. A gold-trimmed leather breastplate covered his torso, his waist was girdled by a gold belt. Anachronistic long boots and gauntlets, and a black cloak completed his ensemble. His hand played around his breastplate in a Napoleonesque fashion as he stopped to reiterate points in his story.

"That's why the Knights Destina were resurrected." Archron halted at the only shelf in the room reverently picking up and stroking the spine of his copy of the Tomes of War. It had been given to him by his mother—the Celestian Knight, Destina.

The Tomes of War were sacred to Archron who studied them over and over. They revealed the ways of the universe and the reason for their existence. And from the Tomes, Archron had come to know that Earth, out of all the worlds in the universe, would hold the key to the universe's survival, the meaning becoming clearer every time he read the Tomes.

Proudly, he proclaimed, "The Knights Destina will destroy the Lore. And we will rule the universe. Earth and Magna Aura will be united under Knights Destina rule. It's a shame my brother is not here now to share in our toast, but he has his own mission to accomplish for our cause. But in time," he said with no irony, "he will return to us. That is why we have come here, built a fortress, this Silver City, for our army of Starguard, human, and Surge allies. But time is catching up to us. Our enemies are coming. Some are already here; those who would try to stop our new universe of peace. There will have to be sacrifices, which is why I've asked you here."

Archron studied the two men, their carefully bemused faces slipping into concentrated determination. Cape swirling behind him he brusquely returned to and sat down behind his stone-carved desk (a personal memento from the walls of Troy he had always bragged), his voidspear mounted horizontally on the gray metal wall behind him; the only weapon Archron held. Handed down to him by Destina, it was part of a matched pair with his brother's nethersword.

The two-and-a-half meter long gray-purple metal staff was inscribed with ancient rune spells from the Tomes of War. They allegedly warded off the Lore. Crowning the staff was a crystal orb encased in a thin lattice. Two sharp pointed blades stabbed out at the centre on either side of the orb, the longer forward-facing blade pointed downwards, the rear blade curved upwards. The voidspear was an entropy vane, a chaos cage, utilising entropic energy to destroy order. Much of the Silver City had been forged using the voidspear, Archron, the chaos-architect, a genius at wielding chaos to create order. That is what he stood for. He was destined to remake the universe in the Knights Destina's image.

He regarded Valtare, who projected confidence and understanding. "I know, my loyal friend, you have been wondering what your role is in the war to come. You may have sensed it already, but you have distant kin out there in the hills."

Valtare nodded in confirmation, his usual smug smile absent from his face as he listened attentively.

"They are the Chryrian survivors from Earth, millions of years ago, the same kind of which inhabit you. I have no doubt they have had a hand in keeping this Guillaume imposter alive for so long." He paused, knowing his next words would be hard to say and hear. "I want you to send L'Coyle and his men to flush them out, see if you can control them. We will need them to both reinforce and counter the Surge should they rebel." His voice took on a more calculating tone as Valtare's realisation grew. "Yes, I want them to inhabit L'Coyle and his men..." He stopped at the shocked look on Valtare's face, but carried on regardless. "This will make them more formidable in battle," he finished with resoluteness.

Valtare was taken aback. "You... you want the Duke and my men to be merged with the Chryrians? That's madness! They won't survive." His shock was palpable, yet tinged with some bout of jealously at having to share his psionic powers with men he considered beneath him. "Does L'Coyle know of your grand plans for him?" He kept his voice even, his face stone-like. His heart burned in anger.

"No," Archron's voice and gaze were hard. "And he won't or I'm sure he'll back out. He'll die anyway in this war without our support. You know it's for his own good, Valtare. The psionics will give him and his men much more power and the ability to survive what is ahead. Besides, if we told him, he wouldn't be able to get near the Chryrians before they read his mind, found out our plans, and killed him. Best if they think they have the upper hand and then you can take over their control and training. Yes?"

Valtare pondered it over. They were sacrificing a lot of men, but Archron made sense. "Yes, my Lord," he said, not meeting his eyes. "For their survival." But he had to ask another question. An important one. And Archron's reply would determine his actions.

"I must ask, Archron, what happened to my wife? She was supposed to be here with us. Is there any word from her?"

Archron's face was still a mask, but had softened somewhat. He could only tell what he knew. "I do not know, Valtare. The deal Lady Elisabeth and I struck was for me to time-port her into the future where she could breed and deliver to me an army of male and female Devouts. I can only assume things did not go well, as I cannot find her timeline after her encounter with the Starguards. I'm sorry."

Valtare was crestfallen, but he couldn't give up hope. He nodded dejectedly. He was alone in his wife's quest now.

I will honour you, my dear, he sighed deeply.

Archron next turned to Decion. "The only way we will know for sure is to ask the Starguards. And that's where you come in, Decion"

L'Coyle's description of his attackers had led Decion to identify Aerl, Urana and Azure. He wasn't sure of the speedster or other male.

Archron edged closer as if studying Decion for the truth. "Your Starguard kin; do you know what Sceptre's plan of attack will be?"

Decion laughed to himself. Here he was working with someone he swore he would never associate with. The Astrals may have saved Magna Aura, but their power and assumption that they could change time whenever and wherever they wanted was dangerous. Yet here he was, because he found himself agreeing with what Archron wanted to achieve. The universe needed to be restructured and the Lore to be destroyed. Decion wanted to be a part of that glory; it was his birthright. He found himself both admiring and loathing Archron's ambition. He didn't need to consider what Sceptre would do. He was an open book.

"I know exactly what Sceptre would do. He will attempt to come here in surprise and talk to us, first. That's his way. Weak diplomacy!"

Archron chuckled. "Hmm, really? So what can you do to stop him?" The Astral was intrigued.

Decion grinned through his thick beard, spooking even Archron. "Can you spare me ten Surge?"

After a little more than half an hour traversing the dry hills and sun-cracked canyons, the Starguards finally arrived at Gordell's hidden cave. He telekinetically rolled several large boulders out of the way revealing a hidden entrance. With alacrity, everyone entered, the passage wide and tall enough so as not to stoop. Once everyone was in, Gordell rolled the boulders back into place.

A lone crystal in the center of the cavern gave off a low light for visibility. As if arriving home from a long day at work masks, visors, and gloves were removed with ceremony. A more relaxed air prevailed.

Or rather, an air of something wafted toward them.

"Shit! What's that smell?" J.J. turned his nose up.

Gordell looked abashed, but indignant. "Pardon the smell, I wasn't expecting visitors." He pointed to a dark corner. "The toilet's open." He concentrated at a hole in the ground and a small boulder began to roll over it.

"No, hold on, I've got to go!" J.J. ran over to the spot to relieve himself. "Don't look!" he shot back at Urana who looked away aghast.

"Once you're finished," Gordell said, exasperated, "I'll give you a tour around our home for a while."

J.J. zipped back up, a smile of relief on his face.

"Anyone else?" Gordell asked. There were no relies. With alacrity he closed up the toilet. "*Alors. Voila*, welcome to my home!"

Gordell showed them around and they were surprised the cave was much larger than they had thought with a couple of short passages leading to extra chambers.

"No back door?" J.J. asked, feeling slightly claustrophobic. "I could make one for you." He itched to show off his powers.

"No need, I can carve things out myself," Gordell said, as small boulders and rocks grew from the ground to form seats and tables for his astonished and impressed guests. "Benefits of having a few extra Chryrians in the head. Not only am I telepathic, but also psychokinetic, besides a few other things I haven't figured out yet. I've been here for so long. I have nothing to do but keep track of Valtare and his movements, plus to practice with my new abilities. But I am glad you are here, I thought I would go insane without more company." He almost sounded lonely, his eyes flirting with the ground.

"How do you know we're not figments of your imagination?" laughed J.J.

"J.J.!" Urana admonished him, feeling sorry for Gordell.

Gordell pondered that, "Hah! I don't mind. I had not thought of that," he said, to more general laughter. "Well if you are just my imagination, then you are surely welcome anyway, and I won't die alone." The laughter was more muted this time. But the mutual company was appreciated all the same.

"I wonder what happen to Altair, Alpha Rion and Chalant?" Urana asked. "Everyone is accounted for except them."

"And the Exmoors," put in Gordell. "My family, how are they?"

Zane could only answer on the future of one of them as she recounted Simon's role in the Axalan War. "He was the only Exmoor I knew or heard of in the twenty-third century and he never mentioned any family. But I can only assume that if he survived then others must have as well." Her voice belayed her confidence.

"We must assume we are the only survivors, here, now. This is our life now, so we have to think of ourselves as a unit and not about the others…" Aerl started.

"Always the pragmatist, Aerl," Urana cut in. "But we need to think of them, of home, and the future. That's always been your problem, cousin, you're too mission-minded; if Altair was here .. ."

"Altair! He's the one who got us here in the first place by touching the Lore Stone," Aerl shouted. "Without him…"

"How dare you blame him!" Urana rounded angrily on Aerl. They stared at each other, Urana's teeth gritted.

"Actually, he was a liability to you guys," J.J. causally added. "We thought he was the weak link with his temper. Almost a psychopath. What was his problem?" He turned in askance to the Starguards.

Urana shot J.J. a look choking any more words back into his mouth. He decided to keep quiet, while Azure and Zane kept their heads down.

"Whatever was going on between you and Altair affected both of your judgments," Aerl retorted, sorrowfully remembering The Goth fiasco. "My brother was always hot-headed and if he were here now he'd probably be fighting someone for no reason or maybe even have joined Archron and his men, who knows."

Urana shook in violent umbrage at Aerl's last statement. But she kept her voice low. "That's unfair, Aerl. You know he wouldn't have joined them. You've always judged him. You never really knew him. Well, I loved him. Your whole family was screwed up, and maybe that affected the both of you; taking it out on each other over the years, but just stop it. Stop it now!" she pointed a finger at him. "New beginnings, Aerl. So stop being so, so... what's that Fifth, sorry, human term... up yourself, and get a personality!" She added for good measure, arms folded, though Azure beside her could see her half-hidden self-satisfied smile.

A collective stifled gasp from the others was the only sound heard, but if any of Urana's words stung Aerl, he didn't show it. He gave Urana a weary look, returned with a frosty glare of her own.

Their host decided to step in and cool things down. "Well, so much for small chat. I think we should eat. Un moment." He rose up from his rocky perch and disappeared into another small dark chamber. A few moments later he returned with some skewered pieces of sweet-smelling meat on a stick.

Mouth watering, Zane asked, "How'd you cook the meat?"

Gordell tapped the side of his head. "I can make fire with my mind, too, and heat up the rocks."

He smiled, demonstrating as he touched a large square rock sitting at the centre of the group, heating it gently. He placed the food on it like a hot plate. The others gravitated to it like cavemen around a campfire. They picked up a stick each and tucked into the roasted meat. It was surprisingly good.

Zane was impressed. "You're pyrokinetic as well? You've got everything up there to survive." She indicated his head.

"Just about." Gordell didn't mention they were eating his entire week's food stock. He'd have to hunt again and find more sticks.

"What is it?" J.J. asked sniffing the meat like a fussy eater. He eyed up the scrawny offerings with distaste.

Gordell lips screwed up. "Some kind of mammal type. It's tasty enough. Try it." He took a bite himself.

"As long as they're not the ultimate descendants of humans." J.J. was decidedly humourless this time eyeing up the spitted roast again.

"Just eat it," Zane laughed, also secretly hoping it wasn't a distant remnant of humanity on a stick. "Lucky Starshina isn't here though!" she joked to J.J.

"She still a vegetarian?" J.J commentated on the Russian E-Corp member.

"Yep, tried to turn me and Lynn, but it didn't take."

"Good for you." He took a bite. "Not bad. Just like chicken," J.J. licked his fingers.

"Hmm, told you." Gordell laughed to himself. He wasn't going to break it to them the meals were just large rats; a delicacy throughout the ages.

"Tera would have loved to see you like this, Gordell," said Zane, in between sucking bones.

"Yes, especially now," Gordell replied, off-handedly.

"Why?" Her question caught everyone's attention.

"Och," Gordell looked at them in surprise. "I didn't mention? We're in what was once northern Africa. It's all changed now, continental drifts and all, but this is the area Tera was born. The Chryrians in these hills have told me the history of when they arrived on Earth. They were the original ones to inhabit the people here, until a war broke out between Tera's brothers and their followers. Many people died and the Chryrians inside them left their bodies, banded with others, and decided to stay unattached. They've lived here ever since and been seen from time to time mistaken for ghosts and spirits good or bad, but not merging with humans, until I came." He noticed the shocked look on Zane's face. "What's wrong, Zane?"

Zane couldn't believe the coincidence, Aaron and Tera, brother and sister? She had thought about it while back in New York, but could it be true?

"What tribe lived here, Gordell? The D'anaa?" she asked excitedly.

Gordell seemed taken aback by the question. J.J. winced as Gordell's eyes blanked out to white, his gaze shifting inward for the answer for a few seconds. When Gordell returned, he seemed shocked. "Yes, one of the tribes was the D'anaa! How did you know?" It was his turn to be curious.

A wave of pleasure swept over Zane. "My brother, Aristedes, he was here, he saved Aranu of the D'anaa tribe way back in 2400 BC. He was dying in the desert and Aristedes somehow heard his telepathic cry for help and brought him to the twenty-third century. He was a great friend to us all and I believe he and Lynn were in love." She looked over at J.J. who seemed surprised that Lynn Kellis could fall in love with anyone. She carried on: "Aaron, as we called him, was searching for his sister, but his brother had tried to kill him. I think Tera, or Chalant, as we know her now was his sister. But who was their brother?"

Gordell's gaze shifted away again as answers came to him from within. The others looked between Zane and Gordell following the story with rapt attention.

"Yes, T'ra was Aranu's sister and their brother was P'ntar. He disappeared and was never heard from again."

"P'ntar?" Zane repeated to herself. "Hmm, didn't come across him." Another thought struck her instantly. "P'ntar. Penthor? Penthor Thane?" She stared at the other in disbelief.

"He did have a guarded past," Sceptre said.

33

Zane shrugged. "It could make sense if he was involved with Van Tager, but he didn't have any powers. Interesting though Thank you, Gordell. I hope Aaron and Chalant caught up with each other. I can see them all now, Aaron and Lynn, Chalant and Alpha Rion—what a great family that would be." She laughed with pleasure which brightened the cavern's atmosphere.

Sadness drew over Gordell's face as something was revealed to him by his Chryrians. The past had not passed as Zane would have wished. But maybe a better future could be rescued.

His thoughts were interrupted by a curious Azure. "How have the Chryrians survived for millions of years? Surely their energy would have dissipated by now?" she asked.

Gordell went quiet, seemingly reluctant to talk about it. But after a while admitted. "Well, for one, they do have tiny amounts of offspring in a way, but there are other ways. They don't talk about it much, but I suppose you can call it psychopophagy. A few volunteers give up their energy to the others to feed on, which lasts for tens of thousands of years. There have been many sacrifices." Gordell eyes fell to the ground in remembrance of past Chryrians he never knew, but felt within himself.

They remained in silence for a while, the sound of last meat, fat and bone chewing breaking the awkward and sombre moment.

"Och!" Gordell's sudden loud outburst startled everyone as he jerked up. He had remembered the mystery which had so intrigued him when he had first come to the cave.

"Aerl, I just remembered ..." gaining everyone's attention as he picked up his distinctive sword. "I found writing on the sword, the blade. Maybe one of you would recognise it." He offered the sword and his meticulous crystalator recordings to Aerl.

Aerl studied the sword admiringly, using the crystalator in his visor to scan the sword and copy data from Gordell's crystalator. He was sure the revealed script was archaic Celestian, but he couldn't interpret everything. But then he reached a name which was unmistakable.

His face opened up in surprise. "Havens Hand of the Celestri Clan, wielder of the Havensword."' he read the inscription. "This was lost in the depths of time and war. Universe!" he whispered in awe. "Gordell, where did you get this from?" His tone was hushed, reverent.

Forgetting his argument with Urana, he passed her the sword for her perusal, who silently, graciously accepted.

Gordell shrugged. "I've always had it. It's been handed down in my family since before we met the Astrals. Our legends say it was the very first sword on Earth, given to an ancestor who aided a strange warrior from a faraway land. We called it the Adamsword. But we never knew about the writing on the sword or the owner's name." He stared at the sword with a new pride. "Havens Hand, who was he?"

A rare smile stole across Aerl's face. "Well, *our* legends tell us that before the first Celestian Knights, there was another heroic tradition: the Celestri Clan. One particular generation disappeared in the midst of a battle, never to be heard from again. Maybe they came to Earth, too. Havens Hand was the father, Haven Mark who in turn sired Teo Venga, one of the missing Celestri who held the sword last. You are certainly very lucky to have this sword, Gordell. It will keep you alive."

Urana passed the sword back to Aerl, ignoring the others who wanted to handle it. Aerl returned it and the crystal to Gordell.

"That is all I can tell you about the sword, but hopefully the crystalator recordings will yield more information. Give it some time."

"Thank you, Aerl. It is a privilege to know the sword's history. Looks like we were all meant to meet together for this final battle."

"I agree," Zane said, glad some peace had returned to the cavern. "And I've been thinking…"

"Uh, oh," Azure rolled her eyes.

"Hey, seriously," Zane took the tease amid the laughter. "For me to have aged so rapidly, I must have gained some temporal powers besides speed and learned to use them by now. If I have, then I can port us right into the fortress, no need for long exposed marches. What do you think, Aerl?"

Aerl thought about it for a few moments. "Test it! Give it a go. Try time-porting somewhere."

Zane brimmed with eager anticipation at the thought of her first solo time-port. "Okay, I'll see if I can reach the other Astrals, get some help."

"What, through all this time? Millions of years have gone by," Azure almost scoffed.

Urana hissed her disapproval at Azure, quieting her. Beside her, J.J. also held his tongue for fear of another scoulding.

"It's a good idea, Zane," Urana encouraged her. "How will it work?"

Zane explained as simply as she could. "The Chronopolis is a state of time. It can be found by an Astral from any point in time," she noted. "I'll be back in a sec…"

She closed her eyes remembering everything she had been taught about time-porting. It was like opening a door first in the mind and then allowing temporal energy to flood in until you were through the door's threshold and in the temporal energy flow. It presented like a shining door in front of her (and like a round flash of white light to the others who gasped). She entered and blinked out of existence before anyone could wave goodbye…

. . . and hit a dead-end wall of compressed time as she emerged in the Astral dimension. Zane rubbed her nose where it had impacted against an invisible force of energy. She couldn't wriggle much against the energy pressing against her. The Chronopolis was nowhere to be seen through the barrier. Zane concentrated and tried to stare through the wall, but her vision could not penetrate beyond the trapped light.

Circumnavigating the time temple she discovered overlapping temporal and exotic energy pressing in around her, buffeting her path, distorting her senses. She couldn't even time-port further back in time to see what had happened—time traps saw to that, reverting her course in loop after loop. There was no secret door, no hidden messages, no nothing.

The Astrals were gone.

"Why me?" Zane slumped in the energy field holding back her tears. *What happened? Where have they gone?* She was truly alone now. She took a deep breath composing herself. Without looking back, she opened a rippling white portal to the awaiting timestream and glided back to Earth...

... to land straight in the middle of another commotion. Her presence was barely registered as J.J. was freaking out over something.

"What's going on?" Zane asked, "I was only gone for a few minutes."

The others turned to look at her with varying degrees of amusement on their faces, except J.J.

He shouted, "Yeah, well you've done something to me," J.J. accused Zane. "My powers have changed! Look!" He held out his hands and rocks started to levitate. He himself rose a few feet off the ground. "See! I'm supposed to be able to turn dirt and rock into bedding or even edible food, not make them fly about!"

"Calm down, J.J.," urged Aerl.

"Easy for you to say ..." J.J. snapped

"I thought you were the tough guy?" Zane tried to humour him, remembering his fearless leadership of the E-Corps.

"Yeah, that was when I could turn bullets into marshmallows," J.J. shot back. "I was famous for that!"

He didn't mention the fact no E-Corps scientist was sure of the nature of the marshmallows or whether they were edible or turn back into bullets one day. And no one had volunteered to eat one even after exhaustive testing. In fact the marshmallowed bullets had been dispatched to and exhibited in museums around the world. As Fusioneer, J.J. had proudly taken a photo with every single gooey bullet. But now he would never get to do so again.

Urana laughed at him, much to his annoyance. "J.J., you've had your powers for a few years, while we've had ours for a generation. You can adapt better than we would."

"Yeah," Azure caught on, flattering him more, "You're taking it bravely; more so than when I was told I had powers, was a Starguard, and the daughter of an evil Celestian Knight, no less. We've all had to adapt and on the plus side, as the best flyer here, I can teach you how to fly."

J.J. stopped squawking, taking a moment to reflect. "Fly? What, like Superman? You think so?" His unshaven face lit up at the thought.

"Of course," Azure assured him.

"Best flyer?" Urana muttered, taking the bait in good heart.

"Yes, the best, Rain. I was a Sky Warrior and am the Goddess of the Darkening Blue. You and Sceptre are better in space, but in the atmosphere, it's me." Smugness hugged her face.

Urana and Aerl looked at each other, Aerl conceding with a shrug.

"Well," Zane said, "Maybe the Lore stone changed me as well since I'm half-human. I was about ten years younger when the explosion in New York happened, now look at me. And my temporal powers seem to work." She was still shocked from her time at the Chronopolis but she couldn't bear to tell them yet.

She continued. "The explosion changed Lynn and Starshina as well. In the twenty-third century, Lynn had no powers when I met her and Starshina had gone from being Angelfire to having winter powers. We called her Winterborne. We all adapted, J.J., you can too." Another thought occurred to her, "Actually, matter manipulation was the power of the leader of the Superions, Mode, but he was Axalan. Anyway, so now you have gravity powers, cool!"

J.J. pulled a face, slowly reconciling himself to the idea of having new powers.

Gordell chuckled, "Well we can't call you Fusioneer anymore."

J.J. recoiled, as if he'd been kicked out of the neighbourhood superhero club, "Whaddya mean? Come on guys!"

"Your name has to match your power or personality," Zane stated, as if she had a superhero rules manual to hand.

"Really?" J.J. thought, seemingly warning to the idea. He loved the name Fusioneer. It was futuristic and unique and he didn't want to ditch it. But he wasn't a Fusioneer anymore. "Hmm, okay, how about Graviteer? Gravitor?" he pondered.

Mute response.

"Airvader?"

There were more nods of dissent.

"How about Force as in the force of gravity?" Zane said, before J.J. could come up with more inane *nom de guerre*.

"Yeah," came the chorus of consent.

"Fitting," Gordell approved.

"Hmm, okay," J.J. mulled it over. "Elegant. Force as in US Air Force, too. That'll do. I suppose I'd better get practising," he said, as more rocks began to float.

They laughed at his tricks as J.J. juggled rocks, "Look, no hands!" He continued with his show.

Azure shuffled over and sat by Zane. "So, how was home Zane," she asked, excited to hear about the Astrals, but Zane's frown told another story.

She drew in a depressed sigh. "I tried going back to the Chronopolis, but there was no one there. It's sealed off and they've gone. I tried another time period, but of course, they think I'm dead, so they would have moved on without me." Azure gave her a comforting hug.

Now it was J.J.'s turn to laugh at someone else's misfortune. "Can't say I feel sorry for you, Time Girl," he laughed sarcastically, ending his display with six rocks piled neatly on top of each other. He sat back on his rock pleased with his efforts.

Urana blasted two of the rocks caking J.J.'s face in dust.

"Ow!" he cried.

Zane and Azure were looking daggers at him.

"What? Seriously, we sound like a comic book: changing powers, time travel, the dead turning up alive. It's like a re-boot of the universe. I wonder who would play me in a movie," J.J. mused.

"I can't say we saw many of those back on Earth," Aerl said, "Nor read many comic books, but I understand your meaning."

There was a general consensus that they were in this together. Despite the shocks to their lives and arguments there seemed to be a congenial mood. Gordell decided it was time to steer them back to the business at hand.

"*Alors*, so what is the plan, Aerl, for the Fortress?" Gordell asked.

Everyone instantly centred upon Sceptre. He sucked in a long breath through his nose When he spoke, the others knew he had already thought out a plan.

"Well, first we get some rest then we need to train as a team, get Force and Zane up to speed, so to speak, then Zane will port us into the Fortress and we'll get some answers…"

"Or kick butt!" Zane finished for him.

"That, too!" Aerl grudgingly admitted.

"By the way, how are you feeling, Rain?" asked Azure. "Past Earth didn't seem to agree with you."

Urana reacted in surprise as if hearing for the first time she had been ill at all. "Actually, I feel okay." She smiled agreeably, head tilted and nodding. "Do you think the Lore stone affected us?"

"It shouldn't have," Aerl said. "Our manoeuvre suits would have protected us against any penetrating rays from the explosion."

Urana made a noise of agreement. "But I am fine," she reiterated.

"Good," Aerl replied. "I'm happy for that." The earlier arguments seemed to have been forgotten between them.

Conversation drifted away in a short silent spell.

"So I suppose it's girls in one bedroom and guys in another," J.J. broke the contemplative mood. "Too bad my old powers have gone, I could have made some decent bedding from the rocks."

"Marshmallow beds?" Zane laughed, everyone joining in.

"Haha." J.J. knew he had been one-upped.

"I believe I can help in that department though," Gordell said.

Suddenly, the cave was filled with a silvery fist-sized mist with snaking tendrils and a pulsating center of light. They all felt faint whisper in their minds. The mist merged into Gordell's head. He shivered for a few seconds, almost convulsed, and then sneezed loudly, taking everyone by surprise.

"Oh, Jesus, no! What the freaking hell?" J.J. was already scrambling away over the sandy floor toward the wall. Everyone else tensed in shock.

"What was that?" Zane shouted out. "Gordell, are you okay?" She tried to hide her disgust.

Gordell shook his head, holding up his hand to calm everyone. "Don't worry. It's a Chryrian. Another one just decided to enter my mind. I'm still not used to it, like an allergy. Each confers me with another ability. This one can manipulate objects. I'll be making the beds tonight, J.J.," he smiled with a wink.

J.J. just nodded silently back. But didn't move from his safe place.

"Whew!" Zane breathed again. "It's weird. After knowing Aaron for so long, I never knew what a Chryrian looked like," she laughed nervously, "Kinda cute and scary at the same time."

Gordell laughed heartily, remembering is first experience with them. "Well imagine being personally invaded by them after centuries of thinking they were the enemy. I haven't apologised enough to them for what I did to merged human Chryrians in the past. I've got five in my head now and quite a bit of power and luckily I haven't gone insane as the first humans they contacted did. Mostly they look like that, those tendrils wrapping around nerves and brain stuff so we become integrated, but there are some Chryrians who have taken on ghostly humanoid forms. I call them Silverwraiths. They're a bit hostile to non-Chryrians, but allies to us at least," Gordell explained. "Mostly."

"Ah, our secret weapon against the Surge then?" surmised Aerl.

"Against them all really, except Lore. Chryrians might not be able to read Starguard or Astral minds, but they can still cause havoc in trying or even just use their psychokinetic and other abilities. We have our own army in these hills." Gordell looked pleased with himself.

"They . . . they wouldn't try and enter me would they?" J.J. whispered, a tinge of apprehension creeping into his voice.

"No, I assure you they will only enter you voluntarily," Gordell said. "Though with myself it was a matter of my survival."

"Good," J.J. said relieved. "Good. But now I have to go to the head again before I piss myself in fear!"

They were all still laughing when Gordell suddenly looked up in alarm as if seeing through the cave walls.

"Get down!" he shouted.

There was no time as tons of rock came tumbling down and buried them.

The average height of a Surge was eight-foot; average weight two tons. Their metallic skin rippled in compressed folds over and over like a living samurai sword combining strength and flexibility. This enabled Surge to absorb as much energy as possible for their sustenance, locomotion, and weaponry. Surge were practically indestructible. Dropped from a great height, Surge could survive the experience mostly down to their physical nature, but also due to the fact that they would absorb any heat and other sources of energy created in order to heal themselves rapidly.

Ten Surge surfed in low orbit, guided psionically by Valtare from the ground. From above they were led by Spearhead, a giant of a Surge, and their leader. Eight other huge Surge flanked him. But the biggest Surge of them all was Chasm.

At twelve-foot and five tons, Chasm was a giant among Surge with large extra armoured platelets covering his torso, arms and legs, and a double-axe-like formation growing upward from his right shoulder. Unusually for a Surge, who were normally monotone in colour, Chasm was three-toned, with his black and silver body shaded in areas with burnished gold, the result of a cataclysmic collision with an asteroid. Chasm had impacted with so much energy he had also absorbed a considerable amount of the asteroid's rich mineralogy. His size and colour reflected the compensation his body had made to heal itself. But Chasm was also a monster, his psychological compass skewed away from the Surge mean of order and justice.

Chasm was a blunt instrument, a weapon of choice, and the first of the group to dead drop from a hundred and twenty miles up to impact the ridges and hills where Gordell's cave lay.

From a mile away and to the east, L'Coyle stood at the forefront of Valtare's force of two hundred men with a hundred Surge awaiting the fallout. His men were nervous, fidgety, standing around in hot armour in the dry wind which had suddenly whipped up. It presaged a growing ominous tone which accompanied an unnerving pressure from above. L'Coyle looked up, shading his eyes from the sun, though it was his ears that told him the story.

An almighty ear-splitting whine announced the arrival of ten supersonic Surge as they dead-dropped through the air. They ploughed into the hills followed by violent ground tremors and explosive eruptions of several mushroom clouds of dark dust which fanned out threatening to swallow the sky. Even then, L'Coyle could see that much of the targeted hillsides had collapsed.

Before the dust could settle, L'Coyle donned his helmet with a fibre face mask to block the dust and took his force into the hills to search for the bodies of the Starguards. The great bluffs and giant rock formations which had risen up hundreds of feet with sheer sides riddled with unexplored caves were now largely destroyed. The Surge combed the area psychically for any signs of life.

One dark green Surge, whose name L'Coyle could not remember—they all looked alike to him—motioned to L'Coyle showing him the dark entrance to a still-intact cave. L'Coyle turned and whistled a signal to a section of men. Apprehensively, they all headed to the cave, scrambling over rocks avoiding slides and tumbling debris.

Just before reaching the entrance there was a thunderous crack from the ground to their north, which trembled. The kinetic bombs had recovered themselves, boring their way to the surface. Each took off slowly, Chasm resembling a rumbling, giant alien bumblebee escorted by nimble wasps.

L'Coyle and his similarly masked men had seen nothing like it and continued watching the metallic fliers as they arched away toward the Fortress. L'Coyle smiled at the sight; one of the wonders of the universe. But time was short and he urged his men on again as they continued into the cave.

"Weapons," he ordered through his helmet comms.

Soldiers drew out laser pistols and rifles; advanced weapons Archron had collected over time. L'Coyle and the soldiers had been extensively trained with them over the past few months. However, every one of them still wore their sheathed swords belted to them. Old habits and tactics died hard even though they knew normal swords wouldn't cut it against the Starguards.

Either way, the Starguards are dead, L'Coyle thought to himself.

The Surge hardly ever ventured into the hills, let alone enter any of the caves. Valtare had gleaned from his fragmentary telecommunications with the Surge that they thought there was something else in the caves besides Chryrians, something which Valtare dared believed made the metal folk skittish or even afraid. That should have been warning enough for L'Coyle, but Archron had insisted he lead Valtare's force deep into the cave systems to flush out or kill the Starguards. For L'Coyle, after all his misfortunes with Gordell Exmoor and then the arrival of the Starguards, it would have been his honour to avenge the Knights Destina. And Surge superstitions were not going to deter him.

Meters into the large cave musky scents assailed his senses, itching his nostrils, eerie noises putting him on edge, but he continued on shuffling slowly through the darkness followed by his men. The Surge remained outside. If he didn't know better, even L'Coyle swore the cave was haunted. Weapons drawn for any sign of the Starguards, he rounded a corner, emerging into a low dark-walled cavern with mist rising from the murky ground.

As he strained to get a better look, a flicker of movement to his right caught his eye. He charged at the shadow. But nothing was there. His men were spooked. Several invoked prayers to the Virgin Mary, some edged their way out. L'Coyle decided to follow them, treading backward lightly. Instinctively, he drew his sword pointing it out front.

A cracking of rock behind them caught them by surprise. Before they could sprint for the exit several large jagged boulders crashed from the cavern ceiling sealing them off. Eerie sounds like stones scraping around the dank tunnels sent the men into panic.

"Aargh!" screamed someone, flailing his arms about slashing the soldier next to him with his sword.

Several men also screamed in abject fear as the denizens of the caves, wispy creatures, materialised from the living rock. Dozens of the creatures phased from the rocky walls, silvery-white in colour, intangible forms flittering around in the dark cave, tendrils brushing against faces and bodies. The knights tried to slash their way out to no avail. It was a desperate fight, L'Coyle treating his cherish sword as a common spade frantically digging his way through a gap in the collapsed wall. He had mercifully crawled half-way out gasping for precious air when something fibrous coiled around his left ankle.

Fear strangled him, making him unaware he had soiled himself. He looked back seeing a snaking tendril wrap further around his legs. He tried to scream, as he was forcefully dragged backwards over jagged rocks into the cave, but a voice in his head told him not to.

He obeyed, against his will.

There were punctuated moments of screaming as dust billowed outside from between the gaps in the blocked entrance.

The Surge had already retreated to the air for safety. There was another earth tremor around the cave.

And then the screaming stopped.

Three miles and a valley to the west, a bright light erupted from a portal and six figures were unceremoniously dumped to the ground. They coughed deeply and spluttered dust from their mouths, inhaling in and gagging on great gulps of hot dry air.

"Geez, Zane, could you cut that any closer?" Force whined sarcastically, retching on all fours.

"Last second rescues are my thing..." she gasped back.

She just wanted to lie on her back and stop her heart from racing up her throat. She was glad her powers actually worked. Without thinking she had created a temporal bubble around them and ported everyone out just in time—destination anywhere.

"Zane, get us to the Fortress, now!" demanded Sceptre, even though he was also on his hands and knees. "We'll have the advantage. They think we're dead. Let's go...!" he panted.

"Oh, classic counter strike," Force grinned, wiping his mouth of grime, in anticipation.

Zane looked around at everyone to see the same expectation on their faces. They were going into the breach.

"Direction?" she asked, having no idea if she could be that precise with her power.

Everyone pointed north.

"Okay," she groaned.

Gordell held her hand gently. With his other hand he held up his crystalator with a holo-image overview of the Fortress with distance and direction. "We're going here. I'll guide you."

Zane nodded. She was getting used to this now. She closed her eyes and felt the exhilarating rush of chronal energy flow through her.

How could I have missed out on this for so long? she rejoiced inside. Her brother, Aristedes had flittered about through time without so much of a care, but she would never take her new-found powers for granted, Zane vowed.

Just as the chronal energy felt it would tear her apart, Zane released it, ripping a threshold into the fabric of timespace where only time flowed. Her own energy was attracted to the portal like a magnet which pulled her in as she held on to everyone else within a temporal bubble, its fields protecting the others from the harshness of the raw timestream. They navigated temporal nodes and streams until Zane sensed the exit portal coordinates she needed, lit up in colliding eddies and flashes of colours and brightness which only she could read.

The trip had taken less than a second in real time, but to Zane it had been like a walk through a park where everything was translated into a temporal landscape. It was a beautiful alien ecosystem to behold as much alive as any natural environment.

Zane was still in the middle of an infinite reflection as the portal neared, but something caught her attention in the void. She didn't know if it was normal or not, but she swore she could hear the word "Stooooop" within her mind in slow motion. But there was no turning back.

The portal's threshold unravelled around them with a blinding flash. None of the Starguards had a chance to react as Gordell's psychic warning came too late when the circle of fifty Surge in the large room they had emerged within bombarded them with a barrage of psionic shocks and close-range energy blasts. The stunned Starguards crumpled easily to the ground, unconscious.

Archron, Decion, and Valtare walked through the encircling Surge, standing over the prone intruders.

Archron grinned and clapped with pleasure, his applause echoing around the large domed room.

"Oh, well done, Decion. Well done indeed!"

INTERLUDE

PROPHESIES OF THE END OF TIME

I had first seen it at the age of five. Waking, screaming, I had ran out of my bedroom and into the warm night. My guardians stood nearby talking and laughing unawares, until I disturbed their evening with my torment.

Urgently, I pointed to the darkening skies. My squeaky child's voice at pains to verbalize my nightmarish thoughts. My guardians struggled with what I could see, which they could plainly not.

"Can't you see? The war, all the fighting?" I waved frantically to the sick blood-spewing sky again.

There was nothing to see. Even Mother Matrix was confused.

As a little girl, I could see and name all the Great Races of the Universe at war against the stars. Only the stars were very much alive.

My Godmother, Zenergy was concerned. At my tender age, I should not know all these peoples. I heard her whisper to the others: "Is she also becoming precognisant?"

If I was, it was a worrying sign, for a terrible war was coming which would engulf the entire universe.

"Let's go see your parents," Zenergy said in a worried manner.

So she and Mother Matrix and even the implacable Colonel Con who for once was astonished enough to agree with both of them, accompanied me back to my other home.

When we returned, there was grave news. I was right. A great war was raging. In the far future. It was spilling backward through time. Changing things. The Universe, the Multiverse, the Hinterverse, and even the temporalverse were all in danger.

The war was coming. And so we prepared; and hoped we were in time.

From Tales of the Time Empress

CHAPTER THREE

Phasia swam in time, trying to tread hard light in currents of chronitons falling in glittering torrents around her. But she could still see the faint buzz of light ahead, a shifting exit which rapidly closed and opened. There was a time storm brewing. She could feel it. It would wash her away from her destination, location unknown, forever lost if she didn't make it ashore to a safe temporal coast.

Since leaving the Chronopolis five months ago, telling Helexius— the erstwhile leader of the Astrals—that she had received a cryptic message, Phasia had leaped into the timestream seeking allies. And now she was two million years away up time or down time, she did not know as the intervening timestreams had crossed and twisted her beyond her experience. She dubbed her surroundings: weirdtime.

There was no sound in the weirdstream, but Phasia sensed there was thunder all around her as charged tachyons and chronitons collided together   unleashing lightning-like temporal strings which rippled violently out into unknown universes.

Who knew what kind of time those dimensions experienced, she mused.

Aching from pain and homesickness, Phasia looked behind her into the darkening abyss of swirling time. That way lay home, safety, and failure. She had to go forward. She was in her Lore energy state, her energy wings and self-spun temporal anchors of energy about to fail.

"Aaaargh!" her desperate cry sailed out into the time void, howling against the injustice and the cruelty of the universe.

Phasia prepared herself to be timewrecked as the raging tides eroded at her tethers.

Then she saw it. Through the surging waves and rapids, a reel of energy snaking her way—a lifeline. She reached out gratefully for the energy coil, wrapping it around herself immediately feeling a sharp tug as she was reeled in toward the blinding light.

The iridescent hole grew closer and Phasia could see it was a portal embedded within the weirdstream fabric. It was like nothing she had seen before, the portal seemed almost crystalline. Just as she reached its threshold, it flashed around her, practically sucking her out of the temporal storm and through into…Somewhere else.

Tumbling helplessly as the energy coil suddenly released itself, disappearing back into the distance, Phasia flopped weakly against a solid surface. Catching control of herself and gaining some semblance of strength, she looked dazedly around. A white-light oasis stretched out to every horizon; the brightness somewhat blinding her Lore senses. There were no reference points or sounds, no smells, breezes of air; only the light texture of the floor. Clear white exerted everywhere, yet she stood solidly on ground.

"Hallo," she called out, her voice falling flat in the echoless, white expanse. "Thank you for saving me." A hopeful chance of a reply was not returned. Forlornly, she looked around for any movement, listened for any sound. She was all alone.

Feeling subconsciously threatening all fired up, Phasia transformed into her physical Celestian state. Her high-cheekboned face framed by long tumbling brown hair was thin and pale from exhaustion. Her usual wide smile and greeting green eyes were absent as she slumped down. Drawing her knees up and hugging them to her chest for warmth, Phasia rested her head against her right arm and waited. It had been a long, hard two-million-year slog through eternity and she was tired.

She drifted off to sleep.

Time passed; how much Phasia did not know, as she awakened. To a bright light. She laughed to herself that in this weirdspace—as she had decided to dub it—there was no notion of time. She was just in a moment, one moment that stretched forever—a waiting room out of time...

Phasia's head spun around.

Something had changed.

She didn't see or hear it, so much as feel it; almost as subtle as a neutrino kiss. But Phasia knew she was not alone. Tilting her head slightly to one side to feel the vibration ripple through her, she turned around and saw the legs of someone standing behind her. She kept looking up to a strong body of a young man, dressed in golden crystalline armour. He walked around to her front offering a hand to pull her up.

Phasia unhesitatingly accepted with an outstretched hand. She felt a strange and unexpected euphoria rising within her. The man was tall, taller even than her, and handsome. And even though Phasia had never seen this Celestian before, she instantly knew who he was with golden armour and the looks, complete with the wild golden hair, of his father.

"Oh, Universe, it's you!"

"Hallo, Mother," he smiled.

"Hellennius," Phasia lovingly cupped her son's cheeks in her hands. "Hellennius," she whispered again as she kissed his face and hugged him to her. "We thought you lost forever. What happened? Where are we? How can this be so?" Phasia wanted to know everything at once, her voice a high-pitched wail of exhilaration. "You were taken from me and your father, Millennius. Do you remember? You just vanished into thin air without a trace." Tears streamed down her face, as she hugged her son again. "Oh, no matter, I'm here now to take you home. I wasn't sure who or what to expect when I received a message I could find help here. Did you send the message?"

Hellennius smiled cryptically. "There is much to tell you, mother."

"Can you travel between temporal planes?" She took his hand ready to go, but he resisted. She looked back surprised.

"What's wrong?" She instinctively searched around for danger, holding her son tight should he disappear again.

"Mother," he said, softly, "It is good to see you, but this is my home," he said, sweeping his arm around him. "This is my Kingdom."

"Kingdom?" She again took in the incomprehensible blankness.

"Yes, I am the Cosmogod of the Zater Jen and all you see around you is our realm of time."

A thousand questions flooded through Phasia's mind, the obvious one first: "Zater Jen? That's my father's name." She was surprised he would even know it.

"I know. He is the one who brought me here," was Hellennius' calm reply.

The magenta hair on the back of her neck rose. "My father ... is he here, still alive?" She looked excitedly around the blank dimension, anxious to see her father. She could feel her Lore-self rearing to be released in joy.

Hellennius walked away from her, maintaining eye contact. "No, mother, he passed long ago. But he saw the storm coming; the future storm, which is why you are here. It was foreseen, your coming was foreseen—the Great Mother's arrival."

Phasia did a double-take. "My arrival? I don't understand?"

A proud smile spread across Hellennius' handsome features. "Your father was searching for the lost Celestri Knights who disappeared during the Hero Siege, but he found something else."

Phasia watched incredulous as a race of colourful crystal beings seemingly materialised out of nothingness.

"Who are they?" she asked, as they continued to fade in from all directions. Far from feeling threatened she felt nothing but benevolence from them.

"Your father befriended them." Hellennius directed his gaze up at them with fondness. "They were a lost, dejected and fractionalised Peoples. Your father gave them purpose, but they were still trapped; he among them. But for his actions and out of deep respect, this nameless civilisation took on his name as their own.

"Zater Jen used his powers to peer into different dimensions. He observed the strife amongst the Celestian Knights, the downfall of his own son, Synther. He could see the love between you and my father. He witnessed my birth. He wept tears of joy. He was so proud of you. Despite this and your efforts to protect me, he had already foreseen the future to come. So with great sadness he took me away from your arms.

"His plan was to bring into being a champion for the Zater Jen, so they could escape this realm. For here, they had been imprisoned by the Lore. Over the years, I used my bond with you to call to you through the portal to help us." His voice was a simple plea: "Can you help us mother? Even with my own powers, the anti-portal you entered is omnidirectional to us; too strong to rend open from inside."

It was everything Phasia could do to not break down. "You have been through so much! I can almost forgive my father for taking you away, because you are alive and well." Phasia regarded him, her first good appraisal of her grown up son. Millennius would have been proud. "Why do you think I can help?" She took another curious glance up at the crystal beings surrounding them.

"Your natural Lore energy may counteract the Lore energy used to create the anti-portal."

Phasia nodded sighing. "I will try, son. I too believe the future storm you talk of is almost upon us." Though tired, she knew she would find the energy within herself to open the portal.

Hellennius nodded solemnly, holding out an crystalline-armoured hand. Out of nowhere, a golden crystal female, taller than she, walked serenely toward them. Hellennius turned and smiled broadly at her. They held hands.

"Mother, may I introduce to you my wife, Celesophia, the Crystal Queen: She Who is in All Things."

Phasia was lost for words. Celeosphia was an undoubted beauty in crystal, but...

"Wife? But you're only forty or so years old, far too young," Phasia blurted out. "No offence," she added to her new daughter-in-law.

Hellennius laughed. "Mother, I have been here for over two hundred years, as you would count them."

"Two...oh, my son, how much we've missed. Celesophia, you are very welcome in my family, such as it is." She stepped forth and hugged the crystal woman feeling the tingle of temporal energy flowing through her.

>*Thank you*< was the reply, a swirling diamond-white light pulsating in her forehead as she psyed.

Phasia was fascinated by this. She looked around at the others who were gathering around. Though they were crystalline, none except Hellennius wore clothing. Phasia didn't consider them to be naked as they had no genitalia to show. She hoped she could distinguish male from female if they all had gender, though they had general humanoid gracile and robust forms. From what she could see they were all over two meters tall, thin, with energy rushing around their heads and bodies. And so many colours, Phasia was dazzled by them.

"Okay, so who are the rest, then?" she asked, hoping none were younglings. She had had enough shocks.

Hellennius grinned with honour. "Mother, as Cosmogod—the All-Supreme and All that is Cosmic, I who rule the Temporal Worlds and walk among the many-armed disc of time—I would present to you, my Court," he announced with pride.

Cosmogod closed his eyes and a call went out:

>*Geomega, the Will of Cosmogod—stand forth*< Phasia heard in her head.

A lean, green crystal being with a sharp-angled face strode forth, bowed to Phasia, and psyed in a male voice >*It is an honour to meet at last, Great Mother. Your will, such as your son's, is my command*< He bowed even lower, sliding backward out of the way.

Hellennius called >*Areigna, the Power of Cosmogod—fly forth*<

A bright silver Zater Jen circled high above Phasia, who was still thinking in terms of 2D blank planes and hadn't noticed she was surrounded now on every plane by millions of Zater Jen. Phasia could tell this Zater Jen was a female even within her gleaming armour. The personal body guard of Cosmogod landed beside him, her jagged skin sparkling like polished armour. Her inner energy coruscated around her translucent body like liquid lightning.

>*My body is yours to command, Great Mother. I am your weapon, your champion, your forsakeable life*< She glided backward to hold position behind Cosmogod.

>*Starmondaus, Time Reader Supreme and Summoner of the Light Guard—shine forth*<

Phasia had to look away while her eyes adjusted to a shock of harsh yellow light which even outshone the white background. This Zater Jen's crystalline body amplified his energy far beyond the others. She understood why:

>*GREAT MOTHER*< his voice boomed >*I FORESAW YOUR FATHER'S COMING AND THIS DAY, AND I CAN SEE THE STORMS AHEAD. WE ARE PREPARED*<

Phasia nodded her greeting, her head still throbbing from his voice. He was a powerful psionic and vision-seer.

Lightstream could learn a lot from him, she thought.

Cosmogod called out once more: >*Arcanaut the Elementor—reveal yourself*<

From out of nowhere, a pure-black Zater Jen faded in beside Phasia. She instinctively leaned back as he inclined forward, arcing his neck toward her as if sniffing her.

>*I sense your Lore-self vying for power. I have cures for such needs*< He seemed pleased with himself.

>*Step back, Arcanaut*< warned Cosmogod sharply. >*My mother requires no such cure*<

>*Ah, but the Synther will*< Arcanaut rubbed his crystal hands together, eliciting sparkling screeches.

"You've seen what has become of my brother?" Phasia was shocked they knew so much.

>*That and much more, mother. We will speak of things to come. But first we must free ourselves*< he psyed.

Phasia was interested in how he had acquired this ability and what else he could do. But first things first. She looked around, searching for any horizon or point of reference.

"Why can't you leave? And where are we?"

Hellennius switched to speaking, "We are in a universe of time. We all exist here as temporal beings, yet our consciousnesses still register ourselves as corporeal beings in a spaceless dimension. Time has been arranged around us to give ourselves a semblance of space. Hence over there, mother, is the portal you came through." He raised a hand toward the blank void.

Phasia concentrated, but could see nothing.

"Here, mother, let me show you." He touched her head.

At once, Phasia's senses were assaulted by a vision of chaos sweeping before her. As if her trip had not been torturous enough, here was time knotted into twisted strands and great rapid rivers, looping, falling, and cascading into turbulent timefalls, barring all ways out of the universe. There were no stars, or planets or expansive clouds of nebulae, just ream after dense ream of temporal sheets, glowing in a myriad of colours.

She caught a brief glimpse of the portal, but it vanished almost instantly.

Helexius explained, "All those temporal fields repel us from the portals. We cannot penetrate the surface of this realm. But worse, in just over one hundred years' time, the temporal entropy of this realm will become unassailable and all will perish in a temporal implosion—"

"A time bang!" Phasia mused.

"Apt. We must leave promptly or be washed back into the maelstrom, never to escape; erased from time!" His voice was a hard edge.

"Universe, no!" Phasia couldn't contemplate such a fate. "But how can we escape, the portal's gone?" Phasia wanted to know.

"No, it's not. The portal shifts randomly in time around the universe. It's an entropic fault, a temporal singularity, where time collapses upon itself, like a time hole into another universe. The temporal singularity's denseness has formed a spatial conduit into normal spacetime. We were able to send an anchor for you to enter, as information can escape, but no more. All we need to do is concentrate our energies onto the fault to rip it open. Your energy is closest to the Lore, so you should be able to get close to the portal."

"But how do we know where to find it?"

"We have help on the outside. She is going to fix it to a position relative to our temporal coordinates then we will blast it open from both sides."

"Help? Who can do a thing such as to manipulate a temporal portal?" Phasia was intrigued.

"The Time Empress, of course!" Hellennius answered, a bit surprised. "Ah, you have not met her yet."

"The . . ." Phasia couldn't speak. She had never heard of the Time Empress, but she thought she had felt her presence. During her long voyage to find her Hellennius she had heard whispers on the time eddies and the scent of powerful temporal energy on the vortices of scarped edges of universal planes. She had been guided here, she now knew. "I look forward to meeting this Time Empress."

"Then here we go, mother. But first, we need more power. >*Starmondaus, summon the Light Guard*<

Starmondaus turned his golden head to the sky and a ripple of energy exploded outward. Phasia had to cover her ears even though the call had been psionic. It was an unintelligible screech of a cry to her, but in an instant the air had unravelled around them and four new Zater Jen had appeared. And they astonished Phasia.

The Zater Jen were a tall, powerful race, but the members of the Light Guard were clearly warriors. Their crystal skins glistened and bristled with extra crystal layers, like armour.

They stood to attention in front of Cosmogod and the Great Mother.

"Mother, may I introduce you to the Light Guard, guardians of the Chronal Stream. He stepped toward a red crystal Zater Jen.

"This is the Glorious Ego Byss, Captain of the Light Guard." Ego Byss glared at Phasia, almost arrogantly. His deep gold eyes capable of piercing the temporal mists. His head seemed afire with red crystal hair. Then Phasia noticed the third eye on his palm, a sigil for fire. Phasia had heard about such sigils. Located in the forehead it denoted psychic energy and in the chest, pure energy. The Glorious Ego Byss was powerful indeed.

Ego Byss tasted the timestream with his palm eye, >*Hmm, a mixture of Celestian, Lore, and Astral flavours*< his telepathic voice resonated through time >*I thought I could smell the time-displacement*<

"You know the Astrals?" A surprised Phasia wondered how.

>*Indeed, the young female kin of Lord Aeon while I missioned for the Time Empress. But that is in the future*<

"Her again. I really want to meet this Time Empress." Phasia was getting anxious now. "And you can really see the future?" Silly question she knew as Ego Byss seemed to challenge her assumptions.

Cosmogod, a knowing smile on his face, carried on with his introductions, "Next is Ax Omen." He was almost as silver as Areigna, but larger, darker, and battle-scarred. Phasia wondered what could scar a Zater Jen.

As if hearing her thoughts, he psyed, >*I travel dimensional realms and planes quite beyond the comprehension of even the most temporally-cognisant. I am a wanderer where darkness holds court; I tread without remorse into places where evil calls its heart. My badges are pledges to those deeds*< He indicated the spidery-web-like thin scars across his torso, arms and legs. Phasia was under no illusions to his power.

Still grinning, despite himself, at Ax Omen's claims, Hellennius felt he should carry on. "This is Adam Finitum, father of the Infinitus."

"The Infinitus?" Phasia regarded the dark blue figure with equally-dark flickering light blue eyes.

>*My children and my future*< was his enigmatic reply. He stood there solemnly. Phasia nodded back none the wiser to his meaning.

"Lastly, Geona Zen—the Quadrassentia." Hellennius introduced a glacial white female. She almost blended into the background.

>*Great Mother, please forgive the rudeness of my brethren. That you are Lore is of no consequence and without you there would have been no Cosmogod. We are his loyal subjects. We shall serve you as we do him*< she gracefully bowed, vibrating with pleasure.

"Thank you. You profess quadrassential powers?" Phasia was impressed. She couldn't wait to see Geona Zen in action. "Are any other Zater Jen quadrassentric?" she had to ask.

>*Alas, no, Great Mother*< Geona Zen psyed in reply. >*I am the only one and have yet to breed*<

Phasia bowed her head in acknowledgement.

"We are now ready to go, mother," Hellennius seemed to order her.

"Great, how many are there of you?"

"Three billion."

"Three billion. . .? How are we all going to get out in time? How can I help so many?"

"The Light Guard and yourself can hold the portal open from the inside, while the Time Empress will do so from the outside. We could only escape now, because of you, Mother. Your Loreself will provide the key energy frequency to rip through the bonds of the portal's singularity. That is because it is the Lore who trapped the Zater Jen here in the first place and only Lore energy can fully open the portal from the inside. We have been communicating with the Time Empress via energised data strands forced through quantum gaps in the portal. However, only you have fully crossed it since Zater Jen and myself."

"And you didn't have enough Lore energy." Phasia was saddened by this; energy shifting was a generations-old family trait they had been proud of; excepting her brother Synther.

Hellennius felt her pain, but had come to terms with it. His mother would have to as well. "Correct. I inherited some of your energy, but it is not enough. I cannot transform my core state into energy like you. And as you can see, in order to survive, I have incorporated crystal into myself. It helps harness the light energy I inherited from father to sustain me."

Phasia understood, but she was a little confused about something. "So, the Lore trapped you here? Why? When?" Phasia asked. The Lore were truly rampant across the universes.

Hellennius' face broke into a mercurial smile. "Mother, do you not know who the Zater Jen are?"

Phasia began to slowly shake her head just as the realisation hit her like a supernova. It couldn't be, she thought, not after all this time. She stared all around her at the teeming billions of crystalloid beings waiting for her to free them, the full shock of where she was and what was to come terrifying the Celestian Knight to her core. The scope of the war became all too clear.

"Oh Universe, Hellennius, I never knew. This goes beyond a final reckoning with the Lore. Are you sure you want this?"

"For the sake of the universe, yes, we must."

Grim determination steeled her into action. "So be it. Stand back," she commanded.

Even the Light Guard fell back, proudly anticipating the chaos to come.

Phasia concentrated and reached inside her for the energy within, her magenta and violet manoeuvre suit and skin shifting in liquidity and texture, becoming hot, becoming fire, becoming energy, until she was aflame with radiant violet energy. Huge wings of energy burned purple, violet, and amethyst as they unfurled gloriously resplendent behind her, fluttering in the temporal whirlpools. Her hair was a fire of deep violet, her eyes glowing like dark seas of indigo.

Phasia flew forth to study the gate. She saw it was the same type of portal her maniacal brother had unlocked millennia ago to free the Lore, but intertwined with crystal. Now she was doing the same to free the Zater Jen to battle the Lore.

Like brother like sister, she thought darkly.

Phasia braced herself against the torrent of tachyons and threw forth her arms channelling temporalmorphic energy at the portal. It twisted and buckled under the energetic attack, but held. Cosmogod and Geona Zen also pitched in, pouring in their combined and considerable energies to slowly unhinge the portal. The portal faded in parts, but temporal patches swept in to shore up the portal.

What an insidious design! Phasia cursed.

The whole of the temporal universe seemed to glow hellish violet as Phasia increasingly applied more energy onto the portal, which flickered like a holographic mirror, reflecting images and memories back toward her. Horrible memories of her brother and the Lore. This was ingeniously temporally-engineered, she knew. Flashbacks designed to dishearten and scare would-be escapees. But she wouldn't give up, even as she saw Magna Aura destroyed over and over again in her mind. She gritted her teeth, ignored the harrowing memories, and waited for just the right moment.

There, an imperceptible quantum flaw just off-centre, she told herself.

Phasia dove for the portal at speed, her energy raining down point-blank upon the portal's centre, energy flaring outward and around her as she crashed through the weakened portal. She rebounded back, undaunted, and immediately dived again. The Light Guard blazed around her attacking the portal, tearing at its edges, getting burned by its energies, yet unyielding in their mission.

Phasia shot barrage after barrage of energy into its heart. Slithers of cracks appeared, Phasia's eyes burned zeroing on the fissures. A third time she swooped down as the portal fractured. This time she was followed by billions of Zater Jen as she breached the portal.

The Zater Jen streaked through as the Light Guard held open the breach with energy shards produced from their bodies. Unbidden, millions of other Zater Jen descended and crammed their bodies within the portal sustaining the opening for others to escape.

Being time travellers, it took all the surviving billions of Zater Jen less than a microsecond to jump through, executing a quantum time jump. All three billion Zater Jen had occupied the same space at once in order to jump beyond the portal's boundary before separating into their individual selves.

With the brave volunteers still holding open the breach, the Light Guard were the last to exit. The conflicting universes exchanged a brief explosion of contrary atmospheres then the portal was sealed once more forever, trapping the doomed millions of volunteers within.

Phasia lamented those millions who had sacrificed their lives so that billions could escape. It was too much for her. She collapsed into her son's arms.

"I'm sorry I couldn't save them all!" she sobbed.

"No matter, mother. It was foreseen. They will not be forgotten."

Not consoled by those words, Phasia slowly withdrew from Hellennius, surveying the environment around them.

With three billion Zater Jen controlling the timestream around them, Phasia found the fearsome weirdtime storm she had fought through to get this far had died down. Calm seas of temporal energy rippled around her. She basked in the energy as she reverted back to her Celestian self. She felt weak, exhausted, having expended a vast amount of energy. And sick over the deaths of millions.

She suddenly looked up, noticing all the Zater Jen were facing toward her and bowing, including Cosmogod. She was about to nonchalantly refuse their praise, when she realised there was someone behind her.

Phasia spun around. A young girl stood amidst the tachyon waves gently lapped up against her.

"Hello, Phasia," she said, with a child's innocent smile.

Phasia was dumbfounded. "Do I know you?"

The girl just smiled, a childish pressing of the lips together, as if that was answer enough.

Phasia scrutinised the young girl; she couldn't have been much more than twelve, but had the bearing of a warrior queen with her pale white skin, long ice-blonde hair, and the unmistakable deep blue eyes of her father. "You're..."

"Yes, I am," the Time Empress confidently replied with a hint of a haughty smile.

Phasia returned her smile. "Oh, my!"

CHAPTER FOUR

To the eyes of human astronomers searching the skies in the twenty-first century, the area of the cosmos known as the Sloan Great Wall was the largest known structure in nature—until knowledge of the Axalan-discovered Grand Immensity was divulged in 2241. If the astronomers had been able to peer closer at the Sloan Wall, they would have seen a thousand-light-year long stellar field birthing stars, assume they would form solar systems, and perhaps life-bearing worlds with civilisations which would one day encounter humanity.

But the civilisation within this stellar nursery was not one any astronomer would have wanted to meet. Significant sections of the star field were not made of stars, but of living creatures of energy; spawning, feeding, growing, searching, flittering through time and space for the one place that mattered.

It took thousands of years to accumulate enough spawn to begin construction. It was one thing to travel alone, but for this journey, something else was needed. There was no rush for they had all the time in the universe. The creatures formed together, interlocking, feeding from the expanse of the super galactic cluster which formed their nursery in order to maximise their strength and temporal capabilities.

When they had finished, a new gigantic star, more than ten times Earth's sun stellar mass, shone in the heavens. Their leader threaded his way through the teeming masses, his golden aura touching every one last of the trillions of them, until he reached the center of the living star; the golden heart of a rejuvenated race.

He gave a command and space warped. A part of the Sloan Great Wall collapsed as the Helstar couldn't resist one last feed for energy. After all, the next time the Lore fed, there would only be one small, yellow star to eat.

"Zane! Wake up! Zane!"

Zane jumped at the deep voice bellowing her name, more out of fright at the instant recognition of the voice than at the realisation she was somewhere in a black expanse.

She turned around and there he was: the red crystal being who had visited her on Earth. They were definitely a long way from her bedroom in Sword Industries.

"Oh, you again," Zane tried to feel friendly, bending her lips into a smile. Inside she was absolutely terrified, trapped as she was with no Astral help.

"Where am I? I was in transit and then, then…" She struggled to remember what her last thoughts were. "Did you attack me?" she accused him.

"No," he responded, somewhat coldly.

Zane's memory struggled to keep up as she recalled her predicament at the Chronopolis. "Did you do something to the Astrals and the Chronopolis?" she asked.

"No."

"What about me? Did you do something to me to make me older than before?"

"No."

"Did you bring me to Earth millions of years in the future?"

"No." For a fourth time.

Don't speak much, do you? she thought.

"No."

Zane thought she could hear amusement in his voice that time.

"Fine, then what are we doing here? And why are you so interested in me?" she asked.

"You must come with me," he said, almost ominously.

"I don't think so…"

Before she could finish, the being held out his eye-palmed hand and Zane felt an irresistible force reach out as she flew into his arms. She thought she'd be crushed up against hard crystal, but his skin was softer than she thought, and soothingly warm to the touch, too. She could see through his armoured exterior and the energy coursing through him. Then she looked into his eyes: Golden, majestic, deep with time. Zane got lost in them, timelines swirling across his orbs, showing her past and future.

Though Zane felt no sensation of movement she knew they had travelled somewhere else. She still gripped her rescuer/abductor around the shoulders, but let go as she looked around her surroundings.

It was temporal space, but not as she knew it. It was still pitch black, but here time particles splashed against each other in exploding spectra, splintering into fractal ripples which twisted away to form bizarre flat dimensional planes in which Zane could see stars and galaxies. As the fractal planes floated away like rotating mirrors, they paradoxically grew larger and larger until at the horizon, Zane could see whole universes. It was a never-ending process, as universe after universe was born and floated away to lead its own life ending up drenched in darkness.

"Holy, sheesh! Where are we?" Zane whispered in awe.

"Nowhere and everywhere," came a familiar and reassuring voice.

Excited, Zane spun: "Phasia!" She leaped from the red being's side and flew over to Phasia, giving her a big hug. "Oh, Phasia, I thought I'd never see you again. Where have you been? Who is this guy who brought me here? What is this place?" Zane had so many questions, but Phasia answered them all patiently.

"Well, first off, you've changed a bit. Do something with your hair?" the Celestian Knight jibed. "You have grown into the daughter your father wanted, I must say. Isn't that so Ego Byss?" She laughed at the crystal being who stood silent and impassively nearby.

"Ego Byss?" Zane repeated. "Sort of makes sense, lots of ego and eyes like deep abysses of time. Who is he?"

"Ah, well. He and his people are the allies I went to find. They call themselves the Zater Jen."

"Zater Jen?" Zane paused, fishing within her memories. "After your father?"

"Well done for remembering. Yes. I found out that when he disappeared he had actually found these beings, brought them back to life, gave them meaning, and so they named themselves after him. And then to top it off, my father brought my son to them."

"Your...?" Zane looked over to her left and saw a man in gold crystal armour glide over to her.

Phasia smiled proudly. "Zane, meet my first-born son and your long-lost, half-uncle, Hellennius the Cosmogod, leader of the Zater Jen."

Zane was lost for words. She stammered, overwhelmed by emotion, not knowing what to say. "Wow! After all this time ... that's so, so . . ." She started to cry. Understanding, Phasia wrapped her arms around her.

"Oh, Zane, we'll find your father, don't you worry about that. Shh, now! I thought you'd outgrow crying by now."

Zane tried to smile, but failed. "I haven't been this way for long. I was as you last saw me on Earth way back when Aristedes and I left to look for my father. I've been to twenty-first and twenty-third century Earth, then somehow millions of years in the future, all grown up, and with temporal powers to boot." Her crying had stopped, though a bit of frustration flared up as she explained her most recent adventures on Earth. "But I think I've been taken out of time somehow, somewhere. I don't know where I've been or why I've aged. Do you?"

Phasia frowned and shook her head. "No, I do not know. It was not us. But don't worry, we'll figure it out, just as we're figuring out what to do next here."

Zane followed Phasia and Hellennius's gaze out into the kaleidoscope of universes.

"So, what is this 'nowhere and everywhere'? It's amazing." Gazing around, she saw shadowy figures in the deep background.

"We're running simulations."

"Simulations? On what? How?"

"There used to be such things called quantum computers. But there are much more powerful machines. Think of this as a cosmic computer, where the universe itself becomes the computer. We're calculating the end of time, the end of the universe which this war will bring."

Zane was speechless, because she knew Lightstream could only dream of doing this. If only she was here. "But the Astrals can help. They can do this, Phasia." Her voice rose in panic as she spoke. "But I can't find them or the Chronopolis. Do you know where they are? Have you been back there?"

"What's happened at the Chronopolis?" a shocked Phasia wanted to know. "Helexius, Spheron and the girls were fine when I left."

"It's abandoned!" Zane replied, still upset from the memory. "The Astrals are gone and the Chronopolis has been sealed with an array of temporal defences. You didn't know?"

Phasia shook her head, but didn't show any sign of shock or surprise. "No, since I left to find allies, I have not been back. But I know this is not the only war front and it's possible the Astrals have retreated to a more strategic location from which to fight, leaving the Chronopolis protected against intruders." She didn't sound entirely convincing.

Zane wasn't sure she understood or trusted Phasia. The Astrals were not here for the big war at the end of time?

Phasia knew what was going through her mind and answered before Zane spoke. "Magna Aura, Zane. The new homes of the children of the Celestian Knights are all under attack. Each is as important as the other. And if one falls the others will, no matter the time or the place. We are fighting for our very survival."

Zane was certain Phasia was terrified, but couldn't figure out why. "Why? How? Surely we can defeat Archron, a few Surge, and the Lore."

Phasia looked sternly at Zane. "You must know what this war really is?" she rebuked the young Astral.

Zane felt a shiver go down her spine at her tone. "No," she replied, meekly.

Phasia's eyes darkened. "Oh universe! None of you know. I'm not even sure if Archron knows the full extent of what he's doing."

"What's happening, Phasia?" a worried Zane's mind tried to imagine the worst that could happen.

Phasia's lips pursed in trepidation. "Archron's not doing this by himself, which is why I was looking for the Zater Jen. It is why I had to find and warn you, through Ego Byss. As he told you before, only you can save the future."

Zane remembered her first meeting with the mysterious red Zater Jen on Earth: "My father. Ego Byss told me he was still alive and can save us. Is this true?"

Phasia didn't say anything, but took Zane a little forward and showed her the images from the universes. They stared at the universal visions until Zane could make out strange, yet vaguely familiar figures.

"But, that's impossible," Zane shrieked, thinking her mind was playing tricks on her. "All of them? Still alive. Are they like you?"

Phasia paused. "No, Zane, not all of them. I can change back into my Celestian form. I have control over my powers, but they do not. Synther made sure of that. It's too late to save them, but now we know what they are doing and they have to be stopped." Phasia had steel in her voice, but not without considerable pain. This was a Celestian Knight mission to end all others, to right the past, and to confront the end of a love which was promised would never end.

Zane was surprised to be hearing and seeing these revelations. No wonder the other Celestians Knights felt they couldn't trust Phasia. What other secrets did she bear?

As if having read her mind, Phasia pointed to the distant horizon to something Zane had not noticed before, or rather someone.

A little girl sat crossed-legged among the warping universes. They bent around her, leaving her untouched as in reverence.

Zane watched in silent awe as the girl manipulated the universes around her, her small hands caressing the outer skies of the cosmoses. The universes glowed back before disappearing over the horizons, perhaps to become full universes with new life.

"That's her isn't it? The Time Empress," Zane whispered.

Phasia confirmed with a nod. "She is the temporally-strongest Astral yet born. I'm her guardian for now. Her parents are in a war of their own, which their daughter cannot be a part of."

Zane was curious. "Do I know her parents? Is she of the next generation or further down the line?"

Phasia smiled, though her voice was a little harder edged. "Just know she's an Astral, Zane, no need to bother with the detail."

Zane looked at Phasia then at the girl. *They've taken her out of her time, maybe like I was,* a suspicious thought running through her head. *No wonder they don't want me to know. What else is there?* But all she said was, "What's she doing?"

"She's reading the universes. As I mentioned, we're nowhere and everywhere. We're standing at the beginning of temporal space where it wells up from the gaps between the great universal branes. From here we can see everything that has been and will be, all the possible futures curving out before us. We just tap into the temporal frame and psionically project all possible outcomes upon the baby universes as they fold out. We can fast-track millions of universes through billions of years in minutes."

"Wow, head-hurting stuff! What are you using as psionic software?" Zane was intrigued.

Phasia pointed her head behind Zane.

Zane turned and a squeak of shock escaped her throat at the sight of a crystal wall that stretched forever. The shadowy figures she thought she had seen in the background were almost on top of her. "What? Who...?"

"That's the rest of the Zater Jen race, all three billion of them, attuned to each other and the universes. They're how we found you and will stay with you. They can concentrate their minds together or work as individuals to forecast the events to come from the events that have passed. But so far, they all say the same thing: We lose. And we don't know why. So, we are gathering time. The Zater Jen are drinking as much temporal energy as they can before we attack and counter the Lore's energy."

"What about the Surge? If they became allies, then they could absorb whatever energy there is and also fend off the Lore." Zane's face lit up thinking she had a brilliant idea, but Phasia shook her head.

"It's not that simple. The Surge are proud beings, both proud of their physical form and proud because they never want to be controlled again. They were slaves once to a race of psi-beings and it was the Lore who freed them from the psis, albeit in a three-way battle. The Surge are the Knights Destina's protection against the Lore and will side with the Knights Destina out of misguided loyalty, and battle for the Chryrians. There's no love lost between any of the races!"

Zane knew she had heard something monumental, but couldn't put it together: ancient myths mixing with her history and the bedtime stories told to her by her father about the People of psi, the People of matter, the People of time, and the dreaded People of energy.

"Holy shit!" The thought thunder-clapped in her mind as she realised everything she had been taught as myth was coming true. But was she just imagining things.

"Phasia, are these Peoples . . . ?" She couldn't bring herself to say their name.

"Yes, Zane, these races, these Peoples, are the Antiqchronals—the first four Peoples: The Lore, the People of fire/energy of the original universe who drove the rest out; the Surge, the People of earth/matter burned into metal by the Lore; the Chryrians, the People of wind/psyche, whose poisoned minds cause insanity; and the Zater Jen, the People of water/time, imprisoned in bodies of crystal and exiled beyond futurecome. Yes, Zane, they exist, scattered as they were around the universes by the Lore. But here they are together with the Fifths about to war again.

"But why are we fighting amongst ourselves, again?" Zane was still confused.

Phasia paused, thinking Zane had already figured out the answer. She pointed to the emerging universes, each one showing a universe wracked and broken at war against twelve distinctive dark round entities.

Zane's breath left her as she sank to her knees in horror and shock. Her senses felt obliterated. Tears rolled down her cheeks as she looked at Phasia for answers.

Phasia only confirmed her worst fears.

"Yes, Zane, they are returning: the Storm of Stars. We are at war with the Gods!"

"Zane! Wake up! Zane!"

Zane sat bolt upright. Her body was being shaken. She felt her mind still wide open to the Zater Jen psi-link, from which she was being awakened. But the vision before her was different.

She saw through a lingering psionic haze they were in the

same room with its high dark dome they had been ambushed in and surrounded by Surge. Archron, Decion, and Valtare stood at the front of the Surge wall arguing with Sceptre and Gordell But Zane couldn't hear them. And she was still being shaken.

Zane's head lolled over to see Azure shaking her, words coming out of her mouth which she couldn't hear, either. Zane shook her head to clear it, but the only thing she could hear was a buzzing in her mind, like the voices of three billion Zater Jen conversing within her head, until it reached a deafening crescendo…

Phwoosh!!

Zane fell sideways. Unable to reconcile all the physical, temporal, and psionic realities assailing her, she retched. There followed a deafening silence, slowly replaced by familiar harsh sounds of people shouting…

"…awake. Zane are you okay?"

Zane wiped the sticky residue from her mouth. She recognised Azure's voice. But she could only look at the Sky Warrior in stunned silence and smile blissfully like a goof.

There was only one thought on her mind: *Phasia's wrong! We won't lose this war.*

***

"… No, Sceptre, you are the prisoners and you will listen to me—join us or die. The universe is changing in our image. We will lead." Archron made it sound like some kind of great game.

Defiantly, Sceptre shook his head, peering over to Gordell beside him who was listening with both ears and mind. His psi-presence was picking up strange chatter from the Surge. They were uneasy; their disquietude reverberating out in distorted psi-waves. But his silent queries for information were rebuffed. Anxious or not, they weren't divulging anything to him. He turned to Sceptre and discreetly shook his head. They were going to have to fight alone.

Sceptre turned to Urana and Azure who were tending to Force and Zane, respectively, both still unconscious. Urana's eyes watched him fiercely—*your fault!*her stare accused him.

He was about to refuse Archron's devil's pact, when he was interrupted by Zane awakening.

Sneering, Archron looked down disdainfully upon his fellow Astral. "So, our dear departed leader's daughter has grown up, but is still weak. Aren't you supposed to be dead?" he smirked.

Zane stood up uneasily, stomach still rolling, still weak from her ordeal. She wished she had a mint. However, after dusting herself down, she regarded Archron in his faux Roman armour, and nonchalantly shot back (breath stinking): "Not as dead as your brother!"

Her words provoked an immediate reaction from Archron who clenched his fists for a fight.

"Don't provoke him," Azure whispered under her breath, spreading out a protective arm.

Zane ignored her, walking forward to Archron, challenging him.

"Not so big without baby brother to back you up, eh, *uncle* Cal?" Zane goaded, knowing Netherlord was dead without totally knowing how, as she hadn't been there. *Had she?* She tried to remember as she grinned at Archron for extra measure.

Archron snapped. Before anyone could react, he snatched up his voidspear, pointed it at Zane, and fired.

Nothing happened. Or rather nothing happened to her.

Zane should have been disintegrated, ripped apart by entropic energy, but it swirled around her and drained away as if sucked into another dimension.

"Spearhead!" Archron spun angrily at the Surge, blaming them for interfering with his powers.

"It wasn't them!" Valtare stirred uneasily, also at a loss. His rudimentary communications with the Surge had confirmed this. He felt the Surge were holding something back, but he couldn't tell what.

Secrets within secrets, he thought darkly.

Inwardly, Zane smirked, silently thanking her Zater Jen guardians for the protection. At least she hoped it was them.

Angrily, Archron stared at his voidspear, stunned, then at Zane who didn't flinch, then back at his voidspear. His helmeted face hid his swirling emotions as he stepped back.

Decion and Valtare looked toward their Lord, knowing the balance of power had shifted. Something was happening which they didn't understand.

So Zane helped them out.

"I want to see her," she demanded. "I want to see her now!" She resisted stamping her foot like a petulant child.

"Zane, what's going on?" Sceptre questioned. He was interrupted before he could get a reply.

A sudden commotion behind them made them turn toward the sound.

"Wha' da Desus goin' on?" a recovering Force slurred himself awake. His eyes widened at the sight of the Surge. "Heh, tin men." Seeing the stern faces of the Starguards staring at him, he shut up.

"Time lag," Zane explained to Sceptre. "His brain will catch up soon." They looked at Force again, tongue hanging out, eyes glazed.

Sighing, slightly embarrassed by the interruption, Zane turned her attention once again to Archron. "As I was saying, why don't you show us, Archron?" Zane goaded the elder Astral, who would be King of the universe. "Show us the secret the Knights Destina have been hiding all this time."

Archron was hesitant, but even Decion turned to his erstwhile Lord. "What is she talking about, Archron? We were promised a war to end the Lore once and for all. We were promised a battlefield on the last world at the end of time. We were promised a new beginning as Gods of a new universe. What is happening?"

"I don't think you would understand, Decion," Archron stated in a low growl. "There is so much more going on than our little battle here with the Lore. There's everlasting peace on the way."

"You could have fooled me," an emboldened Zane retorted.

"Enlighten us then, Archron," Gordell spoke; his Chryrian minds impatient, understanding more of why the Surge were jittery.

Archron regained some composure, smiling as he said: "I'll let someone else do the explaining." He stepped away from them, directing his vision upwards.

The others, even the Surge in their stiff manner, followed suit, all eyes drawn to the top of the dark dome where something large fluttered in the shadows. Abruptly, the figure dropped down, a flicker of green wings circling in the air. Before anyone registered what it was, the figure, a great Lore female, landed beside Archron.

"Wha' da hell zat?" cried Force wildly. He raised his arms trying to use his powers but they wouldn't work. Urana forced his arms down, shaking her head. "Dodal nightmare," he wailed.

Urana smiled weakly at him. "Finally something we can agree on!" She, Azure, Gordell, and Force watched as Sceptre and Zane confronted the new arrival.

Sceptre looked at the creature, at first thinking it to be Phasia, finally betraying them. But as he looked closer, he found he recognised the features of the woman. He recoiled in disbelief, taking a step back. It couldn't be. She was dead. Long dead.

Archron smiled again, knowing Sceptre recognised the woman beside him, even though the others, besides Zane, didn't. They looked at Sceptre, sensing all was not right.

"Yes," chuckled Archron, "that's right, Sceptre. I'd like to introduce you to my mother, Destina, last of the Celestian Knights."

The Starguards stared at the being in front of them. The Magna Auran Starguards could barely recognise the former Celestian Goddess before them, but it was her: Destina, daughter of Millenniar, sister of Millennius, mother to Netherlord and Archron—Lore.

The Celestian Knight regarded Sceptre and the rest of the Starguards coldly. Her ragged mouth of energy twisted open and harsh sounds poured forth with sparks of wispy plasma:

"You are kin of my kin. The Gods have sent you to me. We will all be here together when they arrive and remake our worlds so that we may all live in peace." Her mouth closed.

Sceptre just stared at her. "Gods, we have no Gods. The beings that supposedly made us never existed. Myths!" he dismissed Destina with an angry back wave of his hand.

"You are wrong, Aerl," Archron said, almost compassionately. "This is the truth of the Knights Destina texts. The Gods, the Storm of Stars, are all around us. This will be their home. It was mine and my brother's mission to open the universal portals so that they may pass through. But there were forces ranged against us. You, for instance; the one they call the Time Empress; the errant Phasia, and most importantly, the Lore horde when they arrive here."

Zane shook her head. "Your mother lied to you, Archron. Destina is not trying to unite the Antiqchronals, she is re-birthing the Storm of Stars for war. We're all going to be destroyed."

Urana shouted over them all. "Wait a minute, why would the Lore be against you and the return of the Storm of Stars? They were the Storm of Stars' favourite Peoples," Urana asked, trying to get her head around any of it.

As if in answer, Destina let out a howl of anguish pain, "They are coming," she hissed. "They send forth their emissary," she shrieked frantically, staring up toward the dome.

Again, they all followed her gaze as the dome melted away.

The golden ball of energy plunged through the atmosphere of the once blue world. It was once home, but now it would be a battlefield. It roared through the sky seeking out the silver city on the edge of the world. It could hear the shriek of the enemy and her cohorts; there, there under the protection of the Surge who ringed the sky above in a seemingly impenetrable barrier. But their barrier was no protection. They couldn't absorb the energy from the orb as it brushed the Surge aside in resplendent radiance.

The energy sphere met the dome, crashing through it; hot and unwavering sunshine burst through the room, the bright burning sun shining down like a golden eye of doom.

The golden sphere radiated eye-piercing rays blinding everyone who dared look upon it. All except Zane, who continued to stare defiantly.

As it neared Zane shook her head. "No," she whispered as she realised what, or who, the sun-like being was.

The energy ball glided through the cracked dome, golden wings unfurling to slow its descent, the light alone causing everyone to fall to the ground. Even the Surge struggled to absorb all the energy to keep everyone from being fried alive.

Destina hissed at the newcomer, who turned full circle in a wave of rippling heat. His eyes met with Zane's and there was a moment of recognition—of family. But Zane continued to stare at him, not believing that it had come to this.

"Announce yourself, Lore!" her scream echoed through the searing heat. Her heart beat like a pulsar as she awaited the answer.

There was a crackling as a voice of fire emerged: "Behold," the being spoke. "I have returned—Millennius, king of the Lore!"

INTERLUDE 2

THE EXTRA-DIMENSIONAL ADVENTURES
OF
ALPHA RION AND CHALANT

AMAGESH

"What happened?" Chalant asked, tentatively rubbing her bruised behind.

Alpha Rion, also half-sitting on the ground, looked around. "I think the portal collapsed for some reason."

They had been dumped onto a very hard and parched yellow land. The air had a faint smell of iron, sulfur and another tangy aroma. They dusted themselves off, getting to their feet. They were obviously on a very different world from the weapons fortress dimension and even from Earth.

Luckily their visors compensated, shading their eyes in the brightness of the almost golden sky. They search the horizon, finding themselves in the middle of nowhere with nothing but the cracked yellow barren wasteland all around them. Not a tree or greenery in sight. An eerily quietness persisted with neither birds or insects investing the skies. And it was hot. Scorchingly so. They did not have to look very far for the cause. Above in the sky was an unfeasibly large sun, almost white hot, hanging unimaginably close to the planet.

"Quite a sight!" Chalant whistled. "And look!" pointing to the other direction.

Beyond the horizon on the other side of the planet hung two small crescent moons.

"Not Earth, then," Alpha Rion replied, heaving a sigh.

Chalant looked at him, disappointment in her voice, too. "Nope."

Chalant stared between the sun and moons, her dark eyes squinting as if a memory had suddenly stirred. But she dismissed it; memories playing tricks on her Her blue and silver manoeuvre suit was still dusty. As she attempted to slap more dust from her arms, she stopped suddenly, head shooting up.

Alpha Rion was still cursing their luck, then noticed Chalant wasn't listening. At first, he thought she was angry with him for pulling her unceremoniously through the portal created by the mysterious sword or was ignoring him, but he suddenly realised she *was* listening, but just not to him. Her tall, thin body was still, eyes closed under arching eyebrows, her delicate nose and chin pointed up, her full lips slightly parted all attuned to the task at hand.

"Someone's here," Chalant spoke, still standing motionless, listening not to any physical sound, but to something else.

Alpha Rion stared into the empty distance, heat rippling the alien air. His deep blue eyes off-set the black of his hair and and the red and black of his armour, from which he started to reach for his sword. He thought he could, too, hear something, a faint whisper, spoken not on the air, but in his mind. It suddenly grew stronger, vibrating his mind. Alpha Rion tried to resist, but it penetrated even his strongest mental defences.

"Psi-probe!" shouted Chalant grimacing, trying to protect her own mind.

The sound, like a hurricane of voices, whooshed violently around their heads. They reeled from the din, the oppressive heat conspiring to add to the assault.

And then it stopped.

A little dazed and confused, the two looked around, their minds still ringing, especially in the all-too-eerily quiet.

THOOOM!!

The very air around them thundered savagely, the shock wave knocking them down again as a giant plume of dust covered them. Beneath them, the ground cracked then faulted abruptly, dropping down three meters before halting to a juddering stop, rocks and rubble falling onto them. As abruptly it fell quiet again as the echoing thunder receded.

Up through the dirty haze, on the shallow crater's rim, the two could make out the figures of half a dozen beings standing above them in a circle. The dust swirled and began to clear.

Alpha Rion instinctively reached to his sides to draw his swords from his dimensional sheaths, but nothing happened.

He had no energy. He stared up through the dust waiting for the strangers to attack.

Five of the beings on the crater edge were the like of which Alpha Rion had not seen before——tall, metallic beings with huge wings arcing over them. The last, surprisingly, was an alien humanoid male. His scaly skin or outer covering was the darkest black, neither matte nor glossy, but strangely reflective.

Chalant thought his skin might be metal or an exoskeleton of some kind, but soft organic metal, unlike his surrounding companions. His muscular body betrayed no genitals, but his gender was in no doubt. And while his head was not smooth, but of the same mottled patterning as his body, neither did he have hair anywhere. He was not the tallest of beings and he was thin, but with a strong wiry frame. Pronounced facial features consisted of a sharp nose, protruding brow, thin lips. But it was his eyes which held the life, the spirit of him, shining black piercing eyes. He wore no other adornments or accessories. He held a quiet authority. This was his world.

There was a period of intimidating silence as the two groups stared at each other, wondering what was going to happen next.

But Alpha Rion noticed there already seemed to be some sort of contact between the alien and Chalant. It was a silent, knowing bond between strangers of the mind. Then as suddenly as Alpha Rion had that feeling, it was over.

Chalant stirred, as if released from some invisible grip. She rubbed her head.

Then...

"Understand, I never thought I would meet another *e'fromik* . . . sentient being again," the alien said, in a hesitant voice, as if unaccustomed to being used or having just learned their language.

Chalant had also recovered her wits. "Uh, I'm Tera ZaVoir. From Earth" She didn't know what to say or do, standing in a small crater created by their visitor's forceful landing.

"Earth?" the stranger voiced the unfamiliar word. He tailed off, his thin dark lips stretching into a smile. Then he looked at Alpha Rion, with his piercing black eyes, puzzlement across his features.

"Alpha Rion," he introduced himself. "I'm not from Earth, but Tera and I travel together," he added, just to let the stranger know. "And you?"

"Pleasure to be named Amagesh." His voice sufficiently recovered revealed a deceptively soft, almost lisp-like quality. "Understand, I am from a world you would never have heard of, from another galaxy or universe. You are lost, like I am?" A faint buzz echoed his words.

"Yes," Chalant answered irritably. "And you don't have to keep interrogating my mind for information. Just ask." Her head hurt from keeping him out. He was powerful. She could only wonder if the rest of his race were so.

"Apologies," Amagesh replied quickly. "Understand, I required to learn your language. Being alone for so long, speaking aloud comes hard to me. Forgive my intrusions."

He seemed sincere enough, even to Alpha Rion. Chalant nodded and the stifling mental atmosphere seemed to clear somewhat.

"Um, Amagesh, may we climb up?" Chalant asked.

A look of surprise burst from Amagesh. "Of course, my manners, are *drodro*. You must contemplate me as an alien barbarian. Come, come," he gesticulated to them. He had a funny sort of staccato movement to him. Alpha Rion admired his already increasing grasp of English, as he and Chalant scrambled up the crater's wall.

When on solid ground, Amagesh gestured around him, Chalant noticing his long five-fingered hands had extra short vestigial digits on them as if a sixth finger had been lost opposite the thumb.

Amagesh continued, "These are my hosts on this world. They call themselves the Surge."

The metal beings stood silently, their dully coloured metal bodies absorbing the light. However, Amagesh was even more interesting up close, exuding an extraordinary amount of cold from his body. It made Chalant shiver from a meter away even in the opulent heat.

"We leave before it gets hot," Amagesh added, peering up at the sky. He still imparted an uncomfortableness in the heat despite his seemingly natural air conditioning.

"Gets hot!" chorused Alpha Rion and Chalant. They were already roasting.

"It is only morning beginning," Amagesh seemed to enjoy their mutual discomfort. "Can either of you fly?" The two newcomers shook their heads. "Well then. Sgx, Sede," Amagesh indicated two of the metal beings who came forth. From behind they grasped the two travellers under the arms, as one did with Amagesh. There was an initial jolt and they powered into the air.

An eternity of dead yellow desert stretched below them. Nothing alive, nothing green or watery blue or remotely inviting looking. Parched expanse rolled beyond the horizon, dry gray twisted mountains and black scorched plains separated by deep shrivelled valleys made for an unforgiving domain.

Presently, a flat plain opened up, an old dead seabed. Within a depressingly small area of disturbance presented itself spoiling the natural desolate scenery: habitation.

If that was the word for it. Amagesh's camp was not what Alpha Rion and Chalant were expecting. It consisted of one medium-sized building, built of the same surrounding yellow rock.

"Understand, only I need shelter," Amagesh called across to them by way of explanation. "The Surge live off energy, so they *ugubriathe*, er..." he grasped for a human word, "imbibe the rays almost all day," he pointed to the rising white orb of over-generous energy.

They landed in the middle of the clearing. A few more Surge in the encampment stopped momentarily to inspect their visitors, then returned to the task at hand, which just seemed to consist of basking in the sun rays.

"It is nourishment time for them. We alight inside," Amagesh invited them into his abode.

Chalant took a last look around outside. The world, or at least this part of it, was deader than the Sahara.

Amagesh's dwelling was not luxurious, but it was mercifully cooler than outside. Two storeys contained six rooms, almost identical and entirely of stone with stone-made furniture. There were no decorations to enhance the drab surroundings. There was no electronic equipment, a bathroom, or curiously, any food.

Amagesh sensed their curiosity and again elaborated. "Understand, I, like you two, am an explorer. However, I also, like these Surge became trapped here."

"What do you mean trapped?" Chalant blurted out before the equally alarmed Alpha Rion could. They were thinking the same thing. There was no way they wanted to get stuck on this world. It was creepy. And hot!

Amagesh continued. "There is something about this universe which allows entry, but you cannot escape. Understand, I believe this universe is a . . . prison." He let those words hang in the air then nervously clacked softly at Chalant and Alpha Rion's uneasiness.

Was he laughing at them? Chalant thought down-spirited.

"Understand, I at first thought I was here alone, until I was found by the Surge. They are telepathic and quite empathic, though trapped here, too, lost from their colony after they fell into this dimension from another. They had picked up my thoughts and helped me to assimilate. I tried to escape this

90

universe several times. There are no transgates, mass-ports, di-rifts or substrate-pathways out. I now concede this is my home. I am left alone." His face became downcast. "But how did you arrive here?" he asked abruptly. "You appeared from nowhere. One *trasecc*. . . moment, the psi-sphere was *plaxt* and the next, you were there."

Chalant looked at Alpha Rion; a brief inclination to lie quashed. Alpha Rion reluctantly answered. "I can create portals, sometimes big enough to travel through. I think we landed here by accident, unless. . . there are others here like me!" He was hopeful.

Amagesh had been listening intently, though Chalant now noticed he seemed to have no ears. Slowly he shook his head side to side. "Unfortunately, only myself and the Surge." He stared at them, a strange look on his face. "Food!" he suddenly shouted, with a mild telepathic projection, changing the subject. "You require sustenance. The Surge live in interstellar space and absorb energy, able to refocus and channel energy, like their psi-transfer abilities when you arrived. We just reflected and amplified your thoughts against yourselves. Energy imbibing is how they feed and protect and keep me alive. I have been here for more than a thousand years." He smiled, apparently to emphasise his alien youthfulness.

"A thousand years?" Alpha Rion face could barely contain his surprise.

"I'm impressed," Chalant replied. "I wish I could find others of our kind, ones like us, of the mind." Chalant said. "My mind is in symbiosis with a Chryrian, an ancient psi-being," she explained to Amagesh, who nodded thoughtfully. "However, we were following a signal from one of Alpha Rion's people, but we seemed to have lost the signal en route."

"Ah," mused Amagesh. "Understand, I have not met or known anyone besides the Surge. Perhaps on their travels they have encountered such beings of the mind. This is a large world."

Chalant beamed with pleasure, turning to Alpha Rion. She addressed Amagesh. "Would the Surge be able to confirm any encounters. Could they show us the way?"

Amagesh was quiet for some time. At first Chalant thought he had not heard her, but then she heard a distinct buzzing in her head. An alien murmur. She could only admire Amagesh even more for his abilities. The Surge may be telepathic, but not only did they possess a different and complex language, but also a slightly different psi-frequency. She could only pick up garbled scraps of conversation. She wondered if a Chryrian would be able to converse with a Surge.

As for Amagesh, his mind was either more alien than she could imagine or he was deliberately shielding his inner thoughts from her.

Amagesh tuned back to the physical world of communication. He seemed indifferent to the fact Chalant had tried prying into his mind.

"Understand, first of all, I do not know exactly where this land is, but it is likely somewhere on the other side of an ocean to the east. I have not seen or felt anyone like Alpha Rion, but Siilii sensed others of the *djurnii*. . . mind a series of suns past," Amagesh said, indicating a tall slender blue-coloured Surge. "She does not know where they are now, but they could still be out there. The Surge like to avoid contact with others." He gave a very human shrug by way of an apology.

Alpha Rion sighed in disappointment. Amagesh was doing his best to help them. But even if others were out there, they had no way of getting there.

"Understand, I know what you are thinking, Alpha Rion. Not literally!" Amagesh hastily added as Alpha Rion glared suspiciously at him. "But if I were you, I would wonder how I could get to this land. Well…" Amagesh paused, Chalant hearing the incomprehensible psi-chatter again. "Understand, I cannot, and will not, come with you," Amagesh began, seeing confusion in his guests' eyes. "This is my home, now," he gestured again in his jerky kind of movement to indicate his rock house. "But over the passing of a star's lifetime, things change, even Surge. The Surge are living metal. They absorb, reflect or negate energy. They also evolve. Some can now restructure the energy as when they feed me, but these Surge can also restructure themselves, grow things, make things. Take a piece of them and grow it. Anything you want, any shape, any form."

Alpha Rion and Chalant were baffled as to where Amagesh was leading them, but the alien then announced with a flourish.

"Understand, I will grow you a Surgeship and you can search for this land. Understand, I do this for you, You must promise not to return or divulge to others you found me. Understand, I desire my private oasis of remoteness. *D'vorovikg*?"

"Agreed!" both Chalant and Alpha Rion chimed, understanding his meaning.

"The Surgeship will take some time to build, at least the rest of the day. Please you should rest." It sounded more like a command than an invitation.

"How long are the days on this world?" Chalant asked.

Amagesh considered. "Roughly eighteen of your hours," he said. He walked them to another chamber in his stone house. In it was a large and rough stone bed. "Best room in the house," he announced charmingly.

Alpha Rion and Chalant looked at each other. They had no choice. They were tired and hungry. Amagesh made his excuses and left them alone, off to coordinate the ship's construction. They shuffled onto the bed, deciding to rest. Lying surprisingly comfortably on the warm rock bed, the two travellers did not even have time to talk about the day's events; they were both asleep within minutes, Alpha Rion dreaming of long-gone family and a faraway home.

Chalant never dreamed, not in the usual sense. For some psi's there was nothing, for others there were fleeting glimpses of the future or other visions. Chalant was drifting. She could hear voices, alien tongues, and see shadowy figures. She watched and listened to dark plans she could not understand. Then someone noticed her. And then like a door slamming the voices were cut off. There was blurry movement and Chalant's intrusion abruptly ended. She slept through the rest of the day, undisturbed.

"Morning," Alpha Rion greeted her as she awoke.

"Morning? You mean evening," she yawned, feeling better in the cool of the evening.

"Sure, let's go, smarty pants," he grunted.

Refreshed and ready to move out, they left their room. The stony coolness gave way to rising heat as they neared the entrance. The giant sun hung low in the horizon, a sliver of reddish-brown descending across the sky. A dozen or so Surge stood facing the globe with their huge metal bat-like wings stretched out feeding off its energy. They watched entranced by the almost ritualistic ceremony.

"They are still feeding."

Chalant and Alpha Rion started as Amagesh came up behind them. His thin lips in a facsimile of a grin as if pleased he had sneaked up on them unnoticed. "Understand, I hope you rested well?" he said looking somewhat pointedly at Chalant.

"Well, I did for one," Chalant answered, Alpha Rion concurring with a nod.

"Satisfaction for me. Are you hungry?" He pointed to the Surge, "They can feed you as well."

Chalant was hesitant, though looked interested. Alpha Rion was far more sceptical of the notion. "How do you know it can work for us?"

Amagesh gestured with his hands while he talked. "On the Chryrian part of Tera which is pure psionic energy, she would benefit from raw energy as provided by the Surge. The Chryrian would produce the necessary energy to repair, maintain and rejuvenate her human cells."

"That's why I age slower and am generally stronger and healthier than normal humans," Tera stated.

"Yes, the Chryrians can help you absorb solar energy as sustenance. It is good for you. Would you care to try, Tera?"

Chalant smiled politely. "Thanks, but I'll decline for now, Amagesh. Maybe another time."

Amagesh looked a little disappointed, especially when Alpha Rion waved his hands in refusal. The Celestian could have used his own energy to feed, but was wary of the effects on his portals.

"Very well. Understand, I imagine you are eager to depart. Let us look at how the surgeship is coming along."

Amagesh led them around to the back of the house to where there was a crude staging area of rock and metal. And a small, black, blunt-nosed spacecraft. It hardly looked big enough to hold one, let alone two passengers.

"Notions are welcome," said Amagesh, looking pleased at his achievement.

Chalant was impressed: A grown spaceship—a sleek, black almost organic ship with no discernible exterior features. She looked at Alpha Rion who tried to keep a neutral face, but she could tell that he was impressed too.

Alpha Rion asked the obvious question: "Is it big enough?"

Amagesh almost smirked, as much as his lips would allow him. "Ship is psionically controlled. It will follow Tera's thoughts and conform around her. You communicate your navigation, energy, and other environmental requirements. Like the Surge, it absorbs and expels energy, so no requirement for fuel storage or conventional engines. Command what you require."

"Sounds like you've done this before," Alpha Rion said.

"Understand, I have explored where I have needed. You will be safe. The energy the ship absorbs and harness will enable you to travel as far and as long as you require." Amagesh pointed to the ship, inviting Chalant in. "You will try?"

Bouncing with anticipation, Chalant obliged, stepping up to the living metal ship." She stopped short at the smooth exterior of the ship. "There's no entry hatch. How do I get in?" she asked turning back to Amagesh.

"Control. Control it," Amagesh replied, as if it were an obvious thing to do.

Chalant nodded and thought about getting in. A rectangular hatch started to split the hull open in front of her, like a soundless tear in paper. It lowered down in front of her like a ramp. The cavity inside was absolutely bare. Chalant stepped in, the strong metallic smell hitting her immediately. The hatch closed behind her. There was just enough room to stand up in, a slight luminescence emanating from the metal walls.

There's nowhere to sit! thought Chalant. *Where are the seats?*

Just as the thought formed, a seat rose on a single pedestal from the metal floor. "Oh, cool, that's how it works." She looked around, "Let me see outside," she said aloud as she thought it.

A one meter square section of the wall became seemingly invisible, but as Chalant touched it, she could see that the metal had only become transparent. She could see Alpha Rion and Amagesh outside, Alpha Rion looking somewhat apprehensive. She smiled at the thought of having him at her mercy and she turn as she heard a noise behind her, a low platform rising at the rear of the ship—a bed. She giggled to herself and let the thought flitter from her mind as the bed melded back into the ship's floor. She looked back outside and waved to them, but though they were looking in her direction, they didn't wave back.

One way, assumed Chalant.

Now for the final test. All she did was think. *>Hover<*

There was a gentle jolt and as she watched out the 'window' she could see the ground receding a few meters.

>Turn around< she thought to herself. She only had to picture it in her mind and the craft swivelled a few times. After a few minutes of demonstration, the sensation of flying became unsettling, though rather exhilarating, as she had never flown before.

>Okay, that's enough. Land<

The craft stopped spinning and came to land softly outside the house. Chalant thought the hatch open. The ramp lowered letting heat and dust pour in.

She bounded out. "That was great!" she yelled excitedly. "We'll be fine in that, Alpha Rion." She tried to assure him, but he looked doubtful.

"So, are we ready to go then?" he asked, quite ready to leave, doubts and all.

"Yeah, why not? I'm eager to explore a new world. You don't mind, Amagesh, us leaving so soon?"

"No," though his voice sounded sad. "Understand, I have grown accustomed to my solitude. Though your presence has been… eventfully pleasant. Do not worry about me. Understand I will not be alone." He pointed to Siilii, Sede and Sgx standing beside his house.

"I can see that," Chalant made herself smile. "Well, I suppose then, it's time to go."

She stuck out her hand. Amagesh looked down at it. Comprehending he grasped it in his own, Chalant feeling more than a slight tingle of energy from his very cold pitch-black palm. Alpha Rion likewise shook the alien's mottled hand.

"Thank you for your hospitality and help, Amagesh," Chalant said. "I hope we all find what we need. Goodbye."

"*Bvo.* Journey well," Amagesh replied, splaying out his fingers ahead of him.

The two travellers walked over to the surgeship. Chalant demonstrated her skills to Alpha Rion. She touched the side of the ship and the hatch opened for her. As Alpha Rion stepped in behind her, Chalant produced two seats near the front of the ship which curved downward. She heard Alpha Rion curse beneath his breath.

"Is this it?" he asked, scepticism tingeing his voice. "Is it safe?" He tapped the dark metal walls, trying to be more positive.

"It's alright, Alpha Rion, really. The ship and I 'talk' to each other. I control what it does. Don't you trust me?" She knew he did.

"Of course." He only had to look at her to voice their joint concerns. They trusted each other, not Amagesh. Not entirely.

They sat in the surprisingly comfortable metal seats. Without having to manufacture and manipulate flight controls, Chalant commanded the surgeship into the air and up through the sky though remaining below the clouds. Night was closing in.

Amagesh watched impassively from below as the surgeship disappeared into the air.

A flash of movement to his side caught his attention. He turned to see a figure standing in the shadow of the house, almost a mirror image of himself. The air around him turned colder in the newcomer's presence.

"Techmoses," Amagesh addressed the visitor, his voice firmer and surer. "They arrived, as predicted. Understand, I intercepted them and gifted them with the surgeship, as instructed. They will discover and the others in hiding, as foreseen."

A deep voice answered, bitter cold mist forming as he spoke. "You have done well, Amagesh. With the Astral's Chronopolis sealed off to us, these two will lead us to their home."

Amagesh shivered, but from extreme pride. "As inevitably as you commanded. They will not escape us." He bowed in acquiescence.

"Your vigil is over." Techmoses tilted his head in acknowledgement.

Amagesh bowed again as the dark figure disappeared in another flash of darkness. Amagesh gazed one last time around the compound before following suit, leaving the Surge alone basking in the dying light of the white hot sun.

As they travelled, Alpha Rion wondered about Amagesh and his origins. He was unlike any alien he had met before. But he also wondered if their encounter with a psi-capable being had made Chalant homesick. He decided to broach the subject again.

"So what ever happened to your civilization then? Are there others like you out there?"

Chalant thought about it. Bittersweet memories flashing through her mind. "Well, as I told you before, when I finally returned home, I found it destroyed with everyone dead, and my brothers missing. As far as I knew I was the only one alive, but now we know better. To protect my people and their heritage, I buried the village, sinking it deep under the desert. I used to visit it every few years to make sure it had stayed buried. It's my place of solace, of inspiration, my hideaway and comfort. It's my home and I hope to again some day." She looked sad, not really wanting to say more, but this trip could take months. She knew she had to talk about it sometime. She sighed, continuing her story.

"Years later, I came across the Exmoors and worked with them for a few years until I met you. That's when my life really began." She caressed his cheek. "Of course then Lightstream took you away to the future. I didn't know what I was going to do, but then the Hunters found me again and they had another mission for me. And that took me further away from you and my home." Her eyes were so far away.

Alpha Rion wondered what sort of mission it was. She had never spoken of her time with the Hunters. She looked even sadder now.

He decided to leave her history there. She would tell him in her own time, he knew.

"Don't worry, Chalant, I'll get you home, I promise," Alpha Rion assured her.

"I hope so."

They rode on in the Surgeship in silence thinking of home and new beginnings.

CHAPTER FIVE

Earth. Long ago.

"We won't tell them," Millennius whispered harshly.

He, his sister Destina, and Spheron sat on a grassy hill under the edenite sky of what would become northern Iran. Here they had settled after escaping the Helstar, the living pulsar of dark Lore energy. The Traitor Synther had imprisoned the three Celestian Knights during their failed attempt to escape through Alphatronius' vortex following the end of Celestia. Horrific experiments had followed as Synther had tried to turn them into Lore by infecting them with exotic viruses, using their own Celestian energy against them. But they had resisted and escaped. Or so they had thought.

The Helstar was in constant flux spanning multi-dimensions and temporal planes, a defence mechanism against attack. Feigning illness from the exhaustive experiments, Destina had managed to force her captors into a mistake, enabling their escape from the seething star-mass. Between Millennius' light and Spheron's forceshields, the three had fought their way out of the Helstar and into space. But the combined temporal-dimensional spin of the Helstar had flung the trio into the outer reaches of a young galaxy. With his lightvision Millennius had scanned light-years around them through the dusty vacuum and found a planet suitable for life.

As if having survived the torment of the Helstar wasn't enough, there was more of a shock when they discovered the planet was already inhabited by peoples much like themselves; clearly Fifth, but primitive, making tools and weapons from crude metals. After unobtrusive observations amongst the natives and studies of the Tomes of History on his crystalator, Spheron surmised this to be Adantus' world Destinia. The three agreed that the universe must have been looking favourably upon them, at least sometimes.

The three refugee Celestian Knights filtered into the Fifth groups, hiring themselves out as warriors, healers, and mystics, at which they more than excelled. They moved in and out of disparate cultural groups, as the peoples dispersed from the snowy mountains and into the lower plains, across seas, and deserts, living through epic sagas which would be etched into the Bible and other myths. Finally they arrived in a land which would be called Greece. Over those centuries the Celestians had travelled back and forth, lest their longevity and powers became known.

They could have lived this way indefinitely. But then the past reached out to wrench their lives apart. The results of Synther's experiments had not taken effect for nearly three hundred years; essentially less than a third of their lifespan, but it was long enough, as they were already middle-aged Celestian Knights.

Destina had become the first to fall ill, her body shifting between states of corporealness and pure energy. It took all of Spheron's ingenuity and powers to stave off the attacks as much as possible, even when he and Millennius eventually became infected. The Exegete could only assume Synther had infected them with an unknown Lore virus. The virus had the power to transform even a Celestian Knight, literally creating a new, sentient Lore, which would not be able to be reversed. The three knew it would only be a matter of time before their Loreselves took over permanently. But mostly they feared they would join Synther in his quest to spread his evil across the universe.

Even worse, during their time on Earth they had each fallen in love, taking on Fifth lovers and partners. Eventually, they had decided it was time to have children, before it was too late to leave their legacy upon this world.

At the bottom of the hill Xathanius, Helexius, Zasandra, Lazeron, Cal Xarien, and Halydon played. The two eldest, Xathanius and Cal Xarien, were just e§ntering their teens and learning about their Celestian heritage. Their Fifth parents had long since died. The Celestian Knights took it upon themselves to teach their children all they could about their past. But they could not bring themselves to reveal to them the cost of their escape from Synther and that one day it could affect their children in ways they could not foresee.

"We won't tell them," Millennius iterated. "It would be too dangerous…"

"For who? Us or them?" mocked Destina, sitting between Millennius and Spheron.

She blamed her brother for all that had happened, all because of his and Alphatronius' pride. She could only hope the other Celestian Knights had not survived or were not suffering similar fates.

"Our children are old enough to know such things," she hissed, leaning close to him so their voices couldn't be overheard. "They might need to know for the future. How can we keep it from them, Millennius?" Her face seethed at him, fists clenched.

Her brother sighed, tired of repeating the same arguments. "We already live apart from the Fifths, because of what has happened to us and so they don't get suspicious about our natures. If our children found out, with all we've told them about the Lore, we would scare them away from us and lose them forever. Do you want that, Destina?" he whispered sharply back.

Destina looked earnestly down the hill to where her two sons wrestled each other. Cal Xarien looked up at her, showing off, as he pinned the squirming Lazeron then grinned in his younger brother's face. Destina stopped her eyes from watering up. The love for her sons was too much to lose. She would never want to see that love die in their eyes when they found out the truth.

Relenting, she asked, "What must we do?" Tears finally broke through her resolve.

"We will leave when the time is right," Spheron spoke with the resoluteness of his duty. "The different remedies I have used for centuries will soon wear off. But there is no need to fear. As I am the least infected, I can continue to teach the youngsters for several more years. They will want for nothing and when their powers start to manifest, I will teach them how to use them." His graying features creased as he gave Destina a reassuring smile.

Destina squeezed Spheron's hand, breathing with relief. "I wasted so much time hating you for your loyalty to my brother, Spheron. I should be ashamed of myself. When I look at my sons, I know they'll be safe in your hands. I don't feel afraid anymore. In fact, I feel even more alive." Her winsome face lit up with hope, then her hands glowed.

She suddenly stood up and let loose a hail of energy into the sky. She shrieked in delight and so did the children, the unexpected outburst from Mother and *theía* Destina enough to surprise them all. Destina almost collapsed onto the ground, caught by Millennius, her chest wracked in pain. She coughed wildly.

"Universe! Destina, you could have unleashed more than just a few energy sparks. You have to be careful," Millennius chastised her, searching her eyes for any more outbursts.

Destina looked down weakly to her sons. They returned her gaze back up the hill, collective brows knitted in concern for their mother who seemed ill. As they began to stride up the winding path, she waved them off, giving a faint smile. They glanced at each other, satisfied mother was fine, before Lazeron playfully leaped on his brother. They tumbled and wrestled down the hill, Zasandra always egging on the young Lazeron.

"Our children will be fine, Destina," Millennius hugged his sister, which she reluctantly accepted.

Already Millennius could also feel the strange energy coursing up and down inside him fighting to get free. Spheron had used crystalators to counter and absorb some of the energy, which he then dissipated into the sea and mountains, causing quakes and eruptions from time to time. With great difficulty, he had created an advanced enough laboratory in a mountain hut applying medical procedures to infuse some of his own forcefield energies into the siblings to contain any sporadic energy outbursts. However, Spheron was getting weaker from the constant life-sapping infusions. The crystalators weren't so infinite in capacity no matter how often they were drained, such was the power of the Lore virus.

Millennius sighed inwardly. He knew his son, Xathanius, was capable of leading the others, but secretly he did worry about Cal Xarien and Lazeron, and even his own daughter Zasandra who practically worshipped her cousins rather than her brothers. Millennius knew his dear sister was feeding her sons a diet of Knights Destina heroic tales. They had lived long enough to know that the epic battles of the Greeks, Sumerians, Egyptians, and Hittites, among others had passed into legend and the sons of Destina desired to be a part of their own heroic adventure when they were old enough. And even though her visionary sight was failing, Destina had foreseen that her sons would be part of an epic battle upon this world at the walls of a mighty fortress. But then her sight failed her again. Her sons waited for this time, for upon that day they would come of age.

That day would come at the walls of Troy, but little did anyone know that would be the start of the Astrals and their adventures to the end of time at the walls of another fortress.

***

Millennius and Destina died.

At the moment they knew their time was coming to the end Millennius and Destina walked off into the mountain mists never to be seen again.

The night before, there had been a great family feast of roasted goat, fresh bread, olives, fruits, and wine to celebrate their lives. There was singing of old Celestian battle hymns and re-telling of Celestian and human myths intermixed with the delicious food and strong wine even for the children. The younglings would then be guaranteed to still be asleep when Millennius and Destina departed early.

They exchanged sad farewells with Spheron in the chilly mountain morning. He stood in stoic silence watching as they disappeared around a soaring mountainside.

Over an hour later, Millennius and Destina stopped by a young copse of trees within a shallow valley, a feeble mountain stream bubbling down toward a green plain. They stood not knowing what to say, feigning interest in the scenery.

"Where will you go?" Millennius finally asked, not able to look Destina in the eye. He couldn't imagine saying goodbye to his sister, no matter their differences. His insides were burning from the Lore virus but he was resolved not to let Destina see his pain.

"I don't know. The universe will lead me," his sister replied, coolly.

The three Celestian Knights had talked about what would happen to them once they turned into Lore. They had decided they would leave Earth, never to return, and hope their Loreselves would find a life in the greater cosmos.

"You know, he's probably waiting for us out there," Destina's voice shook a little as she tried to pretend the cold was affecting her and not her fears. She looked up to the last of the stars fading away as the sun lazily invaded the sky.

"I don't think Synther knows where we are. It's been centuries. He would have brought the Lore horde here by now if he did." Millennius was sure about that.

"Maybe, but he might be able to sense and track us when we turn."

Millennius nodded at that. It was more than a possibility. "That's why we agreed to separate," the Celestian Knight leader reiterated. The moment he uttered it, Millennius knew he would miss Destina deeply.

Excited with hope in her voice, Destina suddenly reached out and grasped Millennius' hand. "Yes, I know, but I have been thinking, especially after hearing all the old myths again." She was almost breathless with fervor.

"No, Destina, you can't..." Millennius began to protest.

"I must, brother, hear me! I am not called Destina for nothing. Our foresires fostered at least one believer in every generation and I am of the Knights Destina. I have seen enough of the future to know what I must do." Her mood had swung acutely as she snapped angrily at Millennius.

Millennius regarded his sister. She had never been counted as one of the most beauteous of the Celestian Knights, not compared to the cold-ethereal looks of Elysius or the ravishing sultriness of Ultra Ari, but Destina had a haughtiness about her which drew admirers in, especially among the primitive Fifths. Her guile and charm had been her main weapons and it drove her visions, convincing others of what she had seen. More oft than not they were only her interpretations, not the literal truth. Millennius had to know which was happening now.

"Destina, we have to be resigned to our fates. Your powers have been fading for centuries and you cannot be certain they are true."

"They are true," Destina devoutly protested, arms open wide. "I have seen it; me, you, and the Storm of Stars ... but it's all hazy, as if I am witnessing it through Lore eyes."

"And Spheron? What of him? And our children?" Millennius demanded, not able to resist his sister's visions.

"I did not see Spheron. I do not know. But there is another, your son."

"Xathanius?" Millennius was confused.

Destina's eyes clouded over as she sought the inner images. "No, your first born." She looked at him with her own green eyes, which threatened to brim with tears. "Your first born," she repeated with care.

Millennius was speechless. "Hellennius?" he managed to whisper.

He and Phasia had done everything to protect their new-born son from Destina, lest he had come to harm, due to his sister's hatred for Phasia. But then Hellennius had mysteriously disappeared.

"How? Where?" he uttered, weakly, leaning on a tree. He thought briefly Destina was really just humouring a dying Celestian Knight?

But Destina had more to tell him. "He will kill you, Millennius. I have seen it!"

Millennius scoffed, undaunted. "Then I must find him," he shrugged nonchalantly. "Father and son together again. And then he can do what he wants. I am dead anyway." He gestured from the direction they had travelled from, bringing a little, twisted smile to Destina's lips. "And I must find Phasia, too," Millennius said.

"Really!" Destina burst in anger. "You do not still think of her?" she said with some venom. "How can you still trust her?"

A thin smile touched Millennius' lips. "Because I still love her. And we are in no position to judge her now, considering what we will become. She might be able to help us."

Destina rejected this notion, chopping the air with her hands. "No, she sided with the Traitor Synther. And if you ask me, from what I saw in my vision your son has more of her in him than he does of you, so you would be better off without him, too," she huffed, dismissively.

"Argh!" Millennius lashed out without thinking catching Destina with a back-handed slap, bloodying her face. She recoiled from the blow and went to retaliate with blows of her own, but she screamed doubling over in pain.

A green spark burst from her forehead, evapourating a few meters above them.

"Oh, no, it's happening," she gasped in horror, staring at her hands as they started to phase into energy. "Millennius, help me!" Her eyes were wide with fear. She clutched herself trying to hold onto her physical body for longer.

"I cannot," was all Millennius could say. He looked at his sister with some sympathy, but there was nothing he could do. His look was not returned in kind. She dropped her arms forlornly.

"You brought this upon us; you and Alphatronius and your all-consuming pride. Wanting to live beyond the prophecy. I blame you," Destina yelled, even as her body started to convulse and swell from corporealness into energy. "Heretic! The Storm of Stars will judge you when they awake!" she shrieked.

Destina burned green energy. She felt searing pain, but it was accompanied by soaring exhilaration. It felt normal, like a new skin. Then she felt something else. It poured through her veins, her very soul, burst from her hands; a globule of green energy. It expanded to form a portal.

"Hah!" she rejoiced.

Without a farewell, she leaped into the air and disappeared through her opened portal in a showering stream of emerald shards.

Stunned, Millennius stared at the sky for ages where Destina had disappeared, even as the sun finally edged past the distance hills and into full resplendent view. She was gone, possibly forever. Now he was alone.

There was not much else he could do but follow his own chosen path, even if it would lead to his end. He could feel the pain inside him; the Lore energy wanting to emerge, and he could not hold it back any longer.

Picking a point in the sky, Millennius flew toward it, even as he burst afire, turning into a great winged golden Lore; like a phoenix rising and disappearing into the glare of the sun. It may have been the dawn of a new day on Earth, but Millennius knew it was also the beginning of his day of reckoning.

A few years later, Spheron died. And he went to Hell.

Keeping his oath to watch over the children, Spheron's Loreself, a red energised beast, chose to live out his years in the volatile atmosphere of Jupiter, much as the Lore had done thousands of years ago upon Adantus' Antiqchronals Quest. Spheron couldn't help but think of the irony. He didn't need to eat much, thus Jupiter could sustain him without losing too much mass and without him being detected by other Lore. But at least from here he could sense if the Lore approached and protect the children. Or on the off-chance he might have been able to detect when their powers flourished.

Life continued on, Spheron lazily exploring the gas giant, from its tiny sludgy core to the highest colourful bands of swirling brown, orange, and white clouds of hydrogen, helium, methane and ammonium, from the equator to the poles; round and round like an alien goldfish in an exotic cosmic bowl of metallic hydrogen. But Spheron was happy to be in his self-imposed prison as long as the children were safe.

But only a mere two decades later, something changed. As Spheron let himself drift within the hurricane winds in the upper sky, browsing on the failed brown sun's particles, he felt a twist in the temporal fields. Without his Lore temporal abilities he would not have noticed it, much less have been able to identify who it was. But he could sense it, sense her, unmistakably—the Traitor Synther's sister: Phasia.

Red energised wings propelled Spheron out of Jupiter's turbulent atmosphere, his open portal partially sucking in the poisonous air of the gas giant, which dispersed upon his entry to Earth. But he was too late. Phasia's temporal trail had led him to an enourmous burning fortress on a wind-swept plain. Spheron recognised it as Troy. But the walls had been destroyed by a devastating force—a temporal collision, his senses tasted in the air. There were dead everywhere, human, as Spheron could not see or sense the children as he scanned from the air. He worried for his own son, Halydon.

If Phasia has hurt him, Spheron growled sparks.

Suddenly, a faint temporal echo caught his senses, something like a smell of a memory which hadn't occurred yet. He tilted his head to a direction not known on Earth and listened to a taste coming from nowhere. Spheron closed his eyes and heard the trail calling to him.

Phasia had taken the children.

Incensed at the idea, Spheron thought for what purpose could Phasia have taken them? He took the temporal path open to him and jumped into the timestream. A blink of an eye later he exited over Imperial Rome, having swam in a temporal stream which meandered wildly in an effort to shake him back into normal space. Upon exiting the portal he shifted into phase space; a quasi-dimensional state like a cosmic one-way mirror. Spheron could watch the outer world without being observed himself.

Spheron searched all over the city and surrounding environs, but he could not find them. However, as he flittered unseen past citizens he heard rumours of a strange woman with Phoenician hair teaching children to fight like soldiers before they strangely disappeared.

Again, another scent presented itself. Exasperated, he time-ported again, following the scant trail left by Phasia. However, he heard the same sort of tales in Renaissance Genoa, Enlightened Philadelphia, Buddhist China, Dreamtime Australia, Inca Peru, Easter Island, and countless other places.

Spheron's fears see-sawed at each destination. He could only conclude one thing from Phasia's actions. She was teaching them like he could not. Moreover, she was training them for war.

But for whose side? he thought to himself, as he followed her latest voyage through the centuries.

Though she was careful to hide their temporal trails from casual Lore detection, Spheron had come to discover her tells and techniques. He finally caught up to them on the moon in what would be Earth's late nineteenth century.

The children were standing on the surface of the moon just in their manoeuvre suits. Spheron's inquisitive mind tried to work out how Phasia had crafted the armour. Not that vortexite was hard to manufacture on Earth once you knew the correct chemical compositions with elements abundant on Earth, but she must have possessed extra crystalators with her to as well to power the suits.

Impressive, he approved.

He observed the children using their temporal powers and energy to keep the vacuum at bay around them. They practiced opening time-portals, lateral porting, and temporal mechanics on moon rocks making them decompose or aggregate over time. Not only could Spheron see the original children, but he could also see their own children. And one he could only assume to be his granddaughter. He waited an infuriating few seconds, but he could not see Phasia.

He watched the children, admiring how they had grown and trained. There were Destina's grown children each with their weapons, the nethersword and voidspear. Of Millennius' younglings, Xathanius had a sword forged on Earth, but tempered with Lore energy, Spheron could feel it; while his younger brother Helexius was a conjuror of swirling temporal dimensions. Zasandra was a chaos witch, as Spheron would have called her. At this moment, Zasandra hovered high above the moon. She threw her arms out and a coarse ripple of chaotic, entropic energy shot from her hands and bounced off the bright convex forcefield proffered by Spheron, son of Spheron.

"My mighty son," he spoke to himself, proud of his son.

Spheron, the younger, had grown well. Spheron the elder held his position in phase space, akin to a door half open from time into space, so as not to be detected. He continued to watch the children, more aptly young adults, he realised, practice their manoeuvres and abilities. A familiar sense suddenly clouded around him.

He whirled around. And there was Phasia, all serene and reverted back to her Celestian form. A shocked silence hung between them, both not knowing the others' intention. Astonishment ruddied her face as she recognised the Lore before her.

"Universe, Spheron, it's you! I thought it was Synther hiding and following us from phase space. What has Synther done to you?" she cried, throwing her arms around Spheron, his crimson energy brushed aside by her own. "What happened? Where are the others?"

But Spheron ignored her questions until his own was answered: "What are you doing with the children? They are in my charge!" he growled in an energy-crackled voice, which surprised him, never having heard himself speak in this form before.

"Universe! You don't know!" She suddenly burst into Lore form and before Spheron could shield himself, a cascade of energy burst from her forehead and into Spheron's. Her memories filtered into him, showing him Magna Aura and Synther's destruction of the system.

"Spheron, the children, they are temporally-unbound because of what Synther did to you in the Helstar. They are Astrals. And I am taking them to save their kin at Magna Aura. The last sons and daughters of the Celestian Knights will save the first! Think of it!" Her eyes shone as she slipped back into her Celestian self.

Spheron took a moment to recover from the memory transfer; the Celestian sci-tech in him marvelling more at the ability and the technological possibilities more than the intrusive act. He looked down upon the children: the Astrals. His, Millennius' and Destina's legacy survived in them. Celestian Knight blood would flow heroically through time.

He turned back to her. "Forgive me, Phasia, you can see I'm… not myself these days," he looked down at himself. "You have surpassed my expectations and teachings. They are fine young Celestians and a credit to our peoples. Turning your back on your brother could not have been easy."

Phasia shook her head. "I was never keen to be with my brother, Spheron. I was forced to follow him after The Fall. You all gave me no choice," she lamented bitterly. "I lost my son and the trust was lost. What else could I do? But Magna Aura was different. There was another Golden Era dawning and Synther wanted to destroy it. I could not let that happen. But I was too late, the first time. Now we are going to put things right. And I want you to be there." She stroked Spheron's arm compassionately.

"I cannot Phasia. Not like this," his crackly voice hid his sadness. "I revealed to my son what had happened to us in the Helstar, but only that we were infected and would die, not that we would turn into Lore. The children must never know what their parents have become."

He looked down at his son, who happily embraced his daughter after she had ported herself and several large moon rocks to him. Phasia followed his gaze, knowing his thoughts.

"It would destroy them. I do not even know where Millennius and Destina are. But I do know our children are in good hands with you. Go save Magna Aura and the new Celestian civilisation." He bowed to her.

Phasia nodded, solemnly, looking down in pride at the children. "You could promise me one thing though?" she asked.

"What?"

"Find Millennius and tell him I still love him." Her eyes sparkled. Spheron's Lore heart pulsed.

"It would be my pleasure," he said, his fiery mouth smiling. "Through everything else, through all the torture and the experiments in the Helstar, Millennius never stopped loving you."

She beamed. "Thank you, Spheron, I will never forget this. They are ready now." Phasia looked at the children. "Your son is a fine character and his daughter, Sola, will also be a powerful Astral."

"A daughter? More powerful?" a shocked Spheron gasped.

"Sexist!" she grinned.

"No, I just never imagined. Generation after generation of Spherons have always produced a male line. Earth has changed everything, it seems!"

"It surely has." Phasia pointed out a small, black-haired girl. "She's the youngest of all, Zane. She is special, daughter of Xathanius. She may not be fully aware of her powers, but she has such great potential, Spheron. If you can, watch over this one."

Though he was not sure what Phasia meant, Spheron nodded.

"Goodbye, old sage." She kissed Spheron on the cheek. And with that, Phasia blinked out of existence and in an instant was back amongst her young charges. She gestured and shouted a command, somehow heard by them in the vacuum of space. Portals opened and then she and the Astrals were gone.

Spheron thought about what Phasia had said and her invitation. The more he thought about it, the more he found himself intrigued.

"Hmm, just a little peek!"

Space erupted around him as his portal followed the way Phasia had traversed to Magna Aura.

CHAPTER SIX

Magna Aura. Long ago.

Azure burned blue destruction.

Every single Lore in the Magna Aura system were destroyed in a conflagration of what amounted to anti-Lore fire.

Against the odds, Synther had survived. Blown across the system toward Magna Prime he drifted in space. He came to injured and smarting from the raw power of his Loremaiden daughter.

Synther cursed. He had to escape back to the Lore horde and replenish his energy and forces. Barely able to port out, his vortex shoved him through a weakened conduit. He sighed upon exiting, but he gasped in surprise at what awaited him.

Instead of the Helstar's maw to greet him around the sun, he could not believe his eyes: there was only chaos and death. The shattered remains of the Helstar filled his vision. Azure's power had reached beyond her grasp and years. Dead Lore de-cohered into the universal grave like a cascade of fireworks while other Lore faded like sunlit shadows. His horde was no more.

The Power! Synther had dared not believe the power his daughter possessed. He had come to claim his daughter and take her away from the Starguards, but she had betrayed him. Now he had to act decisively, quickly. There was no time to dwell on his horde's death as Synther was suddenly confronted by Lord Aeon, the Astral leader porting in from temporal space.

Synther sneered. He didn't need to see his enemy as much as smell the energy pouring off Millennius' progeny. The Prime Lore's blue energy burned in rage as his temporal shields and energy thrust him through space. Aeon, on an intercept course, drew his sword ready to smite the Lore leader. The sword sang to Synther; a familiar aura.

No! Synther realised angrily. *A blade honed by my own sister!* The thought pierced through him as surely as a blade to his heart.

Synther reacted quickly. He had been injured badly. His energised form had saved him from certain death, but he ached all over. He swiftly retreated into temporal space, disappearing in a hail of agitated blue rays. Aeon assumed he was escaping to form another Helstar and return with another force. He could not let that happen.

Activating his crystalator, supplied by Phasia and which the Astrals were still getting accustomed to, Aeon commed out: "Archron, Netherlord; with me. The Traitor cannot escape!"

His call had interrupted the brothers who were busy chopping into lingering Lore with voidspear and nethersword. They responded and ported alongside Aeon.

"The Traitor Synther's trail!" He showed them on his crystalator. They synched data. "We finish this now!" The brothers grinned in anticipation.

The three eldest Astrals ripped into temporal space following the ever-shifting path Synther left as he desperately sought to shake them off. He left temporal decoys, traps and false portals, jumped through star cores, and skirted singularities with their jagged chronal landscapes deformed by the black holes they hid within. But still the Astrals followed the Traitor Synther through frightening maws of time vortices, cold timewaves, and convergence interstices, until...

. . . normal space beckoned. The blackness almost disorientated the trio after the kaleidoscopic journey they had endured.

"New galaxy?" Archron guessed.

"Perhaps," Aeon replied.

They knew they were somewhere completely different. They didn't care. All they could see was the world Synther was heading for in normal space.

The three Astrals hovered in space, visually keeping track of Synther's trail with the crystalators. Once they were sure that was his final destination they time-ported to the surface.

"Hnnnnh!"

"Arrgh!"

They had all dropped out of their portals to their knees upon the ground, as if their energy had been switched off. In agony they could only look up.

Before them stood Synther, who had reverted to his Celestian form, grinning from his keen blue eyes and narrow mouth. He had once been one of the more handsome Celestian Knights, but his body now seemed drained as if his energy had been feeding off him. His tall over-lean body was donned in his black manoeuvre suit with dark blue stars and zigzag flashes decorating his torso and chest like medals and scars, lending to his nefarious nature.

But it was not him who had the Astrals' utter attention, but the beings surrounding them; tall metal beings, hundreds of them. The surrounding ground also seemed littered with whole or parts of dead metal beings.

"They call themselves the Surge. And this is one of their worlds," Synther spoke, answering their unasked question, smoothing back his ruffled dark blue hair. His Celestian voice sounded whispery from years of non-use. "And they are negating all our energy. No Lore, no temporal energy, no core Celestian energy."

"Then we will just kill you with our weapons," Archron snarled, jumping to his feet and raising his voidspear for a throw. Netherlord and Aeon also eagerly drew their swords and charged.

"Hold!" shouted a female voice from a ridge behind them.

They froze, the voice sending shivers down the spines of the Astrals. They knew that voice.

"Mother?" Archron turned around, incredulous shock on his face.

He and Netherlord looked around at their staid captors and rushed over to their mother, removing their helmets and dropping their weapons to hug her.

Destina smiled at her sons. "Cal Xarien. Lazeron." She hugged her sons tightly. "Look at my sons. My, that cursed Phasia did a good job!" She caressed their faces and hair.

Her own face was strangely sallow and she looked thin in her green manoeuvre suit, with her one-time mane of brown hair which she had mostly worn up, now hanging limply down her back.

"Phasia?" Aeon spat, still standing ready to cut down Synther. "She was in on this treachery? Archron, Netherlord can't you see what is happening here?" He pointed his sword from Destina to Synther, the later still grinning.

Archron and Netherlord looked at their mother for answers.

"What is happening here, mother? How are you still alive?" Archron asked anxiously, still holding on to his mother's hand. He searched out his voidspear wondering if he could reach it in time if anything went awry.

"They lied to you," Synther started.

"Shush, Synther. I will tell the story." Destina looked back at her sons rather nervously. "Well, Synther is right about that." She stole a daggered glare at Synther. "Millennius, Spheron, and I did lie to you about us dying, as you can see," she shrugged. "But we, well, Millennius wanted to spare you the truth . . ." she trailed off.

"About?" Aeon barked impatiently, not wanting to hear anything of his father's supposed treachery. He still held his sword, ready to strike.

Synther's grin widened. "About what I did to them when they were held prisoner in the Helstar... before letting them escape."

The wind swept around him as if the barren world detected his dark presence.

"We already know you infected them somehow. Phasia told us," Aeon retorted, desiring to wrap his hands around Synther's neck and crush it.

Destina sighed dramatically. "Phasia, hah! She lied to you, too, then. She knew," Destina contended. "Oh, yes, we were infected with a Lore virus . . ." she confessed, "but over time we would have become Lore, fought with you, and destroyed Earth. We didn't want that so we left Earth; we split up and roamed the universe. But Synther found me!" She threw him another disdainful glance. "He offered me a truce in return for a cure for my ailment. Here on this world . . ." She waved her arms around her. "The Surge are a cure of sorts, absorbing my energies, and allowing me to live a normal life, such as it is. But I always had a far grander ambition!" Proudly she regarded her sons, "The Knights Destina will rise and fulfil their mission; such does this destiny flow through my blood. Through our blood!"

It took time for the information to sink in. Archron and Netherlord still stood beside by their mother, exchanging confused glances. Aeon recovered first.

"And that mission?" a fearful Aeon already knew the answer to that.

"Magna Aura of course, to begin with!" Synther spoke out, bursting to reveal this plan. "The firstborn of the Celestian Knights are of no use to us if they will not join us. What better way to seek revenge against the rest of the Celestian Knights for their rejection of us!"

"Us?" laughed Aeon. "You mean yourself. You turned your back on the Celestian Knights. You just want revenge!"

Synther bristled. "Who left you on Earth to rot?" he argued back. "Your father, that's who! Who is giving you back your destiny? I am!" Synther thumped his chest. "Join us," he indicated Destina, "and take what is yours, before you end up like Magna Aura when we attack again." His angry breaths joined the wind, whipping through them all as he awaited his answer.

Aeon stared a hole into Synther. He regarded the other Celestian Knight. "How can you do this, Destina?" asked Aeon, shaking his head. Archron and Netherlord avoided his eyes.

But she ignored him. "And your daughter?" Destina asked Synther. "Has she not joined us?"

Synther looked downcast and then angrily at Aeon. "They turned her against me," he accused Aeon. "The war had been won, Azure would have been mine, but Phasia found your children. Millennius has a lot to answer for: me, you, Azure, Phasia, and more..."

"All this for petty revenge?" Aeon yelled. He backed away from the group, sword pointing forward. "Archron, Netherlord, let's go! We won't be a part of this!"

Destina laughed. "How are you going to leave? Walk to the stars? You have no power." She addressed her sons. "Are you going to let him order you around for the rest of your lives, especially after what his father put us through?"

"Without my father, you would not have escaped after The Fall and had a life on Earth or bore two sons. You can't have it both ways, Destina," countered Aeon, trying not to shout, swallowing down his fear.

"He's smart, Destina, I'll give him that, but tell him the rest," Synther urged.

Aeon look exasperated. He had no way to escape. No way to warn the others. Yet he had no choice, he had to do both. For now, he listened.

None too proudly, it seemed, Destina announced: "There is an alliance between the Lore, the Surge, and the Knights Destina."

"What?" Aeon floundered.

Even her sons balked at this announcement.

"Why, mother?" Netherlord asked.

"Look around you," Destina said. "We have the Lore. And don't you recognise who the Surge are?" She answered before they could: "They are the People of Matter burned to stone. These are Antiqchronals. This is the Knights Destina's universe!"

"Myths, Destina, and superstition," Aeon scoffed, though a deep down fear at the truth petrified him.

"No, Xathanius," Destina scolded Aeon by his birth name. "They are real and we will prove it by summoning the Storm of Stars. We will remake our worlds as they were," Destina proclaimed.

Archron and Netherlord turned to each other realising the import of their mother's news. Their destinies were being fulfilled.

"The Lore have made you completely mad!" Aeon raged, eyes darting around for a way to escape. But they were thoroughly surrounded by Surge.

Destina rebuffed him, shouting, "No, Xathanius, you see, my Lore visions have revealed to me the secrets of the Knights Destina. I saw the Storm of Stars. They are not dead, only sleeping. It is my intention to awaken the Gods, to ask their forgiveness for disobeying the prophecy that the Celestian Knights should not have entered through the Alphatronius' vortex during our war with the Lore, and that we may rise again. But in order to succeed, we will need all the Antiqchronals and the Fifth's energies to open the portals for them and to bath the Gods in enough energy to awaken them. I want to set the universe right," she proclaimed.

Aeon laughed, galled at her insane ambition. "There's nothing wrong with the universe," he said, "Just you. And why should the Surge join you?" he asked. "Surely they would hate the Lore for what they did to them." He looked at the mute impassive metal-like sculptures.

"The Surge are, if nothing, a proud people, full of justice And justice to them would be a reformed universe where all the Antiqchronals were equal as never before. This will be their rebirth," Destina answered smartly.

Aeon sweated. He was running out of arguments and option "At the cost of everything else, including all our lives," he realised glumly.

"Maybe not," Destina threw him a bone. "The Gods may look kindly upon us and spare us," she said. "Who is with me?"

Without hesitation her sons joined her side. Synther crossed his arms in satisfaction, surrounded by the unmoving Surge. The wind had died to a whisper waiting for whatever came next.

Unsurprisingly, Aeon stood alone.

"Zasandra and our daughter, Celestra, will also join us," Netherlord confirmed.

"Naturally," Destina grasped her son's shoulder. "They will be welcomed."

"Over my dead body will my sister join you," vowed Aeon. He wished his powers were back.

Destina considered Aeon for a while. Her lips twisted in a firm but sad smile. "So shall it be. Kill him," Destina instructed no one in particular.

Aeon raised his sword, ready for the attack, pointless, he knew against so many. But he hoped Phasia's tempered blade would protect him.

"Spearhead!" Destina didn't need to finish her sentence as Synther flared up into his blue Loreself, released from the Surge's energy-absorbent influence.

Aeon crouched into a defensive position, searching for any cover or advantage. But before he could defend himself, Synther blasted him with corrosive Lore energy. Aeon seemed to blur in the blast and swayed uneasily as Synther halted his slaughter.

Smouldering and bloodied, Aeon fell to the ground, still clutching his sword. His blackened dead body smelled foul in the wind, which had chosen that moment, as if in spite, to pick up again.

Archron and Netherlord, trying to ignore the stench, stood in silence not sure whether to show shock or to be worried Synther would attack them. Then they felt their own energies return to them as Destina ordered Spearhead to release them as well.

"Mother!" Archron shrunk back in fear. He cried in heaves.

Netherlord shaded his eyes, staring open-mouthed.

To the shock of her sons, Destina herself had transformed into a large green Lore with voluminous wings and a fiery crown of dark hair.

She tried to mollify them. "This is now my true form, my sons." Destina's voice was almost unrecognisable beneath the crackle of energy. Looking down at the burned body of Aeon, and seeing the looks of uncertainty in her sons' eyes, her voice betrayed no emotion. "Bury him," she ordered. "We must leave here, quickly. The Astrals will surely search for him. I have chosen a place and prospective future time on Earth from where to witness the rebirth of the Storm of Stars."

Archron and Netherlord hesitated a split second. The lingering moment was rent by a blast of energy crackling past them as Synther gouged out a shallow grave. He kicked and rolled the semi-cremated body of Aeon into the hole, back-filling it with another gust of energy.

He stood back, landing a look of gloating pleasure at Destina's sons. Neither looked back. Neither said a customary prayer.

"Thank you, Synther," Destina said, a little disappointed in her boys. "Cal Xarien," she continued. "I want you to do whatever it takes to find the Peoples of Time and Psyche, the remainder of the Antiqchronals. Make me an army from them."

Archron nodded swiftly, keen not to seem weak again in front of both his mother and Synther. "We had problems with Psis on ancient Earth. I will search them out for help, willingly or not."

"Good," she said. Turning to Netherlord, she ordered. "Lazeron, I will show you how to open the portals for the Storm of Stars. They will have to be created in precise locations, dimensions, and times. You will have to destroy or manipulate space-time in order to create hyper-dimensional corridors for their passage."

"Understood, mother," her younger son acknowledged.

Again, Destina paused, scrutinising her sons and their commitment. "And as for the rest of the Astrals who don't join us, they will have to be eliminated," Destina commanded.

"Mother, we can't..." Netherlord started.

Destina shot her son a withering look leaving Netherlord feeling ten years old again.

"I will do that," Synther interrupted, gladly offering his services. "But it will take time to find another horde and re-establish the Helstar."

Netherlord glared at him. "Wait until my family have left the Chronopolis," he said darkly, backed up by his brother.

"Naturally," purred Synther. His wicked grin left them less than confident.

Destina continued, "And I especially desire that Millennius' lineage be excised from the universe. No younglings thirsting for revenge." She fixed both her sons with a hard glare of sparks. There was no way to get out of it. Their hands would be getting bloody.

Netherlord nodded silently. Archron embraced his role further.

"We should also take control of Magna Aura negating any resistance. But I'm sure a few of the Starguards would be willing to join us. I believe the Alphatronius Clan are sympathetic to the

Knights Destina, are they not?" Archron asked, knowing the data on his crystalator was correct.

Destina smiled, warming to the idea. "Yes, so the legends say. Try to split the Starguards. Divide and conquer. Our family will rule the universe." Her sinuous lips parted in a cruel smile. "I am so proud of you, my sons." Her Lore eyes couldn't well up, but the emotion was there.

"Don't forget the Lore," Synther added, somewhat less than ecstatic his plans of domination were being suborned.

"Of course," Destina outwardly smiled. "The Knights Destina and the Lore will rule," she affirmed their alliance. "Come." She held out two energised hands. Archron and Netherlord reached out and held one each. "Synther, I will meet you up-time on Earth, once the Chronopolis is destroyed."

Synther hissed agreement. He traced a circular motion in the air with his arm, a blue flash of energy erupted before him. He vanished through the created portal, which snapped shut with a decidedly tempestuous electrical hiss.

With Synther gone, Destina regarded her sons in turn. "We need the Lore, but we don't need Synther. All we need is control of the Lore. And the Surge can do that." She indicated Spearhead and the thousands of Surge around them. "We will take care of Synther once he has completed his side of the bargain. There is no sin in betraying a traitor," she laughed. "Are you ready, Spearhead?" she addressed the Surge leader behind her.

The great red Surge bowed; his forces were ready.

Destina blew into the air in front of her and a portal whirled out of thin air, the temporal vortex within beckoning her to join with it. She soared into the portal followed by Archron and Netherlord. Spearhead signalled to several thousand Surge who streamed into the portal departing the strange little world, littered with dead metal bodies.

Only one Surge was left behind to watch over the dead. In a few days, he would detect a large, unknown object approaching the planet. The jet-black Surge would engage the alien intruder, not knowing his actions would bring the Earth-Axala war into his life.

Spheron fell out of phase space.

Even for a Lore he was exhausted. He had followed Lord Aeon and the sons of Destina, if only to see the end of Synther. Instead of recklessly time-porting down shadowing the Astral trio, he had stayed hidden in phase space as a precaution.

From there, he had witnessed the treachery of Destina, her astonishing alliances with Synther and the Surge, and her plan for the Storm of Stars, which was even more frightening. It had taken all of his power to keep from being detected by the Surge and having his powers absorbed from phase space. And to his ever-lasting bitter regret, he could only watch helplessly as Aeon had been murdered.

Now he glided over to the grave, gently uncovering Lord Aeon's head, looking upon the burnt, almost unrecognisable face of a warrior whom he had practically raised as a second son and who had now died too soon.

"I'm sorry, Xathanius. I failed you." He tried to cry, found he could not, which made him want to cry more.

What could I have done? he thought savagely to himself. Spheron knew he couldn't go back and change time; the Surge would already be here and absorb his powers and Synther or Destina would have killed him, too.

There was only one thing he could do. He covered Aeon's corpse again. Not wanting to leave, but having to, Spheron stretched his arms out and felt space split into the summoned portal. He flew into the portal and imagined his destination.

If he was to help save the universe then he had to find Millennius.

CHAPTER SEVEN

The Astral Dimension. Long ago.

"What do you mean you're leaving?"

A furious Helexius jumped from the throne after his cousins, Archron and Lazeron had suddenly announced their intentions. They stood alone in the central chamber.

"Why in Zeus' thunder are you going?"

Nonchalantly, Archron stated, "We're going to explore, search the universe for answers."

Helexius did a double take. "Answers? To what?" He shook his head in non-comprehension. "With my brother, our leader, still missing, you're leaving just like that?" a suspicious Helexius added.

Netherlord gulped subtly at the mention of Lord Aeon.

"Naturally, we will be searching for him on our travels," Archron channelled his mother's tone. It was becoming easier for him. "But the war is over. Synther is dead. We are leaving!" he stated with finality.

"And Zasandra and Celestra are coming with me," Netherlord confirmed, trying to sound as confident as his brother.

Helexius opened his mouth to contend this, but couldn't speak. A mixture of anger, disillusionment, fear, and confusion gripped him. His blue eyes closed in deep thought. He took a deep breath.

Composed again, he asked. "Are you sure Synther is dead?"

"Yes," Archron replied assuredly. Standing beside his brother in front of Helexius was actually calming for him. He smiled inwardly, finding it easy to lie to Helexius, who was more worried about his own brother than what they were up to.

Helexius sat down heavily. Only a week ago, Archron and Netherlord had returned with a tale of an epic battle on a faraway world where Aeon had slaughtered the Traitor Synther, but had mysteriously disappeared soon after. Presumably Aeon had been returning to the Chronopolis but never arrived. The brothers were conveniently fighting off other Lore at the time And while they saw Synther defeated, they didn't see where Aeon had gone.

Under intense questioning and a time-port to the said lush green world in another galaxy, Helexius had been forced to believe their story. Signatures of the Traitor Synther's potent Lore energy and DNA had been found in a battlefield along a lake, (the substituted world a ruse by Destina with Synther providing the samples) enough to convince Helexius of the truth of his cousins' words.

The Astrals were safe for now in the Chronopolis, watching over Magna Aura. Now the sons of Destina had dropped their bombshell. The timing didn't feel right to Helexius, but what could he do? He couldn't hold them back. They weren't prisoners. And at least they had the decency to tell him face to face, as an equal.

Reluctantly, he only had one option. "Very well," he relented. "But I expect you will report in from time to time and return if called to action." Statement not a question.

"Of course," Archron bowed in response. "We are kin after all. And we stand together," he answered with a crisp smile.

The brothers were about to bow again, but Helexius stood down from the throne pacing toward them. He stopped and held out his right arm. Hesitantly, Archron first, then Netherlord clasped Helexius' forearm. Eyes met, searching for meaning, secrets, and truths. With a last firm pump of assurance, Archron and Netherlord left the throne room for their respective chambers, leaving Helexius brooding on the throne.

A look of utter disbelief set on the face of Zasandra, the Timechantress, after her husband told her of his and Archron's

130

plans. And then came the hard part. Sitting Zasandra down and telling her about her father.

"That bastard! How could he?" she rose angrily pacing their sleep chamber, hands flying about her head. "I hated him, always did for leaving us and now to find out he lied to us—to our faces—his own children!" she fumed. She stood across the room from him, arms folded staring at the wall, while Netherlord sat on the bed.

He knew whatever she said, she was still grieving over a father she despised.

Her breathing was still heavy when she asked: "And Destina can help us?" Her tone said it all—*But she's a Lore!* "I'm sorry," she instantly apologised. "I know she is your mother, but can she be trusted, even if she helped to kill Synther."

Netherlord cringed inwardly. He and Archron had decided to hide the truth about Lord Aeon's death. It wouldn't have been taken well and they needed Zasandra on their side. She wasn't a Knight Destina by blood.

The siblings story had unfolded to the rest of the Astrals that he, Archron and Aeon had tracked Synther. Aeon and Synther had fought. To Zasandra they had added in confidence that Destina had intervened helping Aeon to kill Synther. She had then revealed herself to her sons and they were reunited. While they fought off other Lore, Aeon had disappeared unbeknownst to them. Before her sons had returned to the Chronopolis, Destina had chosen that time to give them their missions to bring forth the Storm of Stars. She thought it was their only option for peace. They had duly accepted and were now prepared to leave. And since their version of events was different to the one told to Helexius to protect him from the truth, it was easier for Zasandra to believe them.

"Yes, my mother can help us, but there is a lot to be done. We'll find Xathanius and restore peace to the universe with the

Storm of Stars, but we have to leave soon," he repeated the oft rehearsed lines. "We need you and I also want Celestra with us. Helexius just wouldn't understand our plans. And Phasia can't be trusted." He paused before continuing, trying to work out how much Helexius would have confided in her. "And where is Phasia?" he asked casually.

Zasandra huffed with mirth. "That is the question of the hour! She disappears as she does and Helexius has been tight-lipped about it." She laughed again, but it was cold and sharp. "I have two brothers who never paid attention to me, a human mother who died when I was too young, and a father who lied to me and now is a Lore. What a family, eh?"

She walked back to the bed and sat beside Netherlord and looked him in the eye.

"You've never lied to me," she purred. "I will follow you where-ever you need me." She looked deeply into his dark eyes. "Have I ever told you how much I love you?" she asked, trying to remember their heady married days back in ancient Greece before they knew about their Astral powers.

Netherlord smiled wryly. "Not recently, but I know." He caressed her chin, any guilt melting away.

"Come, love." She pulled him across the bed, Netherlord obliging.

They kissed gently, lying on the bed, their passion working up, their armour and clothing disengaging themselves from their bodies as they made love for the last time in the Chronopolis.

Weeks later.

"We're leaving, too!" Aristedes stated boldly. "We really want to search for our father! We need him, no offense, uncle." He stood defiantly with Zane beside him, in front of Helexius and his daughter Lightstream with Spheron the Younger and his

132

daughter, Sola. He continued his case, "We all know Netherlord and Archron have abandoned us; you know that!" he shouted in reiteration, punching the air with a clenched fist. "They won't return to help us if attacked; we haven't even heard from them or even know where they are! Any one?" he challenged them to answer him. "Zane and I are of age—"

"Barely," interrupted Lightstream, a little too loudly. Spheron scowled at her, which she ignored.

Aristedes glared at his cousin. She was only a year older than him, yet as the son of Xathanius, Lord Aeon, he would lead the Astrals one day. For now, until it was certain his father was gone—he couldn't bring himself to say the word—then it had been agreed Helexius would command.

"Please, uncle, we can do great good out there." Aristedes pointed in a random direction. "We will keep in touch, we promise, but we have to try!" he pleaded.

Zane was close to tears, her black fringe hiding her eyes as she stared at the floor. Aristedes, headstrong, yet empty of arrogance let his words echo around the throne room.

Helexius sighed, shaking his head slightly. Aristedes took this as a sign of rejection.

"Aristedes," Helexius began, "You have grown up so much in these last few months after the war. I am not disappointed in you," he said with a thin smile and a glint in his eyes. "Your father would be proud of you, both of you, as I am." He studied the two closely, knowing their determination would not be quelled. "Do you promise to keep in touch?"

The siblings' faces brightened in pleasure. "Yes!"

"Do you promise to protect each other?"

"Yes!" they chorused together again.

"Do you promise to find your father?"

"Yes, uncle!" They bowed their vows to Helexius.

Helexius nodded in satisfaction. Lightstream and Sola seemed less than enthused. It meant more chores for them.

Spheron strode forth, clapping the young Astral on the shoulder. "Well done, I am proud of you, too, as my father would have been." He embraced Zane, who smiled broadly back at him.

Helexius had another question. "Where will you start?"

Aristedes answered, "Well, with Lexa's help," he smiled at Lightstream, whose eyes narrowed in suspicion, "we've narrowed it down a few time periods, including twenty-third century Earth."

"Earth?" Helexius grew concerned. "Are you sure about that? Why would your father go there? Synther died a galaxy away." He stroked his chin, knowing not to second guess his daughter's abilities. "Well don't get involved with anyone or change anything—promise?"

"Yes, we promise," chimed Aristedes and Zane.

Aristedes had already seen glimpses of the Earth-Axala war, but neglected to mention it lest Helexius balked at their leaving.

It took a week, but after discussions on temporal diplomacy, shared dinners, and long goodbyes, the two youngest Astrals were gone.

Years later.

Helexius reminisced about times past since Destina's sons and his sister had deserted the Chronopolis, followed shortly after by Aristedes and Zane. At least they had kept in touch, though recently they had been quiet. The war with Axala, he had since learned about, must have been at a critical stage. They still had not found their father.

His handsome face had grown out of its boyish charm; now long and sharp. His long blond hair was braided down to his shoulders, complementing his dark purple, gold-embroidered armour. His belts laid diagonally-crossed at the waist. They would need adjusting soon against his expanding waistline.

He cursed his human genes. *How have we ended up this way?*

The mighty Astrals, time travellers, now divided and powerless. At least he still had his daughter with him, currently patrolling the Magna Aura system; Spheron the Younger manning the Colonnade defences, and the latter's daughter, Sola, rebuilding a comms relay—by hand no less. She was the most technically-gifted of the Astrals. The two daughters had each other for company at least. But most of all Helexius thought of Phasia.

She had confided in him she had been receiving strange messages via a contorted time wave, a signal she suspected originated from her father who had disappeared a generation ago. If he, or someone, he knew was sending a message they could be allies. So she too, had left for destinations unknown. And he had kept that to himself.

I wish I knew where you were Phasia, he told himself.

Just then, Lightstream time-ported in from Magna Aura. Helexius' welcoming smile faltered as her face betrayed her emotions, which she could never hide from him. Her fraught features were a mixture of fear and confusion.

Sola entered the room in good spirits, no doubt sensing the temporal signature of Lightstream returning, such were they attuned to each other. She was so like her father, dark-skinned, inquisitive, and wise beyond her years, but more of an engineer. What that meant for the future of the Spherons, chief exegetes to the Celestian Knights and the Starguards, no one knew.

"What's wrong?" Helexius asked, fearing the worst.

"Where to start?" Lightstream looked tired.

She preceded to tell them of the system field she had discovered around Magna Aura and the fact that Decion and Alpha Rion were also missing, no doubt stolen from the planet by Timechantress. They had been betrayed by Netherlord and Archron.

Sola groaned. "More bad news! Phasia has disappeared, Zeus knows where, and with the universe at stake, it's like the whole universe is falling apart on us!"

"Hades' breath!" Helexius cursed pacing the room.

But then Lightstream had dropped her bombshell, showing them images she had taken on her small diamond-shaped crystalator, uploading the holo images to the main crystalator orb in the chamber.

"What are those?" Helexius squinted at the images.

"Ships," Lightstream said. "Possible alien ships."

"At Magna Aura?" asked a confused Sola, looking at the huge angular shapes.

"Yep, Lightstream confirmed, enlarging the images. "I have looked at all the Celestian files and these ships do not match anything in their records. They're huge, bigger than any swordship I've seen, like city-ships, and without identifying sigils. They might be new Magna Aura designs, but the timeframe is a strange."

"Strange how!" Helexius wanted to know.

"Well…"

BOOM!

The three were violently thrown to the ground as alarms shrieked. The Chronopolis shuddered and tilted.

"What was that?" Sola shouted, scrambling to her feet.

"Sensors are down!" Lightstream yelled back, looking at the crystalators consoles. "Massive temporal disruption. We're under atttack!"

"Impossible!" Helexius shouted wildly.

There were quick heavy footfalls as Spheron the Younger, cape flying behind him, came running into the hall. His face was creased with sweat and fear, his mouth locked on one word.

"Lore!"

Destinia.

Archron had returned to ancient Earth upon leaving the Chronopolis. There he duly sought out the disparate groups of Exmoors, Devouts, and the Chryrian-merged humans trying to forge peace amongst them. Each had their own attributes, but he needed them in one group.

"No!" had been the simple answer from the Exmoors.

Though closely allied to the Astrals, they had rejected Archron's Knight Destina agenda, to his great displeasure. And to add insult to injury they had devised anti-temporal defenses against him utilising their ancestors' crystalators. Adantus' kin would not bend to Archron's will. They took their own path, not interested in world domination, but in guiding from the background. This had led the Exmoors against the Devouts and the Chryrian-merged humans. Archron knew they would be his natural allies.

There had been no unified response from the psi-humans. He knew what the Exmoors had done to them and the rest had simply blended into the human fabric of life. The psis had no love for the Astrals or Exmoors. The early days of the Astrals had been fraught with actions bordering on genocide. He never wanted to think about it again. At first the Astrals and Exmoors had told themselves it had been for the best, to protect Earth, but in reality they had abused their power and compromised their morality. Lord Aeon had convinced Phasia, the other Astrals, and the Exmoors that their actions had to change. And they had. But Archron knew he would expect no help from the Devouts, unless he offered them the one thing they craved—revenge. Revenge against the Astrals and Exmoors.

"You preach against your own people?" The question was asked with intrigue behind it, made all the more potent as Archron lay in bed beside his inquisitor.

"Yes," had been his simple answer. He kissed the woman who responded with affection.

Archron had not expected his ploy to end in love. Much less with a Devout leader. But he had been so taken with her from the very beginning. She seemed so far beyond her years even as a Devout; otherworldly, timeless, and mysterious. She was as volatile as her fiery red hair, as insatiable as her intoxicating beauty, and as mercurial as her intelligence. He knew she had several other lovers, both male and female but he could never resist her summons.

Adra Van Tager was a self-styled Archwitch of the Devouts. She claimed to hold power over a holy object called a Lore stone. As she never judged Archron on his Astral heritage, he never judged her, at least to her face, on the Devouts' worship of the Lore, his enemy—his alliance with Synther notwithstanding.

While Archron had never seen this stone, he believed Adra's claim the Lore stone could manipulate human DNA, giving her the ability to create more Devouts, but crucially, male Devouts with powers. Such powers would give the Devouts an advantage over the Exmoors who only possessed longevity as their natural asset.

As Archron had come and went on Earth over the years, fulfilling his mother's plans, he and Adra had agreed that he should stay in the shadows, not revealing himself to the Devouts to ally their fears he was just another man trying to control women. But it was also to protect Adra's daughter.

In all the years he had known Adra, Archron never knew if her daughter, Elisabeth, was his child. When Adra had told him of Elisabeth's impending marriage to a Chryrian half-breed, he had raged for days; wanting Elisabeth to be pure or married off to Celestian stock. Likewise, Adra had threatened to kill Edgar de la Valtare many a time if he had interfered with Devout ambitions. To placate them both, Adra - the Archwitch, an alchemist at heart had made it so Elisabeth could never have children with Valtare. She had then devised a plot to separate them and advance both their agendas.

Thus had been born the E-Corps plan for the future and the beginnings of Archron's army, through Valtare. Archron had lamented how Adra had never lived to see any of that, killed by the Exmoors soon after he had time-ported Elisabeth to the twenty-first century. He had vowed to protect Elisabeth as his daughter since then. Now he had to inform Valtare he had not heard from his wife.

He could only think the Starguards had arrived on Earth, helped no doubt by the other Astrals and prevented Elisabeth from fulfilling her mission.

Had Synther failed in his plans? he thought. There had been no word from or of him since his mission to the Chronopolis.

But his greatest loss came with the news that his brother Lazeron the Netherlord, had died, at the hands of Aeon's son. He had not been told, had not witnessed the death. His voidspear had felt it, temporal ripples emanating from the nethersword, its matched partner. The power of the ripple had thrown the voidspear off the wall to the ground in his chambers. The ancient engraved runes upon its shaft had lit up in a foreboding glare. Archron had grabbed the voidspear. His hands involuntarily clenched the spear which shook; jolting him with temporal sparks replaying the memory of the nethersword to him through the voidspear's crowning orb.

He saw Netherlord's triumphs in opening the portals and dimensional gateways for the Storm of Stars, Zane being killed, and the final battle with Aeon's son, Aristedes. The scene had ripped Archron apart. He had fallen to his knees in grief, not moving for an hour. The voidspear wept its own eulogy over its lost twin, now alone, bereft of family. The runes finally shimmered away into darkness, the purplish metal blade and bright orb returning to their originals states.

Destina had not been as distraught by the loss of Netherlord as he had been. Her reaction had driven Archron to the edge.

"Weak!" his mother had shrieked. "He was always the weak one; always trying to emulate you. Then he even married Millennius' daughter, the fool. And where is she now? Copulating with that Starguard on Magna Aura no doubt!" Destina sneered her hatred.

Archron didn't want to think about it. Magna Aura had been sealed of from them in an apparent betrayal by Timechantress with Cirrius. But he wouldn't believe she was now with the Starguards. He had to stand up for his brother.

"But Lazeron accomplished his tasks!" Archron had bit back. "Let me travel back and save him, change time," he begged.

Destina brooded. "No!" she forbade him. "Such an event could affect the outcome. It was meant to be! As you state, he has carried out his part. When the Storm of Stars return, all will be restored in peace!"

For the first time in his life, Archron did not believe his mother.

After that day, Destina became more erratic, having even more tumultuous visions about the return of Millennius and the more mysterious Time Empress.

Archron was left with almost nothing. Only Valtare, Decion, and a meager amount of two hundred or so Fifth warriors had arrived at his fortress.

And so Archron drank his memories away. The wine from his ancient home he and his brother used to share, his only comfort. He didn't care if Valtare and Decion disapproved. He could see it in their faces. They were nothing but pawns in his plans. The Storm of Stars would decide all their fates.

Then he had found himself tested even more when the Starguards had somehow arrived in their future time. And most unexpectedly, as predicted by his mother, Millennius had returned at the head of the Lore.

Synther had indeed failed. That thought at least had warmed Archron's heart.

Or is that the wine? he mused with a lopsided smile.

Now more than ever, Archron knew the Knights Destina's fate was drawing close with the awakening of the Storm of Stars.

Deep Space

The Spheron Lore had time on his side.

But it would have still taken him hundred of years to find Millennius in all the vastness of the universe. Spheron could have searched in all the places he thought Millennius could go: back to Earth, around Magna Aura, the Chronopolis, phase space, inter-galactic space. He had searched uncountable reaches.

Then it hit him. He knew where he would be. Millennius and Destina were polar opposites. If Destina had gone to the far future of Earth to await the end then Millennius would go back to...

...the beginning.

Spheron reached the end of the temporal portal. Before he had even exited, a brutal solar storm reached in and wrenched him out. He spun backwards out of control in the vortex's hellish grip before regaining himself. And Spheron found himself at the Great Breach; Alphatronius' gigantic rip in the universe from whence the Celestian civilisation had escaped to Magna Aura and from where the Celestian Knights had defiantly followed.

And there off to his right, hovering cross-legged and staring at the centre of the Great Breach, was Millennius, Celestian Knight—Lore.

"I thought I might find you here," Spheron growled in his Lorevoice. He had to admire Millennius even in his Lore state. He was a golden burning vision.

Millennius didn't acknowledge his presence, continuing to stare at the scar which sealed tight the portal back to their home worlds. It resembled a moon-sized black jagged cosmic string floating free in space. But wherever it orbited, travelled, or landed it would always lead back to their doomed universe.

"Suppose we went back?" Millennius asked, in his own gruff voice, "Would it change anything?" The sadness rang through.

Spheron put a hand on his leader's shoulder. "It's too late for that, my friend."

As if still thinking to himself, Millennius pondered, "What would we find if we opened it up? Would the Lore trapped inside have devoured everything? Will we find any survivors? A new civilisation arisen perhaps?" His voice sounded hopeful, but died as he shook his fiery mane and lamented, "I have failed everyone, Spheron." His golden eyes bore into the Breach's dark heart.

"No, Millennius, you have not. It was prophesied. We would be the last Celestian Knights. But we have a legacy, both from our first born and the last born on Earth. I have seen it. And ... I have also seen Phasia ..."

He was cut off as Millennius turned sharply to him. "Phasia? She lives? And what of Synther?" His golden face grew darker with anger.

Spheron braced himself as he told Millennius of the newly-born Astrals, Phasia's taking of the younglings under her wing, her comforting words to him, the war for Magna Aura, and then the hardest part of all.

"When I followed them to the strange world, well..." he didn't want to say it, "There's an alliance. They... betrayed Xathanius. He is dead. Murdered by Destina, her sons, and the Traitor Synther!" He meant to continue, but didn't have a chance.

Millennius exploded in rage, his aureate light enveloping Spheron and space around them. A roar eclipsing the birth pangs of a supernova boomed from within Millennius and the cosmic background warped into a multi-hued starscape.

There was a sense of unending vertigo.

Spheron had never seen a portal like it as they emerged over the Surge world Spheron had told Millennius about. The ground looked different though, as if it had been recently bombed, with Surge bodies disturbed from their resting places.

Spheron walked Millennius over to where Aeon had fallen. His body was covered with dirt and metal debris from whatever had happened here.

Millennius looked down calmly at his son's body, energy fizzing from his mouth like oral tears. He bent down and gouged a deeper hole in the ground with an energised arm and laid his son in it. He then filled the grave in.

A silent prayer for Xathanius was spoken by both. Millennius then lifted his head toward the heavens and roared again, golden energy spewing upwards as he commended his son, Xathanius—Lord Aeon of the Astrals, to the universe.

His outward mourning over, Millennius asked: "Destina, Synther, where are they?"

"Synther seeks a new Lore horde to attack the Astral Chronopolis and Destina and her sons are on Earth somewhere in the distant future."

"And Phasia?"

"She watches over the Astrals."

Face set in determination, Millennius said, "I shall intercept Synther and destroy him As the dominant Lore, I should be able to take control of the horde and use them against Destina."

"A credible plan, Millennius," Spheron approved. "Then I will observe Destina and discover the Antiqchronals she seeks," confirmed Spheron. "We should then rendezvous over Destina's future Earth and prevent the Storm of Stars from awakening."

They clasped arms, as of old, to seal their mission plans.

Millennius then opened his spectacular portal and to Spheron's amazement it split into two, sending him along his intended destination, while Millennius headed to the Chronopolis.

As Spheron sped through the temporal field, he thought about what Phasia had said about Zane. He was sure Phasia was trying to tell him more than she said. He reminded himself to check on Zane once he figured out the whereabouts of Destina and her sons.

"All the time in the universe and still I am rushing about," mused Spheron.

The Astral Dimension

The Lore closed in on the Chronopolis.

After warning the Astrals in the throne room, Spheron the younger had charged back out to defend the colonnades, the defensive gates to the inner citadel. He could feel the creatures cloying at his neck around his shield, but he held out like his father had taught him. The Lore had come from nowhere. And Synther was at the head of them. It confirmed the treachery of Archron and Netherlord and the probability that Aeon was dead.

Damn them both, he thought. *They were as traitorous as Synther.*

The Chronopolis was a temporal bubble-dimension, built mostly by Helexius' dimensional hexes and Spheron's engineering and forcefield technology. Outside of the Pyrathedral, chronal temples, residences, and courtyards were a series of forcefield walls and colonnades also created by Spheron as an early warning system and buffer trap against any unwanted visitors, such as the Lore. He knew all the little quirks and shortcuts to ward off the Lore, but still the Lore kept coming. He had to do this alone as he knew the other Astrals were inside maintaining the rest of the Chronopolis' temporal integrity and defences.

As Spheron watched, a golden star appeared within the dimensional sphere, above Synther. As it travelled closer and closer at great velocity, Spheron realised it was a Lore, and no ordinary Lore at that. His father had secretly confided in him what he, Millennius and Destina were becoming, lest it became necessary to destroy them if they returned to Earth. Spheron's heart sank when he saw Millennius, for he knew he could not hold out against both Synther and Millennius. Spheron the younger guiltily desired that it was his father coming to his rescue.

Suddenly Spheron saw new hope. To his great surprise and relief, it was Synther who bore the brunt of the attack from Millennius as he ploughed into the Traitor Synther, driving him down into the depths of the pocket universe. The bright light in the depths of darkness was a glow of life. Of justice. Of Millennius. And now Spheron was not fighting just for his life or for the Chronopolis, but also for Millennius.

The Lore had tried to follow and assist their master, but Spheron realised that this was his chance to defeat the Lore and give Millennius a chance to kill Synther. He drew the Lore in, using every ounce of his strength, his powers and body, to corral the Lore around him. He could feel his life slipping away, but he had to give Millennius all the time he needed.

Spheron heaved with all his might, trapping the Lore within his forcefield, dragging them down with him. They gladly burned him. He willingly endured them. He could barely see or hear from his injuries; all he knew he had to do was to keep the Lore away from Millennius. And after almost an eternity, with his last breath, he saw him: Millennius victorious.

The golden Lore rose up from the depths of the temporalscape bathed in the dissipating aura of the blue energy that had once been the Traitor Synther. He roared with triumph. Looking down upon Spheron, there was a moment of gratitude; a connection of equals.

Millennius said something, but Spheron could not hear him.

And then the golden Lore vanished into a portal, which opened liked a golden halo.

"My honour ..." Spheron saluted in return, before collapsing in death.

Millennius was dead.

He had arrived in the thick of battle, the Lore clustered around the Astral forcefield master, Spheron the younger, at the head of the Chronopolis entrance. Millennius saw his target and dove in, focused on Synther who managed to sense him at the last moment.

Synther spun. In a flash of frenzied blue he challenged Millennius, secure in the knowledge his Lore would follow him and rip Millennius' atoms apart. But as Millennius violently clenched him around the neck, using his great wings of golden energy to drive Synther down into the temporal squalls, the underlying foundation of the Chronopolis, Synther sensed he was alone. No other Lore had joined him. Synther shrieked in anger, and not a little fear. Ambitions had to be reshaped.

The temporal squalls were no misnomer. Although the Chronopolis was supposedly sequestered upon a uniform mix of temporal soup, there were areas which were disturbingly knotted up and tangled; time ran in reverse or split or froze. At first the Astrals tried to correct this as the squalls would rotate or move randomly into the only two portal corridors into normal space. However, they realised that the squalls were the perfect additional defence to the Colonnades. No matter Synther and the Lore had bludgeoned their way through the calmer anti-tachyon fields, the squalls had at least protected the underbelly of the Chronopolis, which rode the squalls like a city-ship on the high seas of the cosmos.

Millennius clung fiercely onto Synther in the squalls, wings of iridescence beating like fiery plasma blasts, great jets of blistered matter and energy spewing around them. He could see every twist and turn coming; areas of reverse time temporarily causing Synther to revert back into his Celestian form and thus be burned by Millennius; areas where time would split, tearing pieces of Synther away. It was excruciating pain for a Lore to be so quantumly stripped apart alive and left to drift on the solar winds. But Millennius revelled in what had to do, even at his own expense.

A static temporal wave rolled over both of them leaving them frozen for a picosecond, locked in mortal combat, tumbling in the rapids as a rush of accelerated time washed over them. It threw them through interweaving squalls of slow time, no time, reverse and accelerated time: Millennius was drowning Synther in a temporal quagmire.

Their energies intertwined; thoughts and emotions as fluid as their bodies sifted between them. Synther barred his energy teeth in glee as Millennius glimpsed into his dark mind, seeing the harsh vision of Synther killing Xathanius.

>It was my pleasure to end his life< Millennius heard in his mind.

"Rrrraaaargh!" Millennius tore wildly, clawing and gouging into Synther, who felt delirious with pain, just to see Millennius in more pain than himself. Over and over again, Synther flashed the vision of Xathanius' death into Millennius' mind.

>You took my worlds, my sister, and my destiny from me, Millennius< Synther psyed. *>And I will take everything from you, piece by piece<* He leaned back leisurely deeper into the squalls, giving into Millennius' rage.

Oh, pure satisfaction! he sang to himself.

Synther felt his soul, Lore or otherwise, slipping away. Millennius was going to squeeze the very life out of him and then let his body be torn apart like a nebulous filament in a solar storm. He knew there was only one thing to do to survive; surrender was not an option, but neither was dying.

Synther sensed a large null void approaching, a roiling bubble of nothing. His eyes locked with Millennius' own in mutual hatred. He knew Millennius could also sense the temporal freeze zone coming, but still Synther managed to manoeuvre Millennius toward it to that it would strike Millennius straight in the back.

Millennius could not avoid the trap. He let his voluminous wings take the brunt of the burn as time stood still. But even as time slowed, slower than imaginable before stopping completely, Millennius realised Synther's ploy. But it was too late.

The zero-time wave hit Millennius, his body freezing cell by cell, agonisingly slowly, while Synther wallowed in real time for a blissful nanosecond. And before the time wave possessed Synther, he did what he could only do.

Synther exploded.

Millennius' eyes glassed over as time stopped, his own fires dowsed for a split second as the first explosive rays splashed over him.

Synther felt the release, his energy dispersed toward Millennius. It would not kill Millennius outright—oh no—that would be far too hard. It would not kill Synther insomuch either, that would be far too simple. This would be beyond both their experiences. And Synther preferred it this way.

Time began again.

Millennius felt his Loreself blaze in rage as blue hell spread amidst him. He was being invaded by the core energy of Synther himself, the bio-Lore energy virus which Synther carried within himself from birth and which gave him his power. Mingling with Millennius' own energy, it scoured his mind, embracing his body.

Millennius felt himself going insane. His head burned even more, his mane of flame flaring blue then green then gold. A battle ensued for his will, his mind, his very being, as he felt Synther course through him, violating him, choking, writhing, and corrupting his core.

"You will not have me!" vowed Millennius into the tumultuous squalls.

He fought back, reining in the Traitorous beast, beating it down, suppressing its heart, scorching its soul, shredding the dark Time Knight's energy within himself, even as he tumbled over and over through the squalls.

"Arrrraghhhh!" he roared into the depths of time with an expulsion of finality even infinity would have yielded to.

And then it was gone.

Millennius closed his great Lore eyes, searching inward to find a trace of Synther. But he was gone save for a blue evaporating haze which hung around him. Satisfied, he now had to fight his way out of the squalls and into the Chronopolis bubble. It was a hard fought path through the regions of damaged time, but Millennius surfaced from the squalls as if emerging from a deep, horrific ocean. He roared to announce his entry into the fray. What he saw made his heart sink.

Spheron had just battled to the last. He stood alone amongst the broken colonnades. Lore were still evaporating around him like ghostly corpses within his forcefield.

He looked at Millennius with joy in his heart having given his life so the Lore could be destroyed.

"Thank you," Millennius said. "Your sacrifice will not go unavenged."

Spheron saluted him speaking soundless words, before collapsing dead.

Knowing the other Astrals would arrive soon and discover him, Millennius swiftly opened a portal and disappeared. He had to find the Lore horde, harness them to his will, and then rendezvous with Spheron, whose namesake son had just sacrificed his all.

How many sons will we lose? he sighed with great emotion in his heart.

Onward, Millennius' search began.

An infinitesimal blue spark within the golden universe that was Millennius hibernated. Whatever, whoever, he was now, Synther was a part of Millennius. He was not sure how long Millennius would be able to go without purging him, but Synther knew he would know when the time was right to awaken and wreak havoc.

Yes, Millennius was dead. Synther swore it.

The temporalscape

Spheron the elder had no problems in following Destina. She was careless, either she thought of him and Millennius as no threat or she didn't care. There was also the third option that it was a trap, but Spheron knew Destina wasn't much into subtlety.

But as a precaution he stayed on the periphery of phase space for as much as he could, gleaning Destina had encamped millions of years in Earth's future. There he witnessed Destina's and Archron's building of the fortress from a material Spheron could scarcely believe.

Spearhead and his Surge had allowed Destina to transport thousands of dead Surge bodies, from the Surge world, whereupon the Surge absorbed any residual energy out of the bodies, converted the metal corpses into raw building material, and manufactured different structures. The fortress was almost a living being. It certainly obeyed the will of Archron, or more accurately the chaos spear, who could command the walls or roof to fold open like curtains to allow access and egress. It was an amazing structure, which Spheron's intellect wanted to get his energised hands on, but for now his curiosity would have to wait. He knew what Destina and Archron were up to and they were staying put.

But where was Netherlord? he wondered.

Planet Home. Long ago.

The Multiforce stood against Netherlord who smile curled into an ugly grin.

"Your father is dead," he sneered at Aristedes and Zane. "Believe me, I should know," he ended with a tone of finality, his grin extending.

"That's not true!" Windburst called out, leaving her brother's protective field before he could hold her back. She stood right at Netherlord's chest, staring into his dark eyes, fists clenched, her eyes gleaming with ire.

Netherlord could barely contain himself, laughing scornfully.

"Or else, what? You're a cripple!"

"This!" Windburst yelled, pushing out her arms explosively.

A torrent of energy raged from her hands, Netherlord sent flying through the air landing twenty meters away, smoke spiralling from a gash in his armoured chest. Windburst looked amazed at her hands and then at her brother, who could find no words. It was the first time Windburst had displayed any sign of Astral power besides her speed ability. A smile drifted across her face, tears filling her eyes, as she slowly made her way back to Time.

Then the world crashed into slow motion as Time looked past Zane's shoulder.

Netherlord had risen to his feet. And he was angry.

Before anyone could react, Netherlord reached his hands up above his head, violently casting them down in a throwing motion.

Windburst looked behind her, a cheerful, teary-eyed face turning into one of terror as air-renting energy hit her full force. She hadn't stood a chance. Right before Time's eyes, Windburst disappeared, her body disintegrating into energy—dead.

Noooo!

Spheron had arrived too late, this time.

Netherlord's trail had also been easy to follow as it consisted of dead world after dead world, missing stars, and huge galactic chasms of emptiness which Netherlord had created in order to open the portals for the Storm of Stars.

But distressing to Spheron, was the realisation of the time period he was in. His Lore senses told him he was in the same period in which Aeon had died, but on another world. Spheron wasn't sure how he knew. Temporal fields tasted, smelled, felt, sounded, and looked different to one another, developing characteristics like tree rings or imbalances depending on the energy in the space-time fabric. And this period had the distinctive flavour and energy banding from before, which on Earth equated to the twenty-third century. Spheron knew Aristedes and Zane were searching for their father, but they would have been distraught when they found out the truth. And it was particularly galling of Netherlord to have engaged Aeon's children in this period.

Unfortunately for Spheron, just as he had tracked Netherlord to a world being established by humans and Axalans, he had witnessed the death of the one Phasia had asked him to watch over.

Fortunately for Spheron, he wasn't facing the Lore and the Surge. He was free to intervene as he could not with Lord Aeon. He cycled back on his route through phase space, found the temporal juncture which split off into backtime—the past—and prepared himself to either kill Netherlord and/or save Zane. But just as he entered the new temporal trajectory, an astonishing site greeted him: Zane.

She stood in the temporalscape, her body totally transformed into white energy. She was looking at herself, her arms and body; touching the energy-form she had become.

"What am I?" she asked herself, her voice sounding harmonic and ethereal.

Before Spheron could deal with her, he could feel temporal spools bouncing off his energy. He could see Aristedes again and again trying to change time, his face stretched in agony across the timelines. But Zane's energy repelled him and he failed time and time again. Spheron felt for him. He would not save his sister today. He turned his attention to Zane. She was indeed different; special.

Spheron approached her.

Zane looked up sensing his energy. "Go away," she screamed, not recognising the once Celestian Knight who had raised her.

Undaunted, Spheron hovered closer to her. He wanted to console her, tell her about what she was.

"No!" she screamed. She raised her hands and an uncontrolled torrent of white energy blasted Spheron blinding him, burning him.

The energy suddenly ceased. The light cleared. And when Spheron could see again, Zane was gone. Spheron knew he had to find Zane again. He now knew what Phasia had meant. Zane was special.

Zane was a Loremaiden.

***

Earth. AD 2011

The dogs wouldn't stop barking.

"What the hell's wrong with these mutts?" Fred Jameson yelled through gritted teeth. Sweat played across his graying brow.

"Something's got them riled up!" his younger cousin, Steve, added needlessly. His voice was a pitch higher than was necessary even at the best of times.

Fred and Steve were practically dragged along through the trees. Steve fretted having to leave his nine-year-old son, Patrick back in the pick-up with the deer carcasses, but he didn't want either of them stolen. Plus Patrick had a shotgun and a cell phone to call him if there was any trouble with local do-gooder rangers patrolling for unlicensed hunters.

The duo had just finished tying up the last deer to return to the truck when a bright light had exploded a couple of miles to the north. It had spooked the dogs. Then the canines had started running hell for leather toward the spot, towing their owners behind them.

Fred had his automatic rifle with him and had already flipped down the night vision goggles as the twilight quickly turned to night in the dense forest. Steve wasn't as flash as his cousin and the beam from his hand-held flashlight waggled everywhere, shadows looming out of the forest, causing his heart to jump at every single one of them.

"Whoa, whoa!" Steve cried every few minutes as Rocky, a large black and brown mongrel, lopped along ever faster. "Damned crazy mutt!" he huffed.

They sped along for a good twenty minutes, panting away as the landscape undulated through encroaching undergrowth and exposed roots. The strange light had now subsided and they were working from memory and their dogs' lead.

Finally they reached the area from where they thought the light had emanated.

"Where the hell's that light?" Fred asked himself, scanning the area.

His black Labrador, Poncho, yelped and tried to carry on. Rocky also scraped the ground in eagerness. But Fred held his arm out, his fist signalling 'hold'; something he had seen actors do on TV. He was a keen wannabe-soldier with his green and brown camouflage hunting gear, while Steve stuck out in his usual lucky hunting denims.

Steve looked over to Fred who thrust his arm forward with outstretched palm; 'forward'. Steve rolled his eyes. The former had seen something. They moved at an easy pace until Poncho began barking again, straining at the leash. There was something in the woods to their right, just visible through the undergrowth; something wrapped in a colourful cloth.

Fred inched closer. He stood over the object and poked it with the barrel of his rifle. He jumped and almost tripped backward when the object rolled over. And looked at him.

"It's a girl," he shouted, alarmed. "Some Goddamn girl in a costume." He looked at her clothes, what looked like a purple and pink jumpsuit.

"Christ!" Steve dialled 911. "Hey, Police . . . anyone! We've found a girl out in the woods. Yeah, that's right, you heard me. Yeah, course she's alive! She looks hurt. Get the cops and docs out here!" He continued to give directions.

Steve tromped around in the immediate vicinity looking for anyone or anything else, finding nothing. The girl had remained in and out of consciousness. She didn't speak a word. It unsettled the two men.

A quarter hour later, Steve and Fred heard the whirring of a chopper on the way, which circled them. They could see search beams intermittently penetrating the canopy, but it couldn't land in the dense forest. It was almost an hour before a four-team police unit with two medics found their way on foot.

The lead officer took one look at the hunters, saw their scared faces and state of the girl. After a half hour of grilling they were cleared of any suspicion, but told to report to the police station for further statements regarding the killed deer and their absence of hunting licenses. Fred and Steve were glad of that charge rather than a more serious charge.

The medics tried to recover the girl, who upon fully awakening fought them off, until an almost overdose-level amount of drugs had been administered. The unconscious girl was carried on a stretcher, Fred and Steve also taking turns, through the woods for almost a mile before they reached a clearing. She was then air-lifted by the waiting helicopter to a psychiatric hospital near Blue Mountain.

When she fully regained her senses in hospital two months later, she had forgotten much of what had happened immediately before her arrival. Her near-death experience had been just that, an experience she had been lucky to escape.

She had been diagnosed with retrograde amnesia due to an unknown cause. The doctors were hopeful she would remember more soon, enough help the police with their inquiries and to be discharged. For now, Zane just needed to rest.

Deep space

Spheron was late. He found it infuriatingly embarrassing as a time traveller.

Although time travel seemed an easy feat, timing was everything. Going back in time to prevent or to cause an event or venturing into the future to cause or to prevent an event was not always straight forward. Portals and temporal streams and rifts were temperamental entities, which liked to flow to their own rhyme and reason, and going against the tide was sometimes unpredictable.

But it is what Spheron had to do in order to reach Millennius at the appointed time and place.

Spheron cursed himself.

His encounter with Zane had left him somewhat off-kilter, even lost, and Spheron took a few wrong temporal turns and ruptured unintended timestreams. In return he ended up late for his appointed rendezvous. Millennius was not there.

Millennius had already departed for the fortress. But Spheron was not alone. Alarmingly, he found himself at the head of a large Lore contingent backed up by a Helstar.

However, it wasn't only the rendezvous he was late for. The gathering darkness which was enveloping Earth told Spheron they were all too late.

The Storm of Stars were awakening.

CHAPTER EIGHT

Destinia. Now.

"You are too late, brother. Welcome to the Celestian Reformation!" Destina cried out to Millennius, as he landed in the fortress' main chamber. "The Storm of Stars have heard my pleas. They come!" she gloated with open arms.

"Sister, you have much to answer for," Millennius growled back. "Stop this madness now or I will destroy you and your kin as you have mine." The crackling energy made his voice growl even lower.

"Spearhead." She ordered the Surge to absorb their powers.

But just as Destina tasted victory, another vast portal opened over the fortress. Three billion Zater Jen led by Cosmogod, Phasia, and the Time Empress poured out from the two-mile-wide brightly-yawning tear in the sky, dropping to the ground, like huge crystal snowflakes. The main Zater Jen population surrounded the fortress, while their leader and his court shot through and landed within the open dome.

Spearhead and several other Surge tromped forward to surround Destina in a protective ring. They in turn were surrounded by Arcanaut, Areigna, Geomega, and Queen Celesophia.

>*You are our prisoner, Destina*< Celesophia announced to all; her voice a commanding tenorous tone. Then turning to Spearhead: >*Surge, stand down*<

>*We cannot*< Spearhead answered.

>*Surge, we the People of Time, the People of Energy, and the People of Psyche are united against the Storm of Stars. Why are the People of Matter in league with this errant Celestian Knight and the Storm of Stars?*<

>*We will be remade as we were and the First Peoples will be equal once again*<

>*No, Surge, this will not occur. The Storm of Stars will destroy us all and create a new universe without us. We have to stop them. Then we Peoples will create our own and just universe*<

Spearhead hesitated, caught between believing Destina or the crystal being in front of him. But one look at all the forces arrayed against them told him that logically, he was on the wrong side. He gave an order.

With dread dismay, Destina felt her energy drain way as it was absorbed by the metal warriors. Her Celestian self emerged, weakened, her sharp-angled face more haggard than before.

"Nooo!" Destina screamed in anguish. She sank to the ground in heaving sobs.

The Zater Jen leaders turned their attention to Archron, who belligerently cast down his voidspear in defeat. Even Decion, who sheathed his lancesword, and a dispirited Valtare took on an air of surrender. The fortress was secure from within, at least.

Across the large metal chamber, Phasia, Cosmogod, and the Time Empress flew over to Millennius. The Celestian Knight Lore embracing each other, their bodies, coalescing, their kisses lighting up the chamber as flares and rays emanated from their beings.

"You make a handsome Lore," Phasia joked, stroking Millennius fiery mane.

"I've never felt freer," Millennius replied in a happy growl. "But we must talk later. First we have to stop the Storm of Stars."

"Yes, but first, you have to meet someone." Phasia turned and behind her, standing next to a young girl was a tall, golden crystal-armour-clad man, with familiar looks. "Millennius, meet our son, Hellennius, Cosmogod of the Zater Jen." Phasia beamed proudly, literally, her whole Loreself glowed.

Millennius was dumbfounded. The shame washed over him. "My son," he hesitantly started. "While it is almost beyond impossible we finally meet, I am saddened it is under these circumstances and that you see me as I am; a Lore, not worthy of your presence." He wondered if his rasping Lorevoice conveyed the sadness he felt.

He needn't have worried. "Father, if it's good enough for mother then it is good enough for me." Hellennius embraced his father, energy flaring off his crystal armour.

Millennius remembered what it was like to cry, but his Loreself couldn't. But he felt a coldness wash through his body. He then spied the little girl.

"And who is this?" He approached the girl, who showed no fear. She was dressed in an all-white uniform with blue trim—a short armoured tunic over matching trews, her pale skin and hair almost disappearing in the glow of her inner energy.

"This is the Time Empress," Phasia introduced her.

"An Astral?" Millennius was intrigued.

"Yes," the girl said, swaying from side to side with childish innocence.

"You know of the Astrals?" Phasia asked.

"I know of many things, my love. Spheron told me. He is on his way to meet me here and my Lore horde above us."

"Your Lore horde? So?"

"Yes, Synther is dead! I slew him in combat under the Chronopolis. The Astrals are safe." Millennius couldn't bear to tell the rest about his second-born son and Spheron the younger.

Phasia grieved little for her brother, but smiled warmly at Spheron the elder keeping his word to find Millennius and for trusting her. She wondered then at the time period Zane had visited the Chronopolis to find it abandoned.

Their brief reunion was interrupted.

"Grandfather?" came a voice from behind him.

Millennius' body reversed itself; his front shifting to his back, to peer at the young woman who stood before him.

She stepped forth. "I am Zane, daughter of Xathanius, Lord Aeon of the Astrals," she said proudly.

Millennius' heart both soared and sank or rather his energy knotted within his chest with mixed emotions. "I would know you as my kin anywhere. I can see my mother in you, Zane," Millennius complimented her. "She was a great warrior and beauty. It is an honour to meet you. Your father would have been proud of you." He had blurted it out without thinking.

"Would have?" Zane and Phasia spoke together.

With a heavy heart Millennius forced himself to relate the tragic news regarding Aeon's death at the hands of Destina and the Traitor Synther. He shot his sister a grave look across the hall.

"I buried him on the Surge world," Millennius confessed.

"The Surge world?" Zane plunged her head despairingly into her hands. "We were almost there," she whispered in realisation. She and Aristedes had been so close to their father. His final trail had indeed led them to the right time, but they couldn't locate the right place; the war had seen to that.

Zane's eyes blazed across the fortress. "Destina and Synther will pay for their sins, Grandfather."

Millennius nodded grimly. "The Traitor Synther has already paid. I defeated him in combat. He is no more," Millennius stated with satisfaction. He turned to Phasia. "Sorry, no matter what he was, he was your kin."

Phasia shook her head, unperturbed. "All my kin are here now." They embraced again, their son looking on with pride.

"I hate to break this up," Sceptre spoke up from the periphery with the rest of the Starguards. "But something's happening." He pointed up into the sky.

From the open dome they could see the sky rapidly darkening. Archron summoned his voidspear back into his hands, before he could be stopped, commanding the whole roof of the fortress to retract. They now stood under the sky in the cracked-walled chamber. Above them the heavens darkened with unnatural speed and purpose. It grew noticeably colder, the wind whipping in carelessly around them.

The Starguards, the Knights Destina, the Surge, the Zater Jen, and high above them, the Lore looked upwards and out into space as twelve vast, magnificent, phantom-like orbs of energy began to warp into view. The fantastical super-giant stars: six bright blue-white super giants on the eastern horizon and six black stars on the western front gradually solidified. They surrounded the Earth, so far away, yet as if they were upon Earth's doorstep.

No one seemed to care that such objects should not have been able to occupy such a small sphere of space without destroying Earth, themselves, and local space-time. But these were no ordinary stars.

They were the Storm of Stars: Gods of the Celestians.

Looking at the Storm of Stars in their full glory would have sent even the most ardent Celestian Knight mad. But the overpowering energies radiated away through hyper-dimensional routes. Even the black-hole-like Shadow Stars remained like dormant singularity portals staring into unfathomable depths.

Destina laughed hysterically as the Storm of Stars, mythical no more, circled the Earth; her captors forming a tighter ring around her. The energy of the Gods rippled around the world buffeting all gathered at the fortress with their generated solar winds.

An ominous voice reverberated within everyone's head:

≠*How dare you bring us from our slumber. How dare you act above yourselves, you who we made and can destroy.*≠

"We wish an audience your benevolences," called out Destina in a shrieking pitch. "We wish to ask your forgiveness for our transgressions."

"Speak for yourself," Millennius fired back.

≠*Silence! We will destroy to create; bring death from life; sing chaos over order*≠ sang the Shadow Stars.

= *The new past will be as the future. This will be the new centre*= chimed the bright Prime Stars.

As they watched, the Shadow Stars grew even darker, black upon black heaving as their inner energies stirred to life. As if some cosmic engine had ignited, the Stars began to rotate on their axises, light bending in their foreground, space twisting as the ground began to shake around the gathered mortal forces.

"Yes," shouted Destina, her arms outstretched to embrace the killing Stars. "Take us! Take us!"

"Oh, universe, they're merging into a super black hole!" Millennius shouted, as the noise from their transformation boomed through their heads. "The Shadow Stars will suck in and devour the entire universe from this point!"

"Yes! And the Prime Stars will align as a super white hole in order to release the energy required to rebirth a new universe!" Destina finished in exultation.

Earth was on the precipice of the universal event horizon.

Ten billion Lore, three billion Zater Jen, thousands of Surge and Chryrians, four Celestian Knights, four Starguards, two Astrals, and three humans watched as inch by inch, space around earth was engulfed by the ultra-dense blackness, until a permanent night eclipsed them. Earth lay outside the centre of the black hole's heart, but still they survived.

Zane wondered how they could still be alive. It occurred to her that while the Storm of Stars looked and acted like stars, they weren't. They were something else manifesting themselves as stars and black holes.

At this realisation, with her still-open mind link, she flashed-thought her ideas to the minds of the Zater Jen, the principle shield against the Storm of Stars; their crystal bodies resonating against the song of the Gods, deflecting much of their power.

Cosmogod saw this as his chance, >*Starmondaus, summon the Light Guard!*<

Starmondaus obeyed turning his mind outward.

>*Husband!*< warned Celesophia, >*Your energies will be dashed against walls of infinity*<

>*No, Zane is right. They are not stars, though they are energy beings; they bluff their import for we would be dust by now if it were not so*< he smiled in the knowledge.

Starmondaus had sung his psi-summons and the Light Guard had appeared from nowhere on his flank.

>*Guard, on me!*< came the Zater Jen leader's rallying call.

Cosmogod, the Light Guard, Geomega, Areigna, and Arcanaut, joined their leader taking to the air. Cosmogod enlightened them en route.

>*There were six Shadow Stars, now there is only one. We seek to make them six again and kill them one by one!*<

There was a unified roar of approval as they stared down the black heart of death.

Millennius watched as his son led his small force into the depths of eternity. He could see what Hellennius was about to attempt. He wasn't going to let his first born die in vain, like Xathanius. He time-ported to the waiting Lore circling above the Earth like a second atmosphere. He welcomed Spheron, with gladness, but with a heavy heart over the news about his son.

"This is it, old friend. We will not fail this universe." He clasped arms with Spheron.

"Then let us fight well and long many we live!" Spheron smiled, echoing his friend and leader's words from a lifetime ago.

Millennius gave a mental command. Ten billion Lore obeyed. From the darkened skies, beacons of light shone forth as they ascended into hell; their hellion shrieks threatening to tear the night apart.

From the darkened fortress hall, Zane looked up in awe. Who would have thought the Lore would become saviours? She wasn't the only one. She looked over at the Time Empress, whose serene pale face looked on in wonderment. And then Zane saw it, the resemblance. Just like her mother. At that moment, the Time Empress looked at Zane and smiled.

Family, the word flittered through Zane's mind.

Phasia glided over and held the young girl's hand. They both turned their heads toward the warring skies.

This was the moment. Cosmogod and his forces were only the vanguard; now three billion more crystal soldiers led by Phasia and the Time Empress lifted their bodies and minds arising from the broken fortress dome to assault the Gods.

Zane silently saluted them as they disappeared into the night sky.

In that instant, free of the Zater Jen guard, Decion chose his moment to re-evaluate his decision. He smartly marched over to Sceptre.

"Sceptre, Aerl ..." He hesitated while he choked on his pride. "I wish to renounce my association with the Knights Destina. They are. . ." he harrumphed, "quite mad! I will serve you," he managed to strangle the words out. Sinking down on one knee in submission to the Starguard leader, his lancesword towered over him.

Sceptre looked around at the rest of the Starguards. One by one they silently voted with a nod or shake of the head. The result in, Sceptre gave their answer.

"Decion, your ultimate punishment will be decided once we return to Magna Aura, but for now you may rejoin us and earn a little redemption."

Decion bowed his head in acquiescence. "Yes, Aerl." His voice a gravelly whisper, his brow sweaty.

"But what can we do to fight?" Urana said, none too happy to see Decion back amongst them, shooting him a baleful glance.

"We need the rest of the Chryrians and the Surge," Gordell said plainly.

He glared at Valtare, who attentively stared back at him. Valtare's heart pounded. He had never witnessed anything like this and though he was endowed with power and wisdom well beyond his natural years, he was still essentially a Stone Age man living beyond his time. The end of the universe was something he was not meant to see.

I'd been promised so much, but lost so much more. Elisabeth most of all. He thought of her. And now he had to make a hard choice.

He suddenly smiled ruefully at his own stupidity, realising too late he had psionically broadcast his private thoughts. Gordell smiled back, not revelling in his pain, but in empathy. Gordell had lost much as well.

>The enemy of my enemy is our enemy< came Gordell's sardonic reply. He looked up at the Storm of Stars.

Valtare sighed in resignation. He looked at Spearhead, who in turn gave a small bow of acknowledgement.

Valtare walked over to Gordell, much to the disgust of Archron who could only watch in silence. Facing the Starguards who were still gathered in the recesses of the hall, Valtare awaited his fate.

"Forgive me..."

"Oh, shut up and get in the redemption queue," Force shouted, having regained the ability to talk.

The Starguards looked at him.

"What?" he shrugged. "Look up there!" he gestured to the cosmic battle. "The more turncoats the better, we need all the help we can get!" he loitered in the background, hungry again, and thinking of marshmallows.

A number of nods and murmurs agreed with him.

"Valtare, will the Surge fight with us?" Gordell asked.

"Spearhead will fight," Valtare said. "They have also realised their mistake following Destina. We could do with your side's help though. I could sense them all in the hills. They kept you alive all this time." He almost sounded impressed.

Gordell understood him. He closed his eyes, sending out a psionic signal. He could feel the presence of many Chryrians and Silverwraiths, but to the north, the response felt strange.

In less than fifteen minutes he found out why. From out of the hills, thousands of floating brain-like Chryrians and hovering shadowy Silverwraith emerged, along with an unexpected sight: Duke Fabien L'Coyle and twenty of his surviving men.

They looked fitter and more alive, the Chryrians within them having optimised them to peak human condition.

L'Coyle scowled at Valtare, dismissing him with a wary look. He stood by Gordell's side.

"Gordell, my feud with you is over," L'Coyle stated calmly. The Chryrian within him expressed his depth of sincerity on a level surpassed by mere speech. "Archron and Valtare betrayed both myself and my men. We are what is left and we will fight by your side." He held out his hand.

Gordell could hear the Chryrian within him. L'Coyle and his men were now as he was, involuntary bearers of Chryrians, but they had survived and now they had to use their abilities to stay alive. Gordell took his hand. > *Welcome friend*< he added.

Valtare walked slowly over. He looked L'Coyle in the eye, ashamed. "I am sorry, Fabien. I was also deceived and seduced by the power offered to me. But here, I make amends." He also held out his hand. > *Will my enemy of my enemy be my friend?*< Valtare played with Gordell's words.

L'Coyle smiled warily, turning to his men. They had no choice. They accepted the peace offering, grudgingly.

His depleted force of men were still on edge from their transformation. They stood around L'Coyle protectively, their new acknowledged leader, still wary of Valtare and his betrayal.

Ignoring them, Valtare asked aloud to Gordell. "So what's the plan?"

Archron was torn. This was not the universe he had envisioned. His mother was mad with power. He'd known, but didn't care. All he wanted now was a drink. He had to do something.

Decion and Valtare had willingly abandoned him for Sceptre and the Starguards. They had now formed a circle with the Chryrians who provided a protective psychic shield.

Archron grimaced. *No, this was not what I wanted at all.*

The end of the universe should have been his prerogative. The Gods needed to prevail and rule over them and their new universe. Frantic, Archron searched around him for inspiration.

Spearhead and his Surge stood impassively by. They could see the raw psychic energy emanating from the Chryrians' minds siphoned from the fleshy-ones and directed at the rich energy sources above them. They could feel the power, taste the flavour of the beings who designated themselves Gods. They gratefully fed off it. They couldn't help but gorge on the chaos created by the Storm of Stars, feeling the supremacy course through them. And it was good.

***

Archron, crouched on the crumbling ground, watched first Cosmogod lead the fight, then the Lore, followed by the rest of the Zater Jen. To his right he glanced at Spearhead, who like the rest of the Surge, was a virtual statue, all their extremities, winglets, and protrusions extended fully. It took Archron a moment to remember this was their feeding posture. And they were positively drunk on the energy raining down on them.

He laughed out loud to himself. The Storm of Stars were creating the most potent weapon against them, just by letting off their own energy. Archron realised his voidspear was also as strong a weapon, which could be used against his enemies and save his mother. She was still surrounded by the Surge, her powers rent from her. He knew the Surge would fight. And who better to lead them. He ran over to Spearhead. But never made it.

Destina seethed. Her plan was falling apart. The Antiqchronals were supposed to be on her side and to hell with the rest of them. The Knights Destina had failed to uphold their legacy. Now, in her madness, she could see even her last and most beloved son was going to betray her. She had seen Archron's face when first the duplicitous Decion and then the wretched hybrid-human Valtare had left and now she believed Archron was contemplating an alliance with the Starguards. She could not have that.

Before Archron could reach the Surge leader, Destina threw off her unsuspecting Surge guards still semi-paralysed by their feeding. Bursting into her Lore form, she soared down grabbing Archron by the neck, ripping off his helmet. Her face was so close to his that his skin burned.

He tried to scream, "Mother, I'm trying to help . . ." but his voice was choked off.

Archron tried to raise the voidspear to shoot her off him, but his shot went wild and hit a Surge. Destina plunged an arm of energy into her son's chest, Archron feeling incandescent pain. He stared helplessly into his mother's raging eyes. He couldn't speak. As if in a dream, Destina raised her other hand ready to embrace his head, to kiss him. A metal arm caught hers.

Chasm had been struck and interrupted during feeding by Archron's stray shot. Just in time he witnessed Destina attack his Astral master. The huge Surge bounded over in two steps and wrapped himself around Destina, pulling her away from Archron, who dropped like a rag doll to the ground.

Archron laughed to himself. The ancient Spartans had been wrong. He could see his blood spilling all over his red armour and cape. There was blood everywhere. He coughed blood in agony. He choked, gagging at the smell himself burning.

Destina struggled, even more when she realised which energy-stealing Surge was feeding off her. She exploded with rage trying to shake Chasm off as he rose up into the air under the dome; Destina rightly fearing the worst.

>*Feed, in remembrance of me* < Chasm's thoughts radiated out. Then in one massive shudder, he completely absorbed Destina.

Her Lore face was a silent scream as Chasm's body struggled to contain all the energy, which he knew he could not. Hundreds of Surge flew up to him, just as he ruptured, the nearest Surge in proximity soaking up the excess energy.

Spearhead didn't waste a moment mourning for Chasm. The giant Surge was a part of him now, a shard of memory-energy. He would be avenged on the Gods.

Archron craned his neck in amazement as every single Surge blasted off toward the battle. He slumped sideways, life slipping away. He died alone as war raged around him.

"Jesus!" Force cried out. "Did everyone see that? She killed her own son, the bitch!"

"Almost felt sorry for him," Urana tittered. "Almost!"

Sceptre smiled grimly at his cousin, but didn't disagree.

"Two less enemies to worry about!" exclaimed Gordell, pointedly to Valtare and L'Coyle. "I have a plan. *Allons-y!*"

Deep in the cosmos, six figures looked on with compassionless senses. The Prime Stars were concerned. All their peoples had managed to put their differences aside and fight against them. This had not been anticipated.

One Prime Star mooted breaking ranks, but his brother Prime Star argued against it. They owed their sibling Shadow Stars more loyalty. And the new universe would be remade with more readily pacified peoples. The other four Prime Stars agreed: The creation of the five Peoples would be undone, here and now, despite this singularity moment among the Five.

= *We can begin again; create new peoples and leave these, our first creations, to self-determination*= Prime Star said.

= *They have already possessed self-determination. And then they awakened us when it did not work*= Prime Star replied.

= *They are still younglings*= Prime Star lamented.

=*Even our beloved Lore have turned against us. Look how they feast upon our Shadow siblings*= Prime Star complained.

=*Look how much they love life enough to fight us for it*= Prime Star stated proudly.

The Prime Stars continued to argue amongst each other as the Shadow Stars were attacked.

Shadow Star felt it first; a prickling sensation upon its material surface.

≠*Brother, our Peoples arise in ire against us. What is to be done?*≠

≠ *We are one against them. They cannot win*≠ Shadow Star was concerned.

≠*Continue the Maelstrom*≠ Shadow Star ordered.

≠ *We are vulnerable as one*≠ Shadow Star warned.

≠*But no stronger than as individuals*≠ Shadow Star rallied for battle.

They sang to their sibling Prime Stars for help.

Valtare barely sensed it the first time. Inside the Silver Fortress, he sat on the ground cross-legged, deep in meditation. He didn't mind getting his light silky purple clothing dirty. He was scanning the chaotic background of the psi-scape searching for ways to attack, offering assistance to patch through psi-messages, learning—always learning new psi skills and languages from the Chryrians, Surge, and Zater Jen. Their psi-senses were so different, but still mutually intelligible. It amazed him. He froze mid-smile. Another sensation had intruded his thoughts—a disorientating tilt within the psi-scape; a mind not like their own, neither Antiqchronal, Celestian, or human. It was alien, ephemeral, eternal, yet structured. He instantly understood.

It was the mind of a God.

The Storm of Stars had minds, brains; a hypermind, even if a tenuous physical manifestation.

He immediately flash-relayed his thoughts through all the psis in their circle on the ground and to the Surge and Zater Jen who were fighting within the composite Shadow Star. The Storm of Stars may have been beings of energy, but their vast intellect and ability to manifest in so many forms and for so long, had to have created a structure akin to a physical brain, no matter the supernatural nature of the being. The thoughts of the Storm of Stars could not be read, but they could be felt. And they could be attacked.

But first, they had to find it.

>*Light Guard, locate the hypermind*< Cosmogod instructed Ego Byss.

The Glorious Ego Byss, Captain of the Light Guard called out to his force:

>*Ax Omen, Adam Finitum, Geona Zen we go home to the depths of evil. Long may we live*<

The Light Guard selected the strongest signal and vanished through black-light portals almost invisible against the Shadow Stars. They sifted through the outskirts of the minds of the Shadow Stars. They counted no less than sixteen different dimensions the complex mind was spread out across.

Back on Earth, as the black circle of hell descended, another decision had been made.

"We can attack through the Chryrians," Gordell confirmed, after a quick conference with the psi-beings. "They will take over our consciousnesses and we can take the fight to the Storm of Stars on the psionic front."

"What happens to our bodies?" Force asked, somewhat nervous at being a ghost while he was still alive.

"They will remain here in the fortress," Gordell replied. "There are barracks beyond the chamber. It would be safer this way rather than having to attack physically."

"But consider this," Valtare added in caution to Gordell's chagrin, "We could die here, both bodily and in mind. But if we attack the Storm of Stars and our bodies die, our minds would survive with the Chryrians, almost forever." He grinned knowingly as he looked around at the group.

"Nice of you to be an optimist," Force grimly laughed. "Well, we're on the wrong side of Nevada, my powers have changed, and I'm fighting against Gods, so why not have an out of body experience to boot. I'm in." He put his right hand in the middle of an imaginary horizontal circle.

Gordell and Valtare put their hands on top of Force's. L'Coyle, lis pursed in consternation, followed.

Sceptre, Urana, Decion, and Azure looked at each other. It was the ultimate sacrifice for the fate of the universe.

"And our role?" Sceptre asked.

"You may come with us. Your minds should be suitable," replied Gordell.

"If a Fifth can do it then so can I," Urana said. She placed her hand on the others. "Come on, Aerl, show us some spontaneity. Altair would have done it!" she grinned.

Sceptre sighed. Altair would have done it. He actually missed his brother-cousin. And this was definitely a cousin of an idea. He walked over and placed his hands on theirs.

"What about my lancesword?" Decion asked, fastidiously clutching his most prized possession.

"No material objects can come with you, but you can recreate them in your psionic state. If you want to fight with your lancesword; if you want to be your lancesword, you can," explained Gordell. He knew what the response would be.

"Be the lancesword?" boomed Decion. He grinned. "That I would like to see." His bulky frame lumbered forward and he slapped all the other hands down. "Redemption begins here. For the memory of my brother, Alpha Rion, who I aggrieved."

They waited for Azure to join them, but the youngest Starguard could not. She was staring up at the sky, mesmerised and literally glowing.

"There are too many Lore here." Her eyes were already burning a deeper blue. "I can hear them calling to me and my powers are aching to get out. I can do more this way. See you on the battlefield." She took off into the air and through the open dome, the Sky Warrior Loremaiden joining Millennius and the Lore above the Earth.

The rest watched Azure as her blue radiant energy flared up when contact was made with the Lore. She glowed like a new star.

Zane smiled. "Gordell, what can I do?" She looked at him expectantly.

"Zane, you can't come with us, not like this," replied Gordell.

"Why not?"

"You're an Astral; your mind is not like the others. It is of time, which we cannot inhabit. It is here and there; I cannot explain it."

"But I'm half human," Zane pleaded. "Surely you can hold onto that." She wasn't sure she entirely believed him.

"I'm sorry, Zane," Gordell answered truthfully. "But the temporal unpredictability would be too much. We could lose you."

Zane smarted at this. She'd come so far. "Fine," she kicked the ground. "Go without me." An angry spark of heat coursed through her body, Zane wondering what it was.

Gordell let her be.

Casually, Valtare announced, "We will also need what you call, a pilot."

"That's me!" replied Force excitedly. "What do you want me to fly?" Force was eager to know.

"I will show you in due course," Valtare said.

"*D'accord*, it is time." Gordell called over the Chryrians. He addressed one, the name sounding like a high-pitched whistle.

There was a fluttering as a handful of wispy Chryrians formed a circle above and around the mortals. The Starguards and humans braced themselves.

"Don't worry, it won't hurt," Gordell said to them. *Much*, he thought.

The air was lit up with flashes of light as the Chryrians began to pulsate with energy. They descended upon the mortals and into their heads. There wasn't time for any of them to react to the momentary pain.

The bodies of the humans and Starguards slumped into the arms of attending Surge as the Chryrians embraced their consciousnesses within their own. Gordell let the Chryrian guide his and the others' minds so they got used to being non-physical entities.

>*God, this is so freaky*< Force psyed. >*How am I even hearing and seeing all of this?*< He could see all the others looking like transparent versions of themselves.

> *This is the purest life can get*< Gordell psyed back.

There was laughter as Valtare thought >*And for so long, you thought us abominations, Gordell. How many Chryrians have you killed in your lifetime—hundreds? Thousands?*< The bitterness was in his voice, but he added >*But I find myself privileged to fight by your side*<

> *We will speak later of this, Valtare. There are many things I should tell you about the Chryrians we hunted. But for now, we must fight*< Gordell finished. > *Valtare, please ready Force for his role*<

Valtare guided a floating-bodiless Force to another part of the fortress into what looked like a Surge version of a computer room, full of blocks of metal with crystals embedded in them, which rapidly changed colour.

>*Okay*< Valtare finally said, >*Are you ready?*<

Force was confused. There were no spacecraft anywhere in sight > *What do you want me to fly?*<

> *The fortress, of course*< psyed Valtare without a hint of humour >*The fortress is made from Surge material. It still responds to psionic commands. This is the command hub at the heart of the fortress. One of the Surge who remained, Sine, will be the captain, the rest of us will provide the defence, and you will pilot*<

>*How? Are you kiddin'? I can't touch anything*<

>*I don't know. How do you pilot anything?*< asked a patient Valtare.

>*Ah!*< Force understood. He was in the psychic realm. He could do anything his mind wanted to do. >*Okay, here we go*<

Force concentrated. He had always wanted to fly a vintage World War II bomber and here was his chance to do so. As he thought about it, the outline of a B-17 took shape, the fuselage, the huge wings and tail, all the panels, the engines and propellers, the guns and cockpit, the instruments, the bomb bays, the pilot seat, and even a uniform. Force imagined his body and slid the goggles onto his head.

>*Chocks away*< his mind called. He gunned the throttle and the machine began to move, inching across his imagined runway.

The fortress rumbled on the ground, its metal walls and foundations heaving against the ground. It threw Zane off-balance as she jumped from the fortress to the ground. It finally wrenched itself off the desert, rocks, dirt and sand dropping below, leaving behind a half-mile-wide crater. It rose into the sky, all the open ports, doors, and roof closing automatically.

The rectangular shape became more muted and aerodynamic as Sine moulded the fortress by touching its metals walls. The fortress now resembled a vast, rectangular, metallic zeppelin with short crenelated towers sticking out at various points.

The B-17 took off, Force looking out of the small cockpit windows. He could hear the engines roar as he pulled back on the stick. He steered it straight up toward the blackest storm clouds he had ever seen. But Force wasn't scared; he was having the time of his life.

>*Now this is what I call a flying fortress*<

"Good luck," Zane shouted, waving after them. She was the only person left on Earth. The only Peoples she could fight beside were the Zater Jen, but they were nowhere to be seen.

I will die alone here, she thought.

=*Look how they attack*= Prime Star sang in admiration.

=*They have discovered the hypermind. Our kindred are in danger*= Prime Star fretted.

=*Let them destroy the Shadow Stars, then there will be order*= Prime Star trembled with excitement.

=*No, brother. Without the Shadow Stars there will be no balance. We will be destroyed too. The Five will destroy us*= Prime Star stated reprovingly.

= *That is not true. There is no cause to attack us*= Prime Star inferred.

=*But our kindred call to us for help. Shall we not interfere*= Prime Star questioned.

=*No, their fate is decided. We are content to watch*= Prime Star announced confidently.

= *We are not*= Prime Star rebelled.

There was a thunderous crackle of exploding energy and one Prime Stars broke free of their formation. It hurtled toward the battle, solar flares arcing out into the mortal forces who now fought on two fronts. Four more Prime Stars railed against restraint racing to the Shadow Stars, hurling more flares into the system and the planet below. The remaining Prime Star stood alone stranded contemplating the situation.

Wordlessly, Millennius divided the Lore, engaging each of the incoming Prime Stars. But in the midst of battle, Spheron departed, leaving Azure in charge of his force.

>Where are you going?< she psyed, surprising herself with this ability. *I'm a Lore whisperer*, she mused.

Spheron pointed downwards.

>I won't be long.< He ported down to Earth.

Within Millennius, a part of him surged when he felt Azure so close by. The blue spark began to grow.

The cosmos lit up as fierce energy sliced through the vacuum. The heavens quaked and stars shuddered amidst a battle the likes of which had never before been witnessed beneath the skies of the universe since its epic creation.

Whole waves of Antiqchronal Lore, Zater Jen, and Surge clashed with the Storm of Stars and fell. Space ripped apart with fury as the Zater Jen tore reality. The Lore corrupted, twisted and warped time with unerring death and destruction. The cosmic shock blew atoms apart, system-spanning lightning bolts, brighter than the heavens sheared the stellar darkness, striking down friend and foe, bringing fear even to the mystic hearts of the Storm of Stars as they battled for survival. Space buckled, strangling those unfortunate to be too close, washing over them in waves of temporal energy, sweeping them away into depths of coldest space.

Arcanaut felt ripples of time-shifted dimensions tear at his crystalline skin. He sought the source and was astonished by what he found. Not only were the Storm of Stars simultaneously located in several dimensions, but they were also spread over several temporal zones. These hidden realms were their anchors, their power sources, their manifestation nodes—their Achilles heel.

>*Lord Cosmogod, I sense the temporal nodal junctures of the Storm of Stars, they are anchored through hyper-tesseract space*<

Cosmogod considered this. The Storm of Stars did not just exist in one plane at one time. They were interconnected to the universe in a complex web of temporal, spatial, and psionic strands through multilayered dimensions, which were further warped to extra-dimensional extremes. Their forces would have to cut through every one of the strands, which they could, but not before being destroyed by the Storm of Stars.

A better battle plan was needed or they were all going to die.

CHAPTER NINE

Zane stood upon her ancient home, alone, wondering what she could do to help. A crash of light suddenly split the air before her startling the Astral as a portal opened. Spheron flew out.

She stared at him, her initial shock disappearing, as if remembering something. "Have we met before?" Zane asked, feeling calmer.

"Yes, we have. It is I, Spheron, transformed like Millennius and Destina."

Zane smiled warmly in greeting. "I know that Spheron. And I'm sorry for what Synther did to you. But that's not what I meant. Have I seen you somewhere, somewhen else?"

"Ah, yes. Do you not remember? Just after Netherlord tried to kill you, you appeared in phase space. I frightened you. You fired at me and then disappeared."

Zane cocked her head, confused. It was all a blur, but something was coming through. Whiteness. Pure white energy. She had been covered in it. No, she was the energy. Zane rubbed her head. "I don't understand," she shouted as the wind howled across the darkened skies and dust storms snaked around them.

Spheron wondered if he should be the one to tell her. But she had to know.

"Zane, there are times when a Celestian who becomes a Lore fathers a child, a female. She becomes a Loremaiden..."

"I know, like Azure," Zane said dismissively. "But I am born of a half-Celestian father and a human mother." A mother she barely remembered she realised sadly. She had a sense of an ephemeral motherly figure with long black curly hair, a wide-lipped smile, and always singing. Yes, she remembered her mother's singing—songs about the sea and the creatures that lived within them. They had lived along the coast for a while.

Zane smiled at the faded memory. Spheron brought her back to the present.

"Yes, but by then, Millennius was affected by the Lore virus. It got stronger as time went on and sometimes, just sometimes, random genes inherit energies, which might skip a generation. The epigenetic effects of Millennius' Lore energy have concentrated in you and, yes Zane, you are a Loremaiden," he told her, sympathy in his voice.

Zane shook her head in disbelief. "I can't be!"

"You are, but a different one at that. Loremaidens usually react in the presence of other Lore, but you do not. You are different, special. Once you were of age, your powers reacted to temporal energy. You act as a temporal cluster, absorbing and channelling temporal energies," he thought of an apt comparison, "like an organic Surge."

"You've got to be frigging kidding me?" Zane felt the temptation to scoff at Spheron.

But the more she thought about it, the more it made sense. Netherlord had attacked her with temporal energy. She had unknowingly used that energy to transform into a Loremaiden. It had also given her enough strength to repel Altair's attack when they first met in New York. And then at Thane's, the Lorestone would have been packed with more than enough temporal energy, which she would have absorbed and channelled for their escape from the explosion. Her response had been flight rather than fight.

But why have I ended up here then? Why not the Chronopolis where I would have been safe. Or Zero Star? she thought, as she turned back to Spheron.

"Why have I ended up here in Earth's future? It can't be random. It's like I'm being guided to places," she shouted over the howling winds which in turn were chased by vast charges of lightning searing across the skies above. "And why have I aged so fast?"

"I do not know," Spheron replied in truth. "You may have been somewhere for all those years, but can't remember. Maybe something happened to you? But I believe, Zane, you have been directing yourself, but the temporal loops woven around you have not caught up yet. Your mind is still trapped in a temporal fugue. It will come to you in time."

As if that thought triggered a memory, Zane suddenly remembered her dream about Mindscream. The landscape had seemed familiar, considering what Gordell had said about this being Mindscream's ancestral homeland. This was a coincidence too far. And Mindscream had been trying to tell her something, something about the sky.

She looked up and the first thing she saw was a tiny little star, growing brighter as it battled overhead: the Time Empress.

***

High above in the cosmic melee, the Time Empress sensed her presence being sought. She looked behind her from the depths of oblivion toward the fractured Earth and at Zane, standing, waiting for her.

Phasia sensed the young girl's distraction. "Is something the matter?" Phasia called out, bracing herself against energy attacks.

"I have to see Zane. Hold the line, Phasia. Wait for me." She time-ported out before Phasia could do anything.

The Time Empress ported before Zane. She looked at Spheron as if signalling a command.

But Spheron ignored her dismissal. "She must become what she must," he said, much to the confusion of Zane.

The Time Empress, wide-eyed, contemplated his words solemnly. She understood. "You're prepared to undertake your sacrifice willingly." It was a statement. Her voice was sad.

"Gladly." Spheron smiled as much as he could as a Lore. Pre-empting a response from her, he replied, "I do not need your consent or blessing."

The child laughed, nodding her pale blonde head. Though she smiled thinly, her eyes were cold ice chips.

Before Zane could ask what that was all about, Spheron glided closer to her, almost touching her skin. Zane felt herself almost hypnotised by his energy. And then Spheron advanced even closer, Zane feeling her body evaporate in heat and transform as Spheron melded his energy with hers.

Zane felt exhilarated. She looked around finding herself in a temporalscape all her own, lit brilliant white.

"Spheron, it's amazing." She whirled around in awe. "Spheron? Spheron?"

She looked around for him, but he was no longer there. But she heard a faint echo of his voice:

>*Zane, I have given my energy*—my life—*to you. My time is over. I will be no more. Serve your destiny well*<

The voice faded and was no more.

"What? Spheron?" a traumatised Zane couldn't believe what she had just heard. Sadness threatened to overwhelmed her. But she held back her tears and fears, feeling only love for Spheron.

Zane looked down at herself. She was bathed in resplendent white energy. Spheron had sacrificed his Loreself to her, like a catalyst, so Zane could self-sustain her energy. She could feel the temporal fields pulling toward her, as air to lungs; she wasn't just able to travel time, she was time, more so than her brother. She could go anywhere, anytime. She could see through time, much better than Lightstream could read time. Zane was an avatar of time, its personification and will. Her grieving for Spheron's death gave way to revelry as the young girl in front of her came into focus.

She, too, stood in the temporalscape.

"Who are you?" Zane asked the Time Empress, slightly annoyed. Her voice sounded vibrant and in the fluid medium. "Are you the one really directing me through time?"

The little girl shook her head innocently and looked at Zane with sad eyes. And through those eyes, Zane could see snippets of jumbled time, her own past, her future, and her destiny.

"Oh, I see. I was supposed to be dead, but somehow time was changed. Or I was changed. So confusing ..." She held her head to stop time spinning within it. It throbbed in temporal waves.

Zane knew she was meant to be dead by Netherlord's hands, but fate or someone had intervened—twisted her time for some unknown purpose. Was she in another universe? A parallel one? Was she even in the right timestream? What was her purpose?

Zane desperately wanted to know what had happened to her. *Spheron, if you're still there, help me,* she pleaded inwardly.

There was no voice. But suddenly a vivid flash of her father, Lord Aeon, in his grave on the Surge world almost blinded her. The line of sight centred on his sword. Even from a million years in the future and countless light years away, Zane could feel the energy from the blade. Phasia had tempered the once-ordinary, man-made sword with Lore energy to counter any Lore threat, but now it lay wasted in the ground with its owner. The vision faded away.

"Was I supposed to save my father?" Zane asked herself. She looked at the Time Empress, but there was no forthcoming reply from her; just silent support.

Grief washed over Zane at seeing her father's body and the senseless death he had endured. Synther, Destina, Archron, and Netherlord were already dead so her father had been avenged. Were Spearhead and the Surge as guilty? Yet, here they were fighting against Destina's dream. But Zane was determined to have her father's sword, if only to give it to Aristedes as his birthright.

Her wish was her command as a flash of white energy burst from her mind and Zane found herself portalled to the Surge world beside her father's grave. She gazed down around her. The world had almost been stripped of the old Surge bodies by Destina and Archron for building material; a desecration of death.

This was the home of Solitude, Zane suddenly realised. Instinctively, she looked around for him, but knew whatever timeline she was in, Solitude had long left. She wondered how he was, how the rest of the Multiforce were doing. Most of all she missed Aristedes.

Sighing, she transformed back into her physical body. She looked down at her father's grave wondering what to do. She had no tears though she was as sad as she could ever remember. Maybe she was more grown up now or maybe she was used to death. She didn't like either thought.

"Hey, sis!"

Zane jumped at the voice behind her, hardly sensing the portal open disgourging its occupant.

She couldn't believe her eyes. "Aristedes!" she ran over and jumped into his arms, forgetting she was taller and heavier, knocking them both to the ground.

"Hades' dong, you're heavy, Zane! You've changed!" Aristedes laughed. He sat up and took a good look at her.

Twisting onto her knees. Zane laughed, too, then something occurred to her; two things really.

"Hade's dong? That's an Uncle Helexius curse. Have you seen him recently? Where are the Astrals? We're fighting a war! We need you!" She gushed on, explaining what had happened to her after Netherlord tried to kill her on Home. "And you look... different... older." She saw the guarded look in his eyes, her suspicions confirmed.

Aristedes had taken his time getting up and leaned against a little boulder. "Yes, I'm from sometime in the future." His smile was soft, though Zane could see more lines and strains upon his face. His black hair was a little longer and more curly. And his manoeuvre suit, though still based on the Multiforce uniform Lynn Kellis had issued once upon a time on Zero Star, was fuller and all dark blue, no white trim or flashes.

"Time, the warrior-prince," Zane sang with a flourish.

Aristedes smiled easily. "Something like that." He was regarding her with curiosity, which made her uneasy.

"So, tell me, what's happening with the Astrals?"

Aristedes shook his head.

"Zeus and Hades holding hands!" she cursed, "just tell me!"

"I can't. You know that!" His predicament was as impossible as Zane's statement.

"Ooooh," screeched Zane. "Now I know why people hate us Astrals. How infuriating that's is! Tell me," Zane pleaded.

Another shake of his head.

"So why are you here?" a frustrated Zane asked.

"I came to see you. To say I'm proud of you, that you found father."

Zane's eyes smarted. "Thank you. That's nice. For an end of the world speech. You're scaring me." She held back her tears.

"I forgot, you're still not as strong as me," he joked, both thinking of a time long ago on Consention Base.

"Am, too," came her customary reply, her laughter dying out. Now it was her turn to study her brother. "Stop joking." Her voice was quiet. "You're in a war, too, aren't you?" She quickly held up her and hands in submission. "I know, I know, you can't tell me. But I know goodbye words when I hear them."

Aristedes' smile was a grim line. "I don't know what will happen."

"But you could die?"

Aristedes raised his left shoulder in a shrug. "We all die." A casual statement.

"You're an idiot," Zane complained. "You know what I mean?"

"Anything can happen in this war."

"Is it the same war?"

Aristedes thought about it. "Yes and no." Before Zane could ask, he said, "And that's the truth. A different cause, a different front, a different time, a different foe. But the same war. Ish!"

That confused Zane even more. "There's something beyond the Storm of Stars! Hades' balls!"

Enigmatically, Aristedes said, "There's always something beyond."

"Spoken like a true Astral," she huffed.

"I wish it wasn't always so."

Something in his voice made Zane ask, "Are you afraid?"

Aristedes smiled so happily, it made Zane well up.

"No," he shook his head easily, "Not now I've seen you."

"Oh, shut up!" she guffawed, thinking he was teasing her.

"I'm serious, Zane." His smile had dropped. He addressed her earnestly. "You're the brave one. You've been alone for years, apart from your family, discovered your powers alone, grown up literally with no one to help you. You shouldn't have had to."

"It made me who I am!" she replied more bravely than she thought.

"I know, but you're my little sister and you endured so much alone. I haven't been alone—"

"Oh, so you are with Starshina then?" Zane interrupted, her cheeks flushing at Aristedes' indignant look.

He sighed heavily. "Yes, I'll give you that one—"

"Married? Kids?" Zane pried more in askance.

Aristedes tilted his head, shaking it in amusement. "As I was saying, or trying to say is that I came to find you at this exact time; to see you at your bravest. To be inspired."

Zane realised her mouth was open in shock, surprise, and half laughter. "You must really be on the brink of Hell if you need inspiration from me," she tried not to laugh, seeing how solemn Aristedes was. She stopped short as another thought occurred to her.

"Am I going to die?" she asked softly. Why otherwise was her brother being so nice to her? Complimenting her. Not that he had been anything other than that. But his behaviour...

But Aristedes grinned after a little ponder. "No, you're not going to die. You just have to do what you're going to do!"

"Meaning?" She stared at him in confusion. "I don't even know what I'm going to do. What do I do?"

Aristedes lips curled upward again. "You'll do what you were meant to do." He jutted his chin toward the grave.

Zane followed his gaze, turning back as a glint of light caught her peripheral vision. "Aris..."

He was gone.

"You have got to be kidding me!" Zane screamed at the sky. "Grrrrargh!"

She sat alone for a few minutes. Frightening thoughts suddenly occurring to her.

Was Aristedes really here? Did I dream that? Zane stood paralysed by the grave. *Why would I have dreamed it?*

There was nothing to suggest he had been here even around the boulder where she thought they had fallen. The ground was a mess anyway.

Zane was tempted to cycle back in time, but decided against it. One, she couldn't be bothered. And two, she didn't want to find out she was crazy. The only way to go was forward.

She slowly approached the grave and combed away the compacted dirt from on top the body. She found herself annoyed at how shallow the grave was compared to normal standards.

"Oh!" she gasped at the sight and smell.

Only bones were left now, Zane suspecting the soil was highly acidic with all the Surge metals leeching into the ground not helped by the bombardment from the Earth fleet during the Axalan War. However, the sword looked as good as new. She unwrapped her father's bony fingers from around the hilt and folded his arms back across his chest. The few tufts of brown hair she smoothed back and she kissed his cheek.

Anger flared up inside her. The injustice. The senseless loss. Maybe Aristedes was right.

"No, I won't see you like this," Zane said in a determined voice.

She stood up, brushing the dirt off her clothing followed by her hands. She knew what she had to do; what Aristedes had expected her to do. Energising herself into her white energy state, Zane voyaged back through time. The timestream flowed around her, colourful, silent, sense-tingling. Zane didn't let the branching and twisting side-streams distract her. She had her destination. Not back to Aristedes, but further, back to the point which had changed her life.

And she watched and waited for her moment.

***

"Over my dead body will my sister join you," Lord Aeon was saying.

"So be it. Kill him," Destina coldly ordered.

Aeon raised his sword, ready for the attack.

"Spearhead!" At Destina's command the Surge released Synther's powers and he flared up into his Lore being.

Aeon brandished the sword ahead of him, but before he could defend himself. Synther blasted Aeon with corrosive Lore energy.

Zane intervened. She split the temporal field around her father so he existed in two dimensions at the same time—two potentials in time…

Aeon seemed to blur in the blast and swayed uneasily as Synther stopped.

. . . allowing one of the Aeons to die, still holding his sword, his body smouldering . . .

. . . while the other lived, unnoticed by Synther, Destina and her sons.

Before the Surge's energy-negation fields kicked back in, Zane pulled her father into Phase space. Quickly she time-ported them forward into the future Surge world.

Xathanius, Lord Aeon of the Astrals hardly had time to figure out what had happened to him when he found himself staring down at his alternate doppelganger in his grave.

"It worked!" a delighted Zane sang. She reverted to her Astral form, hugging her astonished father hard around the waist.

"Zane? Is that you?" Xathanius, Lord Aeon of the Astrals looked between his daughter and his dead self in the ground. He lovingly hugged his daughter back, still confused. "What happened?" He tried to get his head around the vision before him.

Zane spent almost an hour recounting all that had happened to her and what was about to happen, especially to him in the nightmare past.

"Those traitors!" Aeon spat, gritting his teeth. "My own aunt! My own sister!"

He had not been prepared for the news of what had followed in the wake of his demise. And his had not been a glorious death. He had not saved anyone with his death. It was unnerving to see himself interred.

He exhaled slowly, calming himself. "I am thankful it was my father who buried me. But I'm sure he would be glad to see me rise from the dead." He peered down at Zane. "But your powers, they hadn't manifested when I last saw you. How did you save me?"

Zane's answer came with a tinkle of laughter. "You were the cat, father."

"The cat?"

"Yes, remember the lessons Phasia taught us about that cat in a box that was alive and dead at the same time?"

"Yes, vaguely." Aeon's brows knitted in remembrance.

"Well you were the cat, I was the box, and the Knights Destina looked in the box where you were dead. See?"

Aeon grasped the image in his head. "Kind of; you're brilliant," he ruffled Zane's hair, Zane still hating it. "But how did your powers develop to such a degree?"

One thing at a time, Zane decided to herself. No need to upset him about Spheron's sacrifice. So she told him the other news she had saved.

"Well, father, it seems I'm a Loremaiden!"

The look of shock on Aeon's face took Zane aback. Then she laughed. "I only found out myself a few hours or millions of years ago in the future, depending on how you look at it." She laughed at the paradoxes. "But it seems Synther's virus experiments affected Millennius, the results of which bypassed you, but ended up in lil ole me!"

Aeon looked down, sorrowful. Zane knew he was blaming himself for some reason.

"Father, you couldn't have known. They kept everything from you." But her face brightened. "But you know what? I wouldn't have it any other way, for I wouldn't have been able to find and save you."

Aeon caressed his little girl's face.

"I'm fine," Zane consoled him. "I'm still me."

They embraced again, before Aeon turned to his grave. "Can we cover me up again, please? It's a bit disconcerting."

The two of them spent a few minutes re-interring Dead Aeon, as Zane dubbed him, building a low cairn-like structure from nearby rocks. Aeon resisted saying a few words at his own funeral. That was just tempting fate.

"Now what?" Aeon asked. He looked up into the swirling skies. The planet wasn't too welcoming and had well-earned its stature as a place of death. He wouldn't miss it.

"We join the land of the living," Zane replied, as eager to leave.

"Let's go."

"Gladly," Zane smiled at her father. She held out her hand for her father to take.

Bursting into her temporal form, to both their amazement Aeon's sword burst into flame, Phasia's magenta fire. He held the sword aloft and the blade sang in vibrant energy, a repeating sound reminding Zane of a heart beat; her father's? Phasia's? She did not know.

Aeon sheathed the sword and the flame extinguished itself.

"That's new!" was Aeon's understated comment.

"Our queue to go, no doubt!"

With that, Zane thrust her arms into the air, a portal spiralling out in front of her. They rode on the chronal streams, slipped through universal fissures, and jumped across temporal fields.

And when they exited, Zane and Lord Aeon landed right in the heart of the war.

CHAPTER TEN

The flying fortress battled through space, flanked by the nebulous brain-like Chryrians.

>*All aboard the Lady Elisabeth*< called out Force, good-naturedly.

>*The what?*< Valtare psyed from the crew compartment, wondering if he had heard correctly.

>*I could see her in your mind, Valtare*<

>Stay out of my mind!<

>*Hey, no problem. Geez, tetchy. All I'm saying is that Van Tager may have gifted me powers for the wrong reasons, but she's brought us together in this war, so I've named our spacecraft after your wife. This lady can also pack a mean punch*<

Valtare rounded on him ready to grab his non-corporeal body, but a flash of memory punched into his mind—a young boy, pushed, verbally abused, bullied in a baseball park by a large man, the boy falling flat on his back at the same moment two fighter jets from the nearby Air Force base fly over, the boy staring up in wonder as he always did, and in that moment wishing he was in one of those metal saviours, flying away, free, escaping—

>*Whoa! That's not embarrassing!*< Force shook his head breaking the memory. He tried repressing the dark memory, even if it was the over-riding reason he had joined the Air Force and then the E-Corps.

Valtare smirked. >*Your father made you like this?*<

>*You want to talk about your wife?*< Violent thoughts swirled around Force's mind.

>*Not particularly*< Valtare scowled.

>*Then let's not talk about my father*<

>*Fair enough*<

195

>*No problem*< Force frowned. >*Now we have to fight this Hyper-God*<

>*Hyper-God?*< Gordell was intrigued entering the cockpit. He had stayed clear of their psy-spat, having no interest in their memories.

>*Well, you know Hyper-this, Hyper-that connected to the Storm of Stars*< Force joked. >*We must be fighting a Hyper-God?*< He grimaced, trying to concentrate on being a virtual pilot flying a living metal castle through space.

There was thoughtful reflection as his musings spread across the minds of the other anti-Storm of Stars forces.

>*Force you may have something there*< psyed Gordell. >*Phasia, Millennius, Cosmogod, and Spearhead split your forces; find and attack the other strands Arcanaut discovered. They may be separate entities, but the Storm of Stars are as Force aptly suggested, Hyper beings; gods nestled within gods, within gods, etcetera, anchored at different points in space and time via cosmic strands, for energy and control yet connected through a single Hypermind. We must find the Hypermind through the cosmic strands—its nerves and control system*<

The Antiqchronals and Fifths re-deployed their forces. Each of the particular capabilities of each of the Five peoples were needed in order to destroy the strands and trace it back to the Hypermind. Arcanaut supplied the best temporal and spatial coordinates he could for the Hypermind nodes finding sixteen such strands. The five Peoples now amalgamated their numbers and the sixteen Hypermind strands came under attack.

Millennius led the largest force of Lore, Surge, Chryrians, and Zater Jen. The Surge could absorb and dispel the Storm of Stars' energy, while the Lore just plainly ate it up. The Chryrians added a psionic element. The Storm of Stars were assaulted physically, psionically, and temporally as the Zater Jen tore into temporal nodes. They kept the Shadow Stars at bay, who also guarded the largest of the cosmic strands, which through the eyes of the attackers sloped off and down a dimensional warren.

The elusive strand reminded Millennius of the Great Rift, all gnarled and lashed together in some great cosmic Gordian knot. The more they hacked at it, the more loose energy filaments cohered together. Millennius knew they had to find the right place to unbind it all like a ribbon waiting to be unwoven. But they didn't have the time. Brute force was required.

The Zater Jen could sense discord in the strand, weak areas of temporal stress. They exploited it to great effect, shearing it apart.

KREEESH!

The sudden shattering of countless Zater Jen shocked everyone, death cries reverberating horrifically through their minds.

>Uni*verse, what happened?*< psyed Millennius across his forces.

>*Resonance*< psyed a Zater Jen called Trittoni.

Millennius understood how the strands were fighting back, producing a resonant frequency vibration pulverising the crystalline skin of the Zater Jen. Their temporal essences leaked out into the vacuum. Yet still more Zater Jen dashed in to battle without hesitation to crush the energy strand.

There was a thundering-like snap as the strand finally broke, the whiplash of the broken energy tie flaying anything in its path, including a Shadow Star, splayed in half. The two black burning pieces of the Godstar drifted apart, the shadow of a God disappearing into infinity. There was no cheer of victory. There was still much to do.

Before the other Shadow Stars could respond, Millennius tracked the other end of the errant strand through time and space back to the Hypermind.

>*Where are you, Spheron?*< Azure psyed as she led another group in Spheron's absence.

She and Millennius knew something had happened to him, but they would have to wait to grieve later, after the war, if they survived.

The strand they sought lay curled up in a dimension of black holes, the ancient cosmos dying of entropy. Navigating through the chaotic mire to attack the node was the worst nightmare Azure could have endured. She choked as black holes clawed menacingly at her energy. Several Lore slipped down forever into a cluster of black holes, their ghostly shrieks disappearing forever, haunting Azure. After what seemed like an eternity fighting against singularity tides, they discovered the strand's base, as thick as a small moon, shining in the distance like a fuzzy sunbeam. They readied for their attack.

Sensing their presence the strand tried to snake off, but the Antiqchronal forces latched onto its spiky end. It violently shook and vibrated trying to flit through temporal fields, much like the Lore did to rid themselves of lore viruses. But Azure's group dug in and valiantly hung on until the end.

***

Cosmogod and Starmondaus found themselves battling the combined Shadow Stars, avoiding the sucking singularity at its centre, sealing the dreaded maw with immense temporal pockets which looped in on themselves. The super massive black hole was trapped within its own bubble. The forces of Cosmogod began to rip it apart from the outside in, while Starmondaus sought one of the almost invisible strands which led from it.

>*Here, my lord*< he psyed, pointing out the filmy sinuous strand angling off into another universe.

Without a word, Cosmogod shot toward it not caring about the Shadow Stars behind him. Flying the length of the strand he spied the misty portal at its end. Plunging in, he was pursued by Starmondaus and their army tracing the strand back to the Hypermind.

Spearhead and his Surge-majority group could not resist the pulsar which hosted another Hypermind strand, a further million years in the red-lit future of a dying solar system. The bright beacon of the wrecked star rotated at an impossible speed, protecting the strand, but the Zater Jen and Lore wrestled the stellar beast to a standstill. Exposed, the strand disappeared into a dark light portal of its own making, the Chryrians tracking its psionic traces through a myriad of torrid temporal and jangled dimensional fluxes.

More than twice they almost lost the signal, but psionic nerves held in distant reaches stretching the limits of even disembodied minds. But they sent out beacons like breadcrumbs signalling the Surge, Lore, and Zater Jen who homed in to bolster their Antiqchronal companions.

Spearhead sunk a giant red spiked fist into the strand. >*Lead us to Justice*< he ordered.

His forces followed him down a portal of unknown destination.

The Time Empress commanded a Zater Jen-loaded force. Her obscene youth, compared to the elders around her, was respected by all of the Antiqchronals. With information on a strand supplied to them by Arcanaut, the Astral time-ported with her group into a temporal cul de sac. Space buckled around them limiting their actions.

>We need room. Find the strand< commanded the Time Empress. She could feel the strand warping space, sending out temporal fluctuations, disguising its location.

But with the combined power of the Antiqchronals, the Zater Jen and Chryrians were able to smooth out the buckled space, psionically and temporally pushing back the folded dimensions before them. Temporal energy spilled out into the universe, cascading over the plain of the alien universe like an undammed flood. Poised outward in all directions, the Lore and Surge were quickly attracted to the energy pulse of the strand which suckled on a nebula of chaotic particles.

They streaked through space, the strand now alerted to their presence. Recoiling, too late, the Time Empress and Antiqchronal units penetrated its portal back to the Hypermind.

Phasia's assembled forces searched for the strand in a thousand-light-year long nebulous cloud. The star factory hid many hazards not least a cosmic strand which brazenly whipped around in the heavenly mists desperately trying to fight back. Despite losing hundreds in destruction to the savage lashes from the strand, Phasia coordinated her Antiqchronal army into subduing the strand creating a counter-temporal vortex. The Chryrians then psionically attached themselves to the slow-motion strand as it spiralled away at a crawling pace through the cosmos. Phasia followed their psi-signal into the unknown.

Celesophia and Arcanaut directed another group into a thirteen-planet system where the strand carefully threaded the sun and its wandering attendants. The Crystal Queen surveyed the dead worlds without compassion. The strand was sucking the essence out of them all. No life would ever grow here.

>*Destroy the system*< came her fateful order. There was no time or emotion to waste on these worlds.

Even as they began razing the worlds with precision strikes, the strand broke free, retreating into the vacuum, the Zater Jen commanders following it wherever it went.

***

Areigna and Geomega's brigade found their strand strung through a vast field of millions of plant-like beings floating through alternate space sieving for interstellar particles.

> *What are those?*< the Power of Cosmogod asked.

>*Space lilies*<

>*Hoh, ugly creatures*< Areigna commented.

The asteroid-sized sentient beings sheltered for warmth against the cold of the vacuum, flat gray bodies huddled around a dark matter cloud, feeding. But they didn't just feed for themselves.

>*I think they're feeding the strand*< Areigna surmised.

>*Agree*< Geomega psyed back. >*I think they worship it as a deity*<

>*Then they are our enemy!*<

Geomega looked toward his sister Zater Jen. >*Agreed*<

When a large alien force interrupted their sacred feeding duty to worship their God, the space lilies tried to fight back.

Areigna and Geomega could see the all-but invisible strand, psionically attached to all the space lilies. To un-tether the strand would kill the entire space lily civilisation. But what was genocide in the ultimate fate of the universe?

>*Attack*< Areigna gleefully cried.

The force descended upon the space lilies burning the foliage of the stars to death. There were great anguished screams from the defenseless beasts as the strand, their God, abandoned its people in self-preservation. The Zater Jen and their cohorts trailed it, leaving behind a dead space field and a universe devoid of its only life.

Only the Light Guard plied their way unaccompanied. The Glorious Ego Byss led Ax Omen, Adam Finitum, and Geona Zen into attack against as many of the Prime Stars as they could, distracting them from aiding the other forces. They hurled themselves into battle.

God blinked first.

One Prime Star hefted itself away from its siblings sliding into a blazing portal. It disappeared. Another blinked out at the last second, the portal snapping shut before them.

Ego Byss roared in frustration. *>Ax Omen, attack Prime Star athwart. Adam Finitum and your temporal brothers, Prime Star zenith. Geona Zen, Prime Star point<* he oriented them to their positions.

The Light Guard fanned out trying to herd the remaining three Prime Stars together to give them less maneuverability, Ego Byss holding the centre.

To his left, Ax Omen was an instrument of destruction pounding a Prime Star into retreat, crystal fists and psi-energy scything across the Prime Star's surface. Flares glanced off his silver form, more scars forming, crusting over in healing, but Ax Omen continued to push the God into submission.

Above Ego Byss, the blue crystalline Adam Finitum had been joined by three other Adam Finitums—future iterations of himself.

>Adam, news from the future. Veer left. Solar cavity. Exploit< Adam psyed to his younger self.

>Adam, quantum shield and quell the flares. Head for the core< psyed the eldest.

Two Adams complied diving and drilling down into the Prime Star. The God screamed, pierced by cold crystal. Exotic energy waves roiled around the Zater Jen brothers, heat squeezed them, crystal started to melt. But the Adams had a mission to accomplish. Now it was up to the others.

Behind Ego Byss, Geona Zen tackled the first Prime Star. The bright white Zater Jen could see her fellow Light Guards ahead and above her even as she ramped up her speed. She ran along the surface of the Prime Star dodging flailing flares and coronal eruptions. She felt her crystal skin melting. Her eyes gleamed and an energy suffused her. Geona Zen, the Quadrassentia, shifted, her body turning into metal—*from Zater Jen to Surge.* She sucked up energy for more speed. The Prime Star tried to roll into its portal, but Geona Zen's rotational speed spun the Prime Star away from its escape route. She steered the gyrating God across toward Ax Omen and Adam Finitum who were achieving the same goal.

Ego Byss readied himself. While two Prime Stars had escaped and with one Prime Star refraining from the war, still hanging above the Earth as if in existential contemplation, the other three were under siege. The Light Guard would bring them together and destroy them. Then they would hunt down their strands to the Hypermind.

In one final effort, the Light Guard cajoled and forced the Prime Stars together. Three burning stars were cast together like cosmic cannonballs. They sparked and flared, churning and gouging at each other, grimly held in place by the Light Guard.

Ego Byss thrust himself like a great red laser straight at the Prime Stars' centre. He snapped up his hand-eye. It pulsed and a radiant beam flashed from the eye. Prime Star shuddered under the beam. It reared against the Light Guard, twisting as one sharply, summoning an inner fury, throwing them off, free to move as one body. It charged Ego Byss, catching the Captain of the Light Guard by surprise. Neither wavered.

They collided.

As if the universe had split open, the exploding energy catapulted the Light Guard across the system. They were shattered. When the light died down, when the temporal ripples cleared, neither Ego Byss or the Prime Star could be seen.

Six autonomous groups of Lore, Zater Jen, Chryrians, and Surge chomped, clawed, burned and destroyed as many of the strands as they could. They were freelancers and fire-fighters, reserves, and cannon fodder, but they knew what was at stake and were ready serve the ultimate sacrifice.

Zane and Lord Aeon had arrived just in time, following one of the autonomous groups' trails into the heart of a red giant where a temporal node was hidden. The core of the star had a seething strand of temporal filament attached to it like a steel fist around a heart. Invisible to anyone but beings like the Zater Jen and Lore, the latter started eating away at the trembling core while the Zater Jen physically un-tethered the chronal attachments. But as the temporal filament broke away, it flailed around through space trying to find another attachment.

Before it could, Aeon flew after it and savagely hacked at it with his sword. A thin filament from the strand wrapped around him trapping his arms to his body. The filament started to fade away taking Aeon down into realms unknown, but the energised Zane and several Zater Jen intervened, grabbing the filament and prising it apart enough so Aeon could slip out.

The two Astrals hung onto the filament, their only path back to the Hypermind. They looked back to the main force beckoning them to trace it back to the source. They faded from existence.

The embattled *Lady Elisabeth* flew undaunted in its mission. Chryrians and Silverwraiths acting as a crucial forcefield were severely hard-pressed to keep out all the cosmic flak and heat from the temporal and spatial journey they were undertaking. The fortress shook violently in duress. But there would be no let up.

>*Force, we need more speed, more power, and weapons*< Gordell urged, feeling his psionic teeth chattering.

>*No pressure then*< Force thought. But he knew exactly what they needed. Before he had been shipped off as an E-Corps leader, J.J. Lundy had been a nifty pilot and engineer. Force did the conversions in his mind adding extra armour and super-charged engines. He thought about bombs, lots of them strapped to the wings, to the underbelly of the fortress, in the bomb bays.

He laughed to himself: *So glad aerodynamics aren't necessary, just my little, ordinary human brain!*

>*Red alert, shields up*< he snapped in his best Star Trek voice.

To his surprise a red forcefield encapsulated the plane, the Chryrians and Silverwraiths actually changing colour.

>*Outstanding!*< he mused.

>*Incoming Storm of Stars*< Valtare yelled out, sounding calmer than he should.

They all cast their minds arrear and sure enough two Prime Stars were bearing down upon the fortress.

>*Ready weapons*< ordered Force, who banked the fortress into evasive manoeuvres. He mentally flicked a red cover on his throttle, a modern fixture to his vintage craft, revealing a fire button.

Various Chryrians and Silverwraiths manned the guns Force provided, protruding from their aft gun ports, waiting upon his order.

>*Fire!*<

Psi-bullets snaked and peppered space in a psionic glow slowing down the Prime Stars with psionic flak. But they were also providing a decoy. Sceptre, Urana, Decion, and L'Coyle who with his men and two hundred Chryrians were poised at a makeshift bomb bay door as psi-paratroopers. Valtare coordinated the troops from the crew cabin

One of the Prime Stars absorbed all the psychic hits to shield the other, which raced around its revolving brother's flank, whipped around by the awesome gravitational forces. The sacrificial Prime Star dragged behind, sucking in surrounding energy to heal itself. But it could not. There was something interfering with its ability to regenerate. It had to carry on fighting regardless and flagged along behind the action. It watched with mute satisfaction as its brother Prime Star gained on the errant Peoples.

Sceptre and his team jumped. From beneath the fortress, a string of pulsating psionic-energy orbs descended quickly executing an upward arcing manoeuvre and sweeping up from below the advancing Prime Star. Decion projected his lancesword ahead of him ready to joust with a God.

The flagging Prime Star began to notice an irritation, an uncomfortable feeling all over. Only when it scanned in the psi-scape did it see the cause.

A group of five thousand Surge had been silently trailing the *Lady Elisabeth*, dormant, like drones in space. As the psi-flak had hit the shielding Prime Star, the Surge had latched onto it, stealthily leeching its energy before the Prime Star could notice.

Now it was too late.

The Surge fed, absorbing all the energy and then the next phase began. Draining a God of its energy was hard work, so the Surge had to dissipate the energy out into space or overload, but the Prime Star could easily reabsorb the rejected energy. A further outer ring of Surge awaited to re-absorb what the first couldn't. Then there was a final ring of millions of Lore eating their emitted energy. There was no lull in their determination, no mercy; the Lore and Surge would feed off this Prime Star forever.

The other Prime Star bore down upon the *Lady Elisabeth*, relentlessly catching up; a race between the speed of thought and the speed of light.

But Force had another surprise.

>*Hold onto your lunches, boys and girls*< he psyed eagerly as he pulled back hard on the throttle.

The *Lady Elisabeth* executed a loop the loop, hurtling in one fell psychic swoop over the pouncing Prime Star. They were now the pursuer.

The Prime Star turned on the spot to fight. Force flicked up the trigger guard and fired. A stream of Lore screamed out from his forward cannons punching into the Prime Star.

>*Hellfire from the Helstar*< grinned Force in the psi-scape. >*Take that, God*< he gleefully remarked, though mentally making the sign of the cross, just in case.

The Prime Star spun again and began to rupture as more and more Lore descended upon it, smelling the scent of a God's blood. But the Prime Star's momentum continued as it slammed into the fortress. The forward hull crumpled.

>*Shit*< Force was thrown from his seat.

The *Lady Elisabeth* lost a wing, rolling out of control, Force desperately clawing his was back to the pilot's seat, simultaneously trying to get his craft to grow another wing.

His passengers tumbled in their various holds and positions, their bodiless forms trying to float among the open areas of the fortress.

The Prime Star smothered itself over the fortress like black cosmic tar; thousands of tendrils penetrating through the walls and ripping backwards leaving sections open to space.

Sceptre and his team had clung on to the Prime Star during the collision imagining their powers in use and striking the

Prime Star. They were hurting it, but the Prime Star continued to slink into the fortress.

Gordell led the charge from within, his non-corporealness ignoring the escaping air rushing through the fortress. He lashed out with a hail of psionic energy.

>*Aaaarghhh*<

A thick tendril struck him down burying itself deep within his massless self, coiling around the psi-beings inside him. Gordell's physical body, hidden below in a fortress chamber, convulsed and blood started pouring from his nose. An attendant Chryrian tried to stabilise his body, but the Prime Star dug into Gordell's mind squeezing the life from it, purging all Chryrians from his mind.

Gasping as he felt his life ebbing away, Gordell focused all his energy and forced through a psionic burst to Valtare who, with other Chryrians, were trapped by and avoiding other tendrils in one of the many sections open to space.

>*Charles, forgive me for not returning*< Gordell spoke to the memory of his son.

Gordell's psionic mass vanished, absorbed by the Prime Star. His centuries' old physical body began to crumble, now free of the Chryrians which had kept him alive, and who had died as well. The other Chryrians mourned. Others poured into the surviving Starguard and human bodies to reinforce them with more energy.

Meanwhile, Force had mentally re-armed and began firing real ammunition made from Surge metal supplied by Sine. The metal limpets attached themselves to the Prime Star draining its energy as Sine sacrificed and cannibalised more redundant features of the fortress in order to fashion weapons. Lore, Surge, and Zater Jen swept from the fortress, attacking from all sides; the Prime Star like a ravenous space monster attacking a ship of the stars. The Chryrians started erecting psionic shields and pushing the tendrils out. The Prime Star had no choice but to retreat from the attacks.

Paralleling the fortress, the psionic Starguards rallied the Antiqchronal forces.

>*We should form psionic versions of ourselves and attack that way*< Sceptre psyed to Decion and Urana. He felt their agreeable replies.

Slowly, their indistinct psi-forms morphed into their familiar identities. They felt their energies rising. Immediately, Sceptre blazed away with his light energy, carving through the Prime Star. Urana's plasma energy rained down upon the Prime Star, while Decion cut huge swathes through it with his lancesword. The combined attack further dislodged the Prime Star, which sought to withdraw. With Valtare directing the energy absorbers and devourers of the Surge and Lore they continued to leech from it. God was bleeding to death.

A huge cheer went up. But many voices were silent, including Gordell's. Finally able to comprehend the carnage left behind, Valtare felt his absence keenly, though the Exmoor's last message to him had been gratefully received. Valtare performed a quick prayer for his missing and newly acknowledged friend. Hastily making his way to the cockpit for a semblance of normalcy, he found Force busy psychically repairing and upgrading some of the smashed instrument instruments. He also wanted it to be personal.

>*We lost Gordell*< Valtare's sad thoughts flowed forth.

>*What do you mean*< Force almost snapped back a joke. But he saw a mental image. >*Oh, shit, no! Now what*< his mind was a flood of sadness.

>*We fight on. How is it going, here? We took some big hits*<

Grateful for a change of subject, Force psyed, >*We're fine, patched up and ready to go. In fact my timescope*< he pointed to a random round spinning dial on the pilot's display, >*says we* *should be about there. Look<* He gestured out the starboard cockpit windows to the starry background.

The *Lady Elisabeth* found its strand coiled tightly around a star about to supernova.

>*Er, if that strand is released, wouldn't that star... like...go...<* his cheeks mushroomed out, his hands mimicking an explosion, >*Kaboom<*

His reply was a wave of defiant assurance laced with humour from the Antiqchronals.

> *We can handle such power<* one of the Surge psyed back.

>*I'm dealing with cocky Surge, now<* Force murmured to himself. He twisted his neck, getting rid of imagined kinks. >*Okay, taking her in<* he warned everyone.

The flying fortress banked and dove down on the black spiky strand strafing and bombing it until the ragged strand gave up its anchor. Force pulled for all his might on the throttle to escape.

The star shuddered, wracked with pent-up rage. It exploded.

At once the Zater Jen shifted the fortress into a temporal portal on an intercept course with the now-free strand, which attacked the fortress like a great whip of energy. But Force maintained his shields and fired, plunging the throttle forward, gunning the *Lady Elisabeth* after the strand. The kaleidoscopic colours of the portal almost psi-blinded Force, but he trusted his instruments and other psis to guide him. Finally the strand broke out of the portal and into normal space, the flying fortress hot on its heels.

>*Now where the blazes are we?<* Force asked, literally seeing red, golden, and orange skies in front to him. They were in some kind of hell.

***

The Light Guard made the breakthrough. They had traced the Hypermind to a region of space far beyond the universal horizon, nestled in the millions-of-degrees heat of the early

Big Bang. Other psionic tendrils snaked away to dimensions and temporal zones, under siege from the rest of their forces, they hoped. And in that cauldron of creation, a single entity awaited.

The sixteen anti-Storm-of-Star forces emerged from their respective disparate dimensions and temporal zones as all the cosmic strands came shrivelling back into the so-called Hypermind. The five Peoples surrounded the Hypermind in a tightening physical, psychic, and temporal sphere, but they could only reach to within a thousand years of the entity before being repelled by primordial energies and psionic blasts.

God was fighting back.

>*Converge for battle plans*< Cosmogod wished to liaise with the other battle leaders in person rather than extend their psionic messages across enemy lines. >*Hold the lines*< he ordered the rest of the forces to maintained their containment.

>*Ho!*< echoed the chorused acknowledgement.

The leaders of the Lore, Surge, Zater Jen, Chryrians, the Starguards, remaining Celestian Knights, and Valtare assembled to the rear of the battle group. Familiar acquaintances and new allies exchanged greetings and experiences. Others were more personal.

>*Xathanius! Hellennius!*< Millennius felt great joy as he embraced both his sons, introducing them to each other. They looked upon their father, a Lore, with a mixture of pride, revulsion, and sadness.

Aeon had described his death in detail and what his own daughter had done to save him.

"A Loremaiden?" Millennius asked, regret in his voice. He wouldn't have wished his curse to affect any more of his family.

"Yes, father, but she was able to save me only because of the gift bestowed upon her through you. She's extraordinary!"

That they could both agree on.

Aeon turned to Hellennius. "So, I finally meet my long-lost half-brother." Aeon was pleased. His natural temporal shielding and armour protected him as he swam in the deadly surrounding environment. "We have much to talk about after, mostly how to save our father."

Millennius laughed as much as he could as a Lore. "Son, with you two, I am saved, no matter what I have become." His body trembled as he felt a weird twinge within him, akin to his heart being drenched in absolute cold. Something stirred within him.

"Haha," Azure laughed happily while catching up with Phasia and Zane. "That was some trick with your father you pulled off, Zane," she complimented the young Astral.

Her next words froze in her mouth. She felt a surge of energy within her. Her vision clouded over in a flash of blue. The last time she had felt that was when…

Dread rocketed through her as she looked around for the source of her ill-feelings and was drawn Millennius. She focused on him not knowing why. Her Lore sight, able to detect Lore energy, delved inside Millennius. She saw through his golden energy. She inhaled sharply. A core of pulsing blue was building around his heart.

Millennius felt the cold surging and grip his heart. He heard a raucous laugh fill his Loreself.

No, it cannot be! He realised his enemy had not been completely defeated as he had hoped.

Synther was re-emerging.

Azure raced over to Millennius to warn them all, but too late.

Millennius' golden hue flickered blue, then gold, then blue again as control was wrested between both Celestian Knights.

Mid-conversation with Hellennius, Lord Aeon's sword flared up, Phasia's tempered blade responding to Synther's energy.

Millennius' golden energy was being snuffed out; blue energy flashing with Synther's features trying to usurp Millennius.

"Kill me," Millennius' strained Lorevoice said. "Kill me before it's too late!"

Synther snarled, "It is too late!" He began to materialise into form from within.

Aeon hesitated, his sword flashing in urgency.

I won't kill my father! he vowed to himself even as he felt the sword being ripped from his hand.

Cosmogod grabbed the sword and swung it around in one twisting motion piercing Millennius' heart.

>*Grrrarrrgh!*< came a long scream of agony.

Hellennius drew the sword out of his father's shimmering heart, the blue essence of Synther's soul perforated upon the blade.

Synther screamed such a heart-rending noise even the Shadow Stars wept for him.

Soaring over, an enraged Phasia savagely blasted the blade with her own energy counteracting Synther's. The blue energy's pulse fizzled out on the blade like a dying beating heart. Phasia then heaved back throwing the sword toward the Hypermind, where the sword with it dying passenger melted into nothingness.

>*Is Synther destroyed?*< Sceptre asked. His disembodied form looked anxiously back to where Millennius was being attended to by his sons.

> *Yes*< Phasia psyed out, trying to sound certain.

"About time!" Azure wished she had destroyed him the first time.

>*How do you know at this point in time and space Synther's energy isn't now the source of all evil in the universe?*< Force psyed from the fortress, keeping pace with the gathered forces. No one thought he was joking.

>*He would love that.*< Phasia psyed without humour, >*But we will always be here to defeat all evil*<

They all seemed to agree to that. But there was an urgency to move on, Millennius' injury not withstanding. He still disconcertingly floated silently in space.

Zane reached out to him. "Grandfather, are you okay?" She touched his arm. His lore eyes slowly held fire once more and his golden hue of energy shone forth in life. "Hell of a time for heart surgery," she quipped.

Millennius nodded. "Thanks to my son," he acknowledged Cosmogod. "Now that Synther's core energy is out of me, I'll be fine. Get on with the battle," he urged in his returning gruff voice.

He wondered if this was the vision Destina had seen or if she had just being spiteful toward Hellennius. Either way, his son had actually saved him by killing his heart.

>*My father is correct. We go on*< Hellennius charted their course forward. >*Nothing but victory. Nothing but our survival. The Storm of Stars must free us from their yoke or perish. Onwards*<

A great roar went up from the Peoples. They reformed into their groups pushing through the primordial stardust and scorching heat. Great pulsing cosmic strings, X-holes, and howling galactic winds pushed them back, lives expiring to dangers of the horrific void along the way. But on they forged.

And then they caught a glimpse; a tantalising peek behind the universal veil at their destination: the Hypermind.

A single pulsing entity awaited them.

"What is that?"

"I can't see it; it's blurred!"

>*A light?*<

"No, it's like a cosmic string, a loop, vibrating ..."

>*It's as big as a planet*<

"Look at the colours, so bright!"

"It's beautiful."

"Is that a face in it?"

>*No, just eyes*<

"A man's face?"

"No, look, it's female … wait, both!"

"No, just a mind…"

> *Wow, a Boltzmann brain*<

>*Shut up, Force*<

"I see circuits and machinery."

The image wavered and shimmered, but there was no disguising its nature.

> *Whatever it is, don't forget it's still the Storm of Stars, with twelve distinct personalities*< Phasia reminded everyone.

She addressed the being. > *Whoever you are, Storm of Stars, we, your children stand against you, ready to smite you. Surrender your reign over us or die*<

There was no reply.

There was only one option.

>*Attack*< came Cosmogod's order.

A great psychic cry oppressed the heavens as the forces tore upon the Hypermind. They believed they were on the cusp of victory.

But, they were fighting Gods after all.

= *We grow weary*=

The Hypermind's outer surface flared violently, engulfing and trapping the Peoples in a bubble of raw primordial energy.

=*No matter what you perceive, we are still an illusion. You have not diminished or defeated us. You see what we want you to see. We made you what you are, but not in our image, not of our nature. We are beyond your imagining. We are Gods!*=

≠*Behold!*≠

A thought rang out from the Storm of Stars and all time stopped—froze. The entire universe ceased at the Storm of Stars will.

= *We will decide your fate. Observe*=

From their positions of stasis, the five Peoples watched as their lives were played out before them.

≠ *We will destroy you. Destroy everything*≠

Watching their lives from some otherworldly experience, the Lore, Surge, Chryrians, Zater Jen, Astrals, Celestian Knights, Starguards and humans were all killed; destroyed—their worlds, galaxies, and the universe unsung into their constituent motes of atomic dust. The atomic universe swirled around in eternity until new worlds formed. The Peoples endured billions of years of existence to see this universe born and die.

But the Storm of Stars soon tired of this state.

= *We will leave you in this state forever; conscious yet frozen in temporal perpetuity. Contemplate your end and suffering in insanity*=

The Peoples endured a million years of unbearable pain and madness, conscious of every waking moment while incarcerated in their temporal trap. Dreams and nightmares combined, days turned to aeons, lives turned to dust, yet they remained all-too aware.

But the Storm of Stars grew bored.

≠ *We will rule you*≠

The Gods ruled. They enslaved their children tasking them over the countless millennia to serve their needs and whims. The Peoples provided them sustenance, amusement, veneration—their very lives. The Peoples were subservient and quelled until the universe died.

But the Storm of Stars grew disinterested.

= *We will punish you for eternity*=

The Storm of Stars delighted in punishments as the Peoples burned in perpetuity. When they did not burn, they feared being burned. When they slept, they burned; they dreamed of being burned. The Chryrians lost their minds, the Surge lost their skin, the Lore lost their fire, the Zater Jen lost their fluidity, the Fifths lost their purpose—all lost hope. Punishment was their reward until the universe died in misery.

But still the Storm of Stars yet grew restless.

≠ *We will choose the People that will live*≠

Through five Great Ages, all the Peoples lived as one race succeeded by the other. First came the Lore, succeeded by the Chryrians, then the Zater Jen, followed by the Surge, leading to the Fifths. The universe bore each People one at a time delivering various fates and destinies, living and dying in peace, strife, disease, and bliss, ignorant of the existence of the other Peoples.

But the Storm of Stars grew weary with one Peoples.

The Antiqchronals were made to exist together, for better or for worse, and the after-thought Fifths had now ensconced themselves within the cosmic network. They were as indelible as the First Peoples.

The Storm of Stars thought about this throughout the ages. Their children were now united in this universe. They had touched the hand of the Gods, endured all their losses, sufferings, tortures, and oblivion. And they had done so for each other over the immeasurable lifetimes of a myriad of nameless multiverses. Their children had shown a crude level of maturity worthy of more attention.

The Storm of Stars deliberated for another short million years and made a decision.

=*Let live*=

Time began again.

It was dark. Everywhere. Uncomfortably so. The trillions of Peoples looked around, but saw nothing, felt nothing. The Hypermind was gone. Or so they thought.

From nowhere and everywhere came their voice.

=*Children of the Storm of Stars. You will remain alive at our pleasure. You will survive and multiply and recover your birthright. To the Peoples nominated as the Fifths, you will be renamed in a fashion deserving of your origins. You will hence forth be the Destina, befitting the child who called us forth in ignorance*=

≠*However, there is a price to be paid; none more terrible than the original price. You, Celestian Knights, who have all denied your end, your fates have expired. You will be commended to the universe*≠

Phasia and Millennius suddenly found themselves next to each other. They held hands in the darkness.

"What do you mean all the Celestian Knights?" Sceptre asked into the darkness. While he could hear everything going on, he could not see anything beyond the penetrating blackness.

Phasia answered back into the void. "Aerl, we were surely not the only Celestian Knights to escape. As you know from Elysius' message to Novan she did not know for certain who else had escaped through Alphatronius' vortex or who had survived on Galatia. But they will join us in the Halls of the Ancestors."

There followed a reverential silence at that thought, before Phasia continued.

"And as the other Celestian Knights on Earth did, any survivors may have also produced kin and they will be alive somewhere. Find them, Aerl. Find them and let them know all what has happened. Reunite all the sons and daughters of the Celestian Knights."

Sceptre didn't have to think twice about it. He bowed to her wishes. "I will. I swear it!"

A swell of compassion so rich in happiness permeated the space around Sceptre, tingling him. As he felt a fervour rise within his chest he couldn't help but cry in the darkness.

>*Father! Mother!*< Hellennius called out, just before Aeon could shout for his father.

"Farewell, my sons," Millennius' gruff Lore voice cut through the nothingness. "You have made me proud. Lead your peoples well. This is my journey now. It's long past I walk the path!" There was humour and sadness in his voice, which neither of his sons looked on for pity.

A chorus of farewells, cries, and lamentations filled the void, from all the Peoples, before the Storm of Stars gently silenced them.

"Goodbye." The sad voices of Phasia and Millennius seemed to fade away into the ever-present void of blackness. And then they were gone.

The Storm of Stars spoke again.

=*We withdraw to the upper echelons of the Exoverse, far beyond your reach. We will be watching. Do not disappoint us!*=

≠Begin again!≠

And then there was light.

The Starguards blinked in the sheer brightness. Around them was a world with blue skies, fresh air, and rolling green hills as far as the eye could see.

It took a while for anyone to speak.

219

"We're corporeal again," Sceptre noted, handling his visor for readings. Nothing had been recorded of the Storm of Stars. He sighed in bitter annoyance.

Everyone else checked themselves. Sighs and laughter of relief reverberated in the air. They looked around the countryside, finding a small clearing to sit in.

"This is Earth," remarked a shell-shocked Force, eyes still watering in the bright light. "I just know it. It's all new again."

If this was Earth it was fresh and new—a vivid green and blue under heavenly skies. The newly named Destina looked at each other in mild shock and surprise.

"What just happened?" Urana asked, trying to gain her bearings.

"I'm not sure," Sceptre replied.

"I think we just survived Revelations and come full circle to Genesis," Force dead-panned, relieved he had a voice again.

"How are we going to get home?" Azure wanted to know. Her being lusted to be in the skies beneath Magna Aura.

"Where are those accursed Astrals when you need them," Decion growled. He cast his dark gaze around as if displeased by the peacefulness.

"Nice to know you haven't changed," Urana sighed. Decion smiled wryly in return.

A bright light flashed before them. Zane, restored to her Astral self, appeared.

"I'll take you all home," she said breezily. "Sorry, I was just looking at Earth from space! It's spectacular!"

"I knew it! Knew it this was Earth!" Force punched the air in triumph, rather to closely to Decion who harrumphed Force into silence.

"Zane, what happened? Where are the Storm of Stars?" Sceptre wanted to know.

"Did we win?" Decion asked.

Zane resisted the urge to shrug. "It looks like the Storm of Stars elected to let us live, so in a way that is a victory. They've sent everyone to where they wanted to be. But it was I who brought you here one last time, before taking you home." Zane looked misty-eyed at them. "I'll miss you guys. And this new Earth is a welcome home to all of you. We are kin, no matter our name or where we are. We are all Starguards."

Even Decion felt a twinge of contentment. He picked Zane up by her waist in his huge hands, holding her high above him.

"Zane, you have restored my faith in the Starguards." He put her down and looked at the others. "I have wronged you all, my family, and I will forever serve as the Starguard I ought to have been."

Sceptre looked at Urana and Azure, but it was Urana who said it for them, "Welcome back, Decion." She gave him a surprise hug around his broad shoulders. They gathered in the moment.

"And what about you, Zane, where will you go?" Azure asked her fellow Lore maiden.

"I . . . I don't know." Zane kicked absentmindedly at a small rocky outcropping. "I feel I have a duty to do something, but I'm not sure. But first, I have to find out what happened to me and who I am now."

"And this Time Empress?" Sceptre asked.

Zane thought about it. "I think she's watching over us all, wherever, whenever."

"Cool, so like a Homo *Destinas* guardian angel," Force quipped airily.

"Shut up, Force," Urana tittered, though with a playful glint in her eye.

"Well, he's kind of right," Zane said.

"So where are everyone else?" Sceptre asked.

"Yes, the Antiqchronals, Valtare, and your father, Zane? Where are they? Where were the Astrals in all of this?" Urana responded with questions of her own.

Zane shrugged. "I'm not sure about the Astrals, but I think they are fighting this war on another front. However, the rest are out there, somewhere," Zane answered, looking out to the stars. "All safe and sound where they desired to be; living their own lives, content and animosity-free. They warp the temporal fields. I can feel them." Though Zane was not sure about the Time Empress. Had she even been born yet?

"So these Storm of Stars have been God all along; I mean humanity's God," Force asked. "I fought for my country, I fought for God, glory, and gun metal. So who's Gods were they?"

Zane could only shrug again. She didn't have all the answers.

"I suppose they're everyone's God, now," Urana whispered, fearful of any perceived blasphemy. She shivered, feeling oddly content.

Sceptre concurred, "Once we're home, I have to honour Phasia's wish and start the search for the other Celestian Knights' kin. We might have half-kin out there."

"Agreed," said Urana. "I can't believe our parents might have survived, Aerl, and we'll never get to meet them again! Why didn't they tell us sooner?"

Sceptre could only shake his head. "The Will of the Universe, Rain. I think we know better than to question it now."

Urana wasn't happy, but Sceptre was right. She had to live with it. "So, ready to go home? I can't wait to see if Altair's back, too!"

Azure sighed in agreement, ready to be flying under the blue skies of Halcyon.

"Force, where do you want to go?" Zane asked, turning to the only pure human Destina on Earth.

He thought about it. "Well, there's no one here on this Earth. It's all new again; ready for new life. And as much as I've had fun with you guys, I wouldn't mind being around humans, maybe reunited with Lynn and the others, wherever she is."

"So be it," Zane said, wishing she could see Lynn again. She threw her arms into the sky, her body shimmering into resplendent white energy.

Zane took her charges into her large energy bubble and for the first time sprouted energy wings. They whipped the air around her into a portal, through which they all disappeared.

Earth was left alone in its new destiny.

Valtare, L'Coyle, and a half-dozen of their surviving men walked through a field of tall green grass. The day was warm, speckled sunlight playing around them, melodies from a cacophony of birds reminding them of the Earth of old.

"Where are we?" L'Coyle asked, anxiously looking around at the massive trees in the distance and a line of far off mountains.

"I do not know," answered Valtare. But he had his senses on full alert. He peered up in the sky. "This isn't Earth, however. Look!" He pointed to the two faint moons in the sky, half crescents shining against the sunlight from a star which was slightly whiter than Earth's.

They stared at the miraculous sight. Even after seeing the wonders of the universe and fighting Gods who had created it, they were still in awe of the power of nature to surprise them with such glorious sights.

Stopping to contemplate the views, a distant look in his eyes, Valtare said, "I think I know where we are."

L'Coyle cocked his head at him expectantly. But Valtare's mind was closed to him.

"Just before he died, Gordell showed me a place in his mind—this place." He spread his arms out encompassing the scene. He laughed, a bitter sound invading the serene pasture they walked through. "For so long I hated the Exmoors. It was well known they exterminated us half-Chryrians. Or so I had thought." He breathed in deeply then out in a cathartic exhalation. "It seems the Exmoors didn't kill all of our kind. They and the Astrals put them here; Chryrians, Devouts, and other undesirables alike, on a new world they had discovered, so they wouldn't harm the normal humans. A myth was perpetrated against the Exmoors or maybe they started it themselves to scare us into submission. But this is a new world, a world full of people like us. I thought about being here. Maybe we were sent here by the Zater Jen."

"Redemption?" queried L'Coyle.

"Perhaps," Valtare concentrated on the distant vista.

As he had spoken, the green-hilled horizon was crested by four people, dressed in Bronze Age garb, followed by a few small groups. Then a veritable crowd of people topped the hillside. Valtare could sense all of their Chryrian minds inquiring about them.

L'Coyle smiled tightly. "No more Marquis. No more Dukes. This is our home." He breathed the fresh air in deeply.

Valtare thought about this, returning a cynical shake of his head, "Or the place from where we return to Earth," he said. He thought of his wife, his desire to be with Elisabeth again.

They were soon surrounded and welcomed to their new home by a peoples with a myriad of questions for the strangers. L'Coyle regarded Valtare and his words. There was still restlessness within him, too, a dark edge waiting to spill out like the Plague. But L'Coyle hoped this world would be a cure for both of them.

The billions of Surge gleamed in the overwhelming sunshine of the triple star system, grazing upon the rays and cosmic particles. For aeons they had been nomadic voyagers searching for meaning and revenge. Now they were free.

They had communed among themselves praising the Storm of Stars for their continued existence. They were about to embark upon a new adventure. The tri-star system held a large rocky world in its protective grip. They would settle and build. It would be the new home of the Surge Civilisation.

The Lore were leaderless. They should have run amok through the universe devouring stars and energy. But the essences of Millennius, Spheron, and Azure had flowed through them. They were no longer impulsive, errant creatures. They could co-exist and devour energy not used by other beings. They had all the time in the universe and everywhere to go. Wrapping themselves together to form a Helstar the trillions of Lore disappeared into a portal to dimensions unknown.

The Zater Jen constructed their own Temporal Court on the edge of Phase space, a glittering edifice of portal planes and vortexes. Cosmogod held a memorial for his mother, last of the Celestian Knights. There was also a grieving time for the Glorious Ego Byss, Captain of the Light Guard. He had mysteriously disappeared in the last battle against their strand. Ax Omen and Geona Zen were no more. Adam Finitum had survivors from the past and future. But almost a billion Zater Jen had perished in the Reckoning of the Gods, as it would be called in their Tomes of Time. Now it was time to settle and live a free life. Cosmogod looked over to Celesophia on her throne. They had lost so much. But having the young Time Empress among them had shown them what they had been missing: It was time for a new generation of Zater Jen to arise.

The pocket dimension had a new visitor. After leaving the Starguards, Zane had thought about her father. He too had been ported by the Zater Jen to another destination without her knowing where.

Bloody infuriating, she had thought, just having got her father back.

But as if by some cosmic intuition, Zane had shifted into her Loremaiden energy porting almost randomly into the universal timestream following unknown temporal paths and reading unfamiliar energy signatures, yet somehow connected to her father. Exiting the portal she found herself face to face with the Chronopolis. More than anything she had just wanted to see home. But—

"That's not..." she whispered to herself, staring in disbelief at its virtual twin. "Bloody Nora!" She drifted closer still not believing her eyes.

This dimensional shrine with its temples, pyramids, other structures, and defences was different. Twice as massive as the Chronopolis, it reminded Zane more of the Magna Auran City-States, with a blend of both Grecian and alien architecture mixing into an impressive fortress. Though the colonnades were missing, a great forceshield erupted from the bowels of the dimensional bubble encompassing the entire temporal realm. A bright small silver sphere spun impossibly fast around the whole fortress.

Zane kept her distance. The defences would not be easy to penetrate, the temporal fields tasted hard and bitter. But she longed to have one last look; one last contact with her kin.

Using her energised eyes her sight was greatly increased beyond the visual spectrum. Her vision sifted through the forceshields.

Beyond the defenses were more private chambers, spacious plazas, common areas, and even space ship hangers. The latter surprised Zane, wondering why time travellers would need ships. But what grabbed her attention was the gathering in the throne room. The set up was almost the same with crystalator stations lining the wall and holo-imagers projecting visions from all directions.

However, this space was almost entirely inhabited by strangers; people Zane didn't recognise, but whom she assumed could only be time travellers themselves. She thought so because they were all surrounding her father with Helexius, Lightstream, and Sola. She didn't see Spheron the younger, but she knew his fate through Spheron the elder's energy memory. The inhabitants of this Chronopolis all stood around with smiles on their faces making a fuss over a baby.

There were no Lore tears for Zane, but her energy flared in joy. Her brother, Aristedes and Starshina, once her Multiforce teammate Winterborne had had a baby. Zane laughed aloud at her memory speaking to Aristedes on the Surge World. How he had teased her. And now she knew the truth.

Zane was proud of her brother, what he had accomplished, and what he had brought into the cosmic sky. Zane took one last look and smiled at the memories yet to come. Hers was now a solo existence. Someone had led her to this place, but not allowed her to interact with her family. Somehow cruel, but there was a reason for that. Zane knew she had many missions to accomplish, not least to find out what had happened to her in her lost time.

Without looking back, lest she lost her nerve to go, she opened a portal and disappeared into the temporalscape.

Lord Aeon proudly held his grandchild as he blessed the baby's head. He wished Zane was here to see this. He thought he had sensed her close by. But he knew the Zater Jen would take care of her and that she would find her way back to them.

"Oops!" He felt the baby spew on him, gurgling its own pleasure.

Everyone laughed as he handed the baby back to Starshina, his new daughter-in-law. He had only met her a few hours ago. He had only met the new Astrals hours ago.

Dead one day, alive the next with more family. He held back his tears. His father and Phasia were also in his heart.

The baby's mother and father gathered around, looking more mature and grown from the battle they had endured, but the war was far from over. With family and allies gathered around, Aeon was rightfully proud of Aristedes. He had shown he was a leader. And now he and Winterborne were the parents of a beautiful pale-skinned, blue-eyed baby girl. They named her Sky.

In the deep void of temporal space, Zane flitted around tasting and feeling the various time fields warp and pop as they flexed around worlds and each other. She could smell new timelines forming and see the oceans of colour swirling around her. But there was a new element in the mix, a searing shaft of red following her.

She turned around and there he was.

"Why, it's the Glorious Ego Byss, Captain of the Light Guard," she said, slightly surprised at his presence. "Come to say goodbye?"

He glided over to her. He seemed hesitant—shy almost. >*No, I have come to join you*< he finally psyed.

Zane was stunned. She thought her duty was a solo mission. "Why?" she could only ask.

>*I find your temporal presence ... harmonious*< He looked at her in earnest through his golden eyes.

Taken aback, Zane felt her cheeks flush. *Was he flirting with her?* He was handsome, in a crystalline sort of way. "Oh, right. Er ... thank you. I thought everyone was sent to where they wanted to be? Won't you be missed?"

>*I desired to be here, Zane Astrak* His golden eyes twinkled. >*And the Zater Jen think I am no more*<

Zane sensed her energy rushing to places she had only felt when she was a young girl thinking of a certain dashing officer during the Axalan war.

"Okay," her voice wobbled, not realising until now how she did miss Paolo. "I guess I could do with the company." Zane smiled back. "Let's go see what's out there!"

Ego Byss beamed back in acquiescence.

Zane transformed into white energy and took Ego Byss' hand. A portal opened and they vanished through it.

***

Force dropped out from the brightness of the portal and into the blackness of space. His manoeuvre suit provided an instant forcefield against the hard vacuum. There was nothing in front of him except empty deep space.

"Oh shit! They've stranded me!" His heart jolted in panic. "No, no, no, no!" He breathed deeply, calming himself down. *Why would they do that to me?* he thought. *Think!*

He rotated a hundred and eighty degrees and gasped at the sight.

"Oh! Okay!"

He found himself looking down at a world not unlike Earth. His improved visor could detect nascent cities on the ground with large terraforming projects still ongoing on much of the other side.

With his new gravity powers lending decent thrust he orbited around for the best place to land and find out where he was. The glint of four spacecraft approaching him from starboard caught his attention. A smaller object darted from one of the craft. Force realising it was a person flying toward him. As the individual closed in on him he recognised the newcomer, even in his new forcefield protected manoeuvre suit.

"Venture?" he called through his comms, which had automatically tuned into the prevalent frequency around him. "Warren, it's me, J.J.!"

"J.J.? Hey! My God, Fusioneer, where you been?" He drew up to Force, a wild grin on his unmasked face, and shook his hand with an added shoulder bump, sending them into a gentle clockwise spin.

"We came up to investigate a time portal! We've had issues with those before!" he grinned under his forcefield. They steadied themselves from the spin.

"Tell me about it. I've had enough time travel to last me a lifetime!" he laughed.

"How are you here, dude?"

"Long story, you wouldn't believe me if I told you."

"Hey, me too. Plus they call me Venturion, now."

"Cool. Call me Force, I guess; new powers and everything. So when and where am I?"

"Ah, man, we are in the twenty-third century, the blessed year twenty-two twenty-one, four years after a war with the Axalan Empire. But now we're all friends, now." His smile was more a lopsided grimace. "We're around a planet called Home, a joint world of peace." He gave Force a brief overview of how the rest of the E-Corps team, Thane, and some of the Devouts had ended up in this new time and the Axalan war.

"Jesus, that's mental!" Force stared off into deep space, wondering how to tell his friends the kind of time he had endured. Fighting Gods was off the small chat menu for now. "How're Lynn and Starshina?" he changed the subject, as they flew toward one of the ships.

Venturion rolled his eyes. "That's another long story. Come on, let's go see Lynn. I don't know who'll be more surprised to see who. And she's has the cutest little baby girl!"

Force looked over in shock. "Lynn had a baby?"

"Don't ask, man. That's just another weird story!" He looked sideways at Force with a knowing smile. "I knew you had a thing for Lynn."

J.J. rolled his eyes. "That was long ago. Another lifetime."

They reached the ship and Venturion cycled the air lock with a control on his forearm. "Might as well ride in style," Venturion said as they entered.

"We do have some catching up to do!" Force said.

They entered through a sliding hatch into a spacious octagonal airlock chamber. There was a brief anti-contamination mist bath.

Venturion leaned toward him with a conspiratorial grin. "Oh, and she's foreseen a rogue planetoid is on a collision course with Home in around thirty years or so!"

"Foreseen? Seriously? You've got to stop dropping all this on me!"

The inner door opened and they stepped out into the ship proper. A long battle-gray corridor stretching either side of them awaited, Force's eyes taking in this new ship; well-lit, portless, quite silent, with wall comms and data panels at various points.

Not a patch on the Lady Elizabeth, he thought sadly of his flying fortress, wondering what had become of her.

Venturion directed Force to his right as they walked. "So, much to discuss, but now you're here you can turn that planetoid into a huge marshmallow, right?"

"Uh, about that. . ." Force started, but before he could finish they were met by a military officer.

The tall handsome officer greeted Force with a salute. "It's an honour to meet you Colonel Lundy. I've heard a lot about you."

Venturion guffawed as Force glanced at him sideways waving a hand casually, "Enough of the Colonel, please. Just call me J.J." He smiled at the younger man with copper-coloured skin and almond-shaped dark eyes.

"Hey, Paolo, say hello to mine and Lynn's long lost buddy, Jay Jupiter Lundy." The two men shook hands, Venturion smiling away as the spacecraft turned toward the planet below.

"Welcome to Home, J.J."

Sceptre, Urana, Decion, and Azure burst out of their twisting temporal portal. It vanished behind them in an inward rush of energy.

"Universe!" Urana exclaimed. She grinned from ear to ear. The sight was an emotional view for them all.

Magna Aura beamed away majestically in salutation to her returning heroes. Far in the distance, they could make out the ruddy orb of Placia. Below them spun Halcyon, its bright northern floating ice cap shimmering in the sunlight.

"We're back!" sighed Azure, feeling a shiver of excitement run through her.

"Looks like Zane could penetrate whatever forcefield my idiot brother put up," Urana said scathingly.

"Or maybe he was expecting us?" Sceptre tried reasoning, but it rang hollow with them all. "And no Altair to greet us." He exchanged glances with Urana.

"Or my brother," Decion stated coldly. He silently cursed the Astrals.

None of them wanted to open old wounds. In silence they floated for some time, admiring their world as if seeing it for the first time. They hardly noticed the uncharacteristic black clouds which darkened the far side ocean. There was a storm on the way.

"Let's go!" Sceptre said.

From their lofty perch they descended toward their destination, Sky Command, and a long-awaited reunion with their kin.

The Starguards were home.

Epilogue

The Storm of Stars watched.

They had decided in secret they would not sleep. They would transform. They would walk among all their Peoples throughout all the universes as one of them. They would be of them, live like them, die like them, and begin again. It was not the Antiqchronals who needed watching, but the Destina; they who were destined to rule or destroy the universe. Their war was far from over.

There were others out there. Ones from before. Dark forces. And they were coming.

And one day the Storm of Stars would gather again to decide the fate of the universe.

Post-epilogue
Home: Thirty-One Years Later

It was over. They couldn't win.

"What do we do now, mother?" Brightness Marie asked, voice emotionless but direct.

Kellis looked at her daughter, still so young and innocent, yet unperturbed in the midst of war. There, she had admitted it to herself. They were at war.

The thing, the potential world killer of a space rock had hurtled through the cosmos towards Home. It had defied long-range analysis throwing up some kind of natural scattering field. Or so they had thought. Home's Planetary Defense Council had been in agreement with the Constitutionate leadership in deciding to greet the alien visitor three years before it was due to collide with Home in 2255. But even with their best deflectors and weapons, the planetoid could not be destroyed or diverted. It was back to the drawing board. The next rendezvous with the rock would come with one year to go. And from then onwards, it would have a constant escort until some reasonable proposal to avoid the collision could be implemented.

And naturally, Lynn Kellis, the Constitutionate's roving Xeno-Specialist at large, retired, was suborned by the Emperor-General himself, Xaul Relentus, to re-form the Multiforce and covertly investigate the planetoid on the edge of the solar system.

And that's when things went wrong.

"It did what?" Kellis spun in her chair spilling out of it to see the readings for herself.

"I'm telling you, Lynn, the thing has just sped up. Velocity increase!"

"I know what that means," Kellis snapped back at Force in the same sarcastic tone.

"How much so?"

"At this velocity, about eight months," Venturion confirmed from his place at navigation.

"Give us a mo," Kellis spoke to Force.

"Sure, I'll be here. Force out."

The *Esprit de Corps*, refitted and modified over the past decades rocketed through space ahead of the huge rock. It was at times like these that despite the *Esprit* being one of the fastest ships in the Constitutionate fleet, it was still not fast enough for what Kellis wanted. She missed Aristedes and his temporal abilities. Hell, she missed Zane and Starshina, too. But Time and Winterborne had disappeared into the unknown, and Zane, according to J.J. and his encounter with Zane in Earth's far future, was now some type of energy-being.

Whatever a Loremaiden was, Kellis thought to herself. She could have used them all now, especially Aaron. But the Multiforce were a different team now.

They were still a secret from most of the general population of the Constitutionate, with Earth still preserving a ban on superbeings, though some still persisted for better or for worse. Home was more tolerant, but Kellis wanted her privacy. Her orders came only from the Emperor-General himself, these days practically living in the new fortress-like U.N. Headquarters on Earth. Kellis just wanted to out-live the Emperor-General then she would be free, she hoped. Now here she was, out saving her adopted home, again.

After settling on Home thirty-one years ago following the birth of Brightness Marie, Kellis had tried acclimatising to life on a new world amongst other humans, Axalans, and Bions. She had been so used to space and her own micro-society on Zero Star that she missed the constant adventure. But while she missed her labs and the people of Zero Star, managing to keep in contact with the still-classified installation, she was a mother now. She had responsibilities.

Working in Home's Defense Force in various roles, planet-bound, daughter in tow had raised a few eyebrows at first. But her work ethic gained Kellis a reputation as a hard-nosed miracle worker, able to successfully build consensus between the three aliens races.

Kellis wasn't above using her burgeoning psi-abilities to get the job done. She had reconciled herself to 'inheriting' Aaron's psychokinetic powers. She had been training herself; training Bright to hide her powers; training for the day she might be called upon to use them. And on rare occasions she would accompany Venturion and Force on missions of state. The Constitutionate still had malcontents and required extraordinary contingencies for extraordinary situations.

In her Multiforce guise Kellis now called herself Zenergy.

Kellis had tried to blend into Home life. However, her reputation had elevated her to celebrity status among the Home elite, military, and political circles. And with it the unwanted attention from the media. Her real personal history, life, and her E-Corps past in the twenty-first century had already been classified by Xaul personally. Her role in the Axalan War at Zero Star and with the Multiforce had been redacted. She had plausible deniability on her side and a new life.

However, the dogged author, Hermes Daracales—'that hack'—as Venturion called him, was determined to write the definitive biography on Kellis. The Constitutionate's foremost historian and biographer had Kellis in his sights, but she had resisted any official or unofficial books about her. Daracales had faded away lured by an irresistible mythical story. But he was never shy to send her his salutations and offers. Kellis hoped never to see him again.

"Hey, any ideas?" Force commed impatiently in from his station, flying alongside the planetoid.

There was a strange crackling over the line.

"What was that?" Kellis inquired. The crystalators should have been clear of any interference.

"What..." Static played again. "...say?"

Kellis shook her head. "Never mind. I'm still thinking here. Just keep comms clear," she ordered.

"'Kay," came the reply.

"What happening?" Paolo turned to her, his dark features worried.

Venturion stayed silent concentrating on keeping the *Espri* within range of Force, out alone against a killer rock. Bright sat in the back listening, learning, but otherwise calm. Kellis wondered how the years had passed by so quickly seeing herself on a planet-saving mission with the new Multiforce consisting of three middle-aged men and her kid.

And they didn't even have costumes, she laughed to herself. The Emperor-General had insisted they wear standard blue and gray Constitutionate uniforms lest their mission became compromised. Plausible deniability.

Kellis leaned over to Paolo. "Our crystalators shouldn't be affected by any other signals. They work anytime, anywhere, unless damaged, but..."

Her face changed in that way Paolo knew from decades of working with Kellis, though she had hardly aged a day over the thirty-odd years he had known her. His hair was now gray and no matter how much he worked out his spare tire was growing. Even though Kellis had told Paolo about Zane's heritage, he wondered if she would ever return to see him. What would she think of her former lieutenant, now a retired Colonel; the one-time Duke of Dare Unit Command? But he was content, wanting to spend more time with his wife, Beth, four children, and new grandchild. Kellis had told him to move on and not to wait for Zane. Besides, Zane could return to his past and live happily ever after with him. Paolo wasn't sure how he'd feel about having his family and life re-written. He hoped he wouldn't find out. Zane was a dream from the past. This Multiforce mission was a favour to Kellis, his last mission. Then he was retired for good.

"Having a brainwave?" he asked Kellis.

She smiled absentmindedly and spoke more to herself than to the others. "We already know T'Non'Za," she named the rock by its Axalan name meaning World-ender, chosen by the Constitutionate, "is an alien rock of unknown material; dense as hell and resists all our best plasma torpedoes. It even prevents Force from using his gravity powers against it. It could also have other properties such as exotic energy affecting comms."

Paolo studied her. "You mean jamming? Deliberately?" He looked at her aghast. "Do you think it's alive?" The thought horrified him.

Kellis shrugged, shaking her head, putting thoughts to words. "Don't know. This rock seems more engineered then alive. And I don't sense anything like that from it. I can barely sense Force out there!" She was grateful for that part of her powers. "Origin unknown, unknown material, it changes speed, destination Home. I don't think it's a coincidence it's coming here. But who could have instigated this?"

Paolo didn't need to say it, but it was on Kellis' mind as well.

"No, Mode is dead. I saw him die along with Aaron. No one else has the power to transform molecular structure. He had Force's old powers, remember?"

Paolo nodded almost automatically. There were still aspects of the whole E-Corps, Multiforce, Superions saga he never understood.

"Okay, so what, there's another enemy out there, alien or otherwise?"

"Yeah," Kellis exhaled nosily. "Looks that way." She was still studying the readings. Something was bothering her about T'Non'Za.

What did humanity do to deserve this? she thought. *Or the Axalans or Bions?*

As far as everyone was concerned T'Non'Za was an accident of the cosmos with Home in the way.

Kellis' mind was racing at the thought that higher powers were at play. Force's description in his debriefing thirty-two years ago of the Storm of Stars and their capricious natures against the Zater Jen, Surge, the Chryrians, and of course the reviled Lore made her think of her suspects, motive, and opportunity. But why would any of them do this? Revenge for the future war? But that wouldn't make sense. Unless...

Was this the last action of Netherlord? she asked herself. His previous attack on Home had failed. Had he orchestrated a failsafe? Did he set this motion?

"Holy shit!" Kellis jumped in her seat, tying her crystalator into the science station.

Everyone in the *Esprit* turned to Kellis, startled, energised, braced for action.

"What's up boss?" Venturion pitched in from his controls. He monitored Force's vitals and location, making sure he didn't get too close to the rock.

"Time," Kellis remarked, thinking it all through aloud. "This rock came from nowhere, right? Wrong, it came from somewhere we just couldn't conceive of its origin—the future!"

"The future? I don't get it," confessed Paolo. "Surely this could still have been tracked no matter from where it came?"

"Not if it's from the future," Kellis said, revealing the screen she was working on. "See?" Her brow instantly furrowed in puzzlement. "Oh." Her voice wavered between disappointment and intrigue when the results appeared.

"What's that?" Bright crowded over Kellis' shoulder. She was tall and lanky like her father with light brown skin and the brown eyes of her mother.

Kellis frowned, confused. "Um, well, I was looking for a temporal signature. Something to match the Astrals or Netherlord's. It's minuscule, but this," she gestured at the screen, "this is a temporal signature, but nothing like I've seen before." She caressed her neck brushing her hair back.

"Different as in alien temporal signature?" Venturion asked, concerned.

"Yes," Kellis answered with reluctant acceptance. "An alien temporal signature. *Great!* she thought with gloom. *Another damn enemy to fight.* "Kellis to Force, status?"

The crackle seemed to be mounting up. Venturion tight beamed the signal for more clarity.

". . .Totally gravitating the ass off this thing, but it's still coming. Ain't slowing down. And that ain't right. Even I know that!"

Kellis could hear the strain in his voice as he manipulated gravity to slow T'Non'Za down. But the black behemoth spun inevitably toward Home.

"Acknowledged, Force, come on back in. We've discovered something. We need a Plan B."

After a twenty second delay. "Sure, I can do with the break!" he laughed halfheartedly.

"And Plan B?" Venturion asked, once Force was off comms.

"Haha," Kellis let loose, "that would be telling."

"You don't have a plan?" he smirked.

"I always have a plan; it just hasn't revealed itself to me, yet."

There was a collective groan in the cabin.

More than annoyed, Kellis hit back. "Hey, I don't see any of you coming up with brilliant ideas. Don't worry, I've got this!" A blast of static over comms interrupted her. "How you getting on, Force? Stop mucking about, chop, chop!"

A prolonged string of static-infected expletives punctured the *Esprit.*

"Force, what's going on?"

"Some. . .zzzzzz. . . happening! Can't disengage!" His voice wavered in and out over the static.

"Seriously?" She shot a look over to Venturion. He nodded back confirmation. There was a moment's silence as they digested the news.

"Talk to me," Force's strained voice called. "Thing's . . . got me!"

"Stand by, we're trying," was all Kellis could come up with. Plan B was out the window. So were plans C, D and everything else, too.

Venturion spun up a holographic image of their location, T'Non'Za and the red dot that was Force. A faint veil of energy enveloped Force from the planetoid.

"What the hell is that now?" Paolo gasped.

"Gravity," replied Venturion. "Gravitons being absorbed from Force and redirected at him?" He was uncertain, guessing. He looked at Kellis for her interpretation.

"Gravity? But shouldn't Force be able to counteract his own power?" Bright asked. Her expressionless face still relayed her concern.

An explosion of pain erupted from comms.

"Hnnnn. . . being crushed. . . hope done expositionin'. . . help me!"

"Dammit, Venturion, what's happening?" Kellis tried to stare out the port, but she could barely make out T'Non'Za in the darkness and it was only a few kilometers behind them. She'd have no way of seeing Force.

"Increasing gravity. . ." Force's voice spluttered over comms. "Try and batter. . . thing!"

"Be careful!" Kellis said.

His reply arrived a few seconds later than expected. "Hey. . . survived. . . end. . . universe. . . . survive this!"

"Mom!" Bright was by her side, almost excited with an idea. "What about the Astrals or super-assed Great Races helping us? Where are they?"

Great question, thought Kellis. Here was a temporal catastrophe heading for Home and no one was coming to their rescue.

"It seems it's just us, honey," she replied. She wouldn't even know how to contact any of them, even Aristedes and Starshina. They hadn't left so much as a forwarding address or emergency contact. "It's just us!" she repeated.

That thought gave her confidence. "Look," she addressed the others. "This could only mean the powers-that-be out there have faith that we'll save ourselves so have left us to it. It's already history for them." She didn't want to think of the alternative. But others did.

"Or that we're not worth saving," Venturion stated.

"Or what has happened has happened badly and they won't change time for us!" Paolo jumped in straight after.

Kellis regretted telling him about the Astrals. She stared him down.

"Okay, stop it! We're not going to think that way," she fumed.

Venturion laughed. "You always told us Home was cursed!"

Only Kellis didn't laugh. She had always thought that. And for good reason.

"Update, Force," she snapped out.

It was a while before his reply.

". . .'date? Crystalator almost shot, too much data. . . crash. . . hold on. . . hold on!" he gasped in pain.

He was gone for so long, Kellis thought comms had indeed crashed.

Then Venturion yelled: "Force, look out, it's doing it again!"

Kellis didn't have to ask what had happened. She could see for herself both outside the *Esprit* and on the holo display. The dark shadowy form of T'Non'Za had changed velocity again.

And not in a sedate manner. It had shot off into the distance impossibly fast.

"That has gotta be a spaceship!" Venturion stood up and whistled. He sat and stared vacantly in awe.

"Chase it then!" shouted Kellis, clicking her fingers, angry at Venturion's distractedness.

Venturion snapped out of his wonderment. Fingers flew over control consoles. *Esprit* responded instantly lunging into lightdrive, thrusting space behind it in great warped waves.

Paolo, the erstwhile ship's science officer was calculating "Shit, Kellis, at this velocity we'll be at Home in less than five days. We'll have to stop T'Non'Za, even if that means shooting it out of the sky!" He turned in horror to her knowing what that would mean for Force. For all of them.

"Five days? But we were a year out! How?" Bright asked.

Paolo tied in his station to the holo display. Data began spewing out. He shrugged, not sure what he was seeing.

"Is that...?" Venturion began.

"The strongest gravity drive I have ever seen or heard of," Kellis finished. "The power T'Non'Za must have to do that..." she tried to think of some words, but failed.

"Unimaginable," Venturion supplied his own.

It reminded Kellis of something but she couldn't think what.

"Well Force better think of something quick out there," Paolo said. His lined face then creased more. "Oh, no, we have incoming." He placed the image on holo.

The outlines of the twenty approaching vessels were unmistakeable. And more were on the way. They lay in the path of T'Non'Za, the *Esprit* trailing the planetoid.

"Constitutionate destroyers," Paolo added needlessly.

"But Force?" Bright protested. "He's still out there!" She looked between her three elders for any plan.

Before Kellis could contact the advancing fleet, an incoming signal arrived. The *Esprit*'s screen came to life with the image of a young Axalan warrior. His blue face was unmarked from war, but was handsome, his dark blue hair cut almost to the scalp. His stern features belayed the hunger in his dark eyes. Kellis shook her head. The new generation of Axalan warriory were so eager to prove themselves. This one would be no different. And it could cost them more than just Force's life.

"*Esprit de Corps,* Captain Lynn Kellis commanding, I am Tier-Commander Eklogar of the Constitutionate Fleet, commanding the Claw *Semblance of Vengeance* for the Home Forces Battalion. As per Constitutionate orders, T'Non'Za has substantially exceeded the perimeter threshold deemed safe to for diversion."

Kellis listened with horror, knowing what his orders were.

"We have orders to destroy it!"

"With what?"

"You can't"

"No, no, no!"

Everyone spoke at the same time.

"Shush!" Kellis demanded. The *Esprit* went quiet. She turned back to the screen. "Tier-Commander, we have an asset, a crew member, out there on T'Non'Za. You cannot fire!"

Tier-Commander Eklogar nodded. "Standby."

The screen went dark reminding Kellis of an old-fashion screen-saver. She quelled another reminiscence of the past. It never helped.

Silence followed for a full two minutes.

They're going to fire, Kellis knew. They were just getting final orders from Relentus, whether Force was on the rock or even Kellis herself. One person was not worth a planet full of people.

"Mom?" Bright was at her side. If she was afraid, she didn't show it. "What can we do?"

Kellis shook her head just as comms suddenly returned, Tier-Commander Eklogar's youthful face almost filling the screen.

Behind him, Kellis could see his crew readying for action on the bridge.

"Captain Kellis," he spoke, his Axalan-accented English startlingly compassionate, "With regret..."

Kellis cut him off immediately. "Force! Force, get off that godforsaken rock now! The bastard Constitutionate fleet is going fire. You will be destroyed. Move it! That's an order!"

No reply. No Static. No sign of life.

"Force!" screamed Kellis closer into the comms as if volume would make a difference.

"Dammit!" cursed Venturion, who then laughed out loud. "I bet that joker is already on his way back and is keeping radio silent to surprise us!" he continued to chuckle. "Idiot."

Everyone instinctively looked out the portals and at the rear compartment door for his arrival.

"They're firing!" Paolo leaped from his seat from looking at the holo display to stare in disbelief outside through the port. Bright sparks were thrust into the night from the fleet.

"Forty seconds to impact," Venturion counted down.

"Take us out of range," Kellis ordered. Venturion navigated them out the way. "Force respond... respond..." Kellis sweated, pleading for his voice, a joke, anything.

"Twenty seconds!"

"FORCE!" screamed Kellis again.

She tried to reach out telepathically. But nothing could be sensed.

"Ten, nine, eight..."

"Please, please...!"

Unbearable silence.

"Six, five, four..."

"Force?" A whisper.

"Three, two, one..."

"J.J."

Incandescent fury erupted in the distance. Upgraded plasma torpedoes and thanium missiles, had detonated in blinding explosions.

"Kellis!" called out Venturion. He was at the console monitoring the strikes and aftermath.

But she knew there was nothing she could do. She watched terrified with the rest of them, memories of the Christmas Day Massacre on Consention Base flashing through her mind as if it had been yesterday. Then she remembered something. It was the month of Legens on Home, Vag 19. The years, months, and days were different on Home with a combination of human, Axalan and Bion terms for dates. New traditions had began with old festival dates and religions only practiced locally. But Kellis had almost forgot. On Earth it was Boxing Day, December Twenty-Sixth. Her world was falling apart again. And outside the *Esprit* the fire works were dying down.

The glare started to dissipate. Paolo rubbed his temples and eyes. Bright sat silently in the cabin, stunned.

"Kellis!" Venturion shouted again, breaking the calm solemnity.

Kellis heard the summons in his voice this time. But she didn't care to see what had happened. Why should she see what she already knew? Force was dead.

But Venturion was pounding at the controls, venting his frustration. "Kellis, something's wrong!" he finally concluded. "The explosions..." he tailed off.

"They didn't hit T'Non'Za," Paolo was already studying the holographic screens. "They were repelled and . . . the fleet's gone!" He pointed at the screens showing over twenty ships all afire in the depths of space.

"Hell, what!" Kellis examined the data herself. "Gravity again," Kellis stated quietly.

Information buzzed at the back of her head still unable to coalesce into a valid concept.

"How come we weren't attacked?" asked Bright, eyes wide with more questions no one could answer.

"No idea, maybe because we didn't attack it. But let's not look a gift horse in the mouth. We have to figure out what to do next."

They all jumped when their comms sparked back into life with enough feedback static to jolt the dead to life.

"Tell the fleet to leave, Lynn. They'll be destroyed."

There were a few seconds of realisation over the familiar voice. They looked at each other in overwhelming relief.

"Force? Oh my God, you're alive. Thank God! What happened?" Kellis asked, a great smile lighting her face.

But Force continued. His words were a rush of data.

"Warn the fleet. Warn Home. They have to evacuate."

"Tell me something I don't know. Didn't you see the explosions? Where are you? Get back aboard and we'll warn Home!" She started looking out the port for him.

"We've got this all wrong," Force's voice continued in a chilling fashion. "This isn't a planetoid. It's not a ship. And it's not a rogue encounter. Lynn," his voice was a forceful tone, "someone has thrown a chunk of solidified black hole at us."

"What? A piece of black hole?" Suddenly it hit Kellis: Gravity. Dense gravity. It was the missing piece in her mind. Kellis looked at Venturion and Paolo who both shrugged even as Force continued.

"I'd never heard of such a thing! No wonder we couldn't get sensors on it!" Force's speech quickened as if out of breath. "There's no hawking radiation, no information coming from it. It's an impossible middle existing between quantum physics and general relativity. It's getting more. . . gravimetrically active, stronger, as it closes on Home. S'why comms were affected. Time dilation. The friggin' thing's ramping up with power. We are under attack!" he wheezed.. "Evacuate Home! Let them know!"

"Force, can you hear me?" Kellis asked. Fear started trickling down her spine.

"Oh, by the way, Lynn," he hesitated for a while. "I think you think we're having a conversation, but we're not. I'm. . . I'm already dead."

Kellis looked in desperation at the others. It couldn't be true.

A coarse laugh escaped him ending in a coughing fit. "By the time you hear this I've been dead for a good ten minutes. Crushed most likely. Hope I don't suffer," he wheezed. "I'm sorry I let you down. My powers would never have defeated this gravity monster. It's sucked my powers right out of me. Wish I could have turned it into a giant fluffy marshmallow, but, you know." He was silent for a while longer.

Kellis didn't make it to a seat. Her knees buckled to her chest as she sank down the hull. She closed her eyes tightly trying to blank everything out.

"Don't worry about me, Lynn, you'll never retrieve my body in this denseness. Just warn Home!" He made a noise of pain as if fighting for breath. "Lynn, Lynn, I lo…"

Everybody listened for his next words which never came. The line was dead. The fleet was gone. Force was…

Kellis compelled herself to stand up. All eyes were on her, stunned, glazed, sad. Kellis didn't look into any them.

"What do we do now, mother?" Bright asked, her voice raised to break the grieving atmosphere rather than an emotional outburst.

Kellis looked at her daughter, thoughts rolling around her head. This was war.

"You heard him," Kellis' own voice was quiet. "Warn Home, now!" She found herself shaking with anger. "We live to fight another day!"

Paolo reacted quicker than Venturion, contacting Home's Council headquarters in Relenta City.

"Venturion, cut us a wide berth around that fucker! We're running for Home," Kellis ordered.

Venturion complied in silence.

It was a quiet flight back to Home.

On Legensvag 19, Home Year 32 (Earth year 2254), the Constitutionate world of Home was destroyed. Or was it? Experts from all over the Constitutionate did not know T'Non'Za had slammed into home, but with no apparent destruction. Had T'Non'Za enveloped Home? Perhaps absorbed the planet? It just resembled a large black swirling storm in space. No one could elucidate the mysteries of T'Non'Za.

The planet had barely been evacuated in time with refugees heading to Earth and her colonies on Alphas Centuri and Proxima or to Axala and her worlds. The Bions only repatriated their own residents.

Home was now just a black mass, a seemingly planetary singularity at the heart of a black hole which didn't grow or emit any radiation. There was no way of piercing its dark heart for information. No way of saving Home.

The Constitutionate banned all travel to within a light year, but kept remote sensors in orbit to monitor the phenomenon.

Kellis had vowed one day to return and defeat the enemy who had visited this atrocity upon them.

***

From within the denseness of the black gravity storm, several tall dark figures emerged from portals. They surveyed the destroyed land before them; the air a seething mass of millions of black tornadoes.

Standing amongst the spiraling deathtraps, cold air coiling around him, Techmoses announced with throaty satisfaction:

"Threshold complete."

APPENDIX A

FAMILY LINES

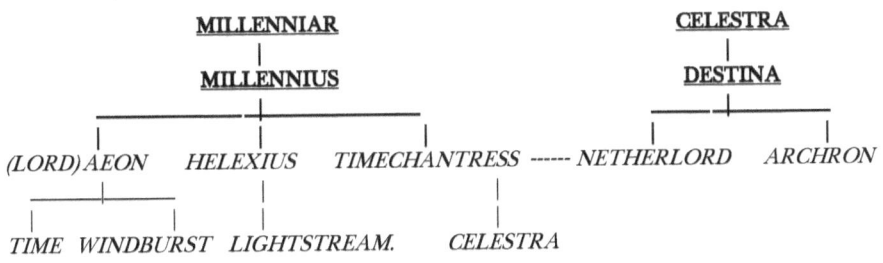

```
        MILLENNIAR                              CELESTRA
           |                                       |
        MILLENNIUS                               DESTINA
   _____|_____                 _____|_____
  |           |            |                |          |
(LORD)AEON  HELEXIUS  TIMECHANTRESS ------ NETHERLORD  ARCHRON
 ___|___        |            |
|       |       |            |
TIME WINDBURST LIGHTSTREAM. CELESTRA
```

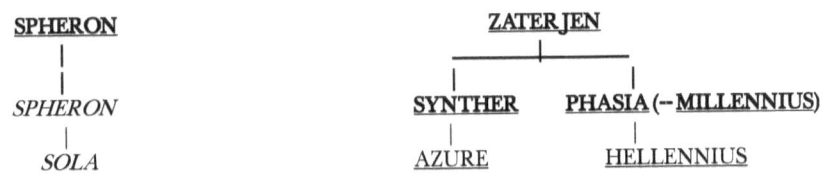

```
 SPHERON                    ZATERJEN
    |                   _____|_____
 SPHERON               |              |
    |                SYNTHER    PHASIA(--MILLENNIUS)
  SOLA                 |              |
                     AZURE        HELLENNIUS
```

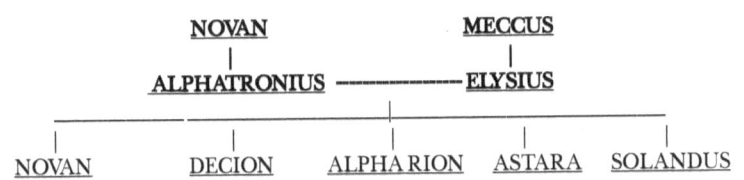

```
      NOVAN              MECCUS
        |                  |
   ALPHATRONIUS --------- ELYSIUS
 _____|_____
|           |          |        |        |
NOVAN     DECION   ALPHA RION  ASTARA  SOLANDUS
```

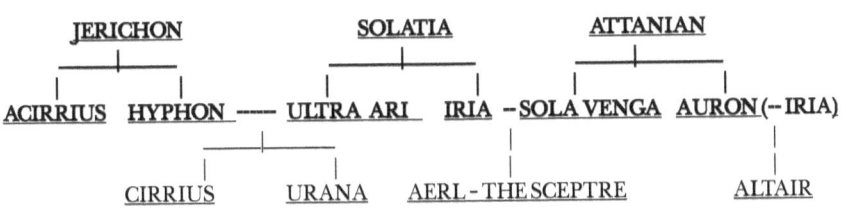

```
   JERICHON           SOLATIA          ATTANIAN
  _____|_____      _____|_____      _____|_____
 |         |      |          |     |          |
ACIRRIUS HYPHON --- ULTRA ARI  IRIA –SOLA VENGA AURON(--IRIA)
      _____|_____          |                |
     |          |          |                |
   CIRRIUS   URANA  AERL - THE SCEPTRE    ALTAIR
```

CELESTIAN KNIGHT
STARGUARD
ASTRAL

Have you enjoyed this book?
If so, why not write a review on your favourite website?

THE STARGUARDS

continues in

BOOK 5 - THE CELESTIAN ODYSSEY

www.ingramcontent.com/pod-product-compliance
Lightning Source LLC
Chambersburg PA
CBHW031231120726
47905CB00002B/545